Cassie blinked at her sister, nonplussed. After a moment she began to pace about the room. "I don't know, Eva," she murmured worriedly. "Even if this Jeremy is the paragon you describe, I can't put aside the feeling that the age difference is too great."

"Your daughter *loves* this man. Truly! She is barely aware that there's a difference in their ages. He is the man of her dreams, I tell you! The circumstances are not at all the same as yours. You were *coerced* into wedlock against your will, but Cicely *wishes* it more than anything. If you refuse your permission, you will break the girl's heart."

"Will I? Oh, dear!" Cassie sank down on the chair again and twisted her fingers together nervously. "Are you sure it's not a case of puppy love?"

"Give your daughter credit for a little sense! She's no longer a child. She knows what she feels." Eva leaned back in her chair, satisfied that she'd weakened Cassie's resistance. "Wait till you see them together. Cicely's eyes positively shine when they look at him."

"Very well, then," Cassie said with a surrendering sigh, "give her my blessing." But her eyes—and her heart—remained troubled.

Eva reached out and took her hands. "Don't look like that, dearest. Everything will be fine, I promise you. Wait till you meet Jeremy. You're going to *love* him. Take my word."

Books by Elizabeth Mansfield

Mother's Choice

Elizabeth Mansfield

JOVE BOOKS, NEW YORK

If you purchased this book without a cover, you should be aware that this book is stolen property. It was reported as "unsold and destroyed" to the publisher, and neither the author nor the publisher has received any payment for this "stripped book."

MOTHER'S CHOICE

A Jove Book / published by arrangement with
the author

PRINTING HISTORY
Jove edition / May 1994

All rights reserved.
Copyright © 1994 by Paula Schwartz.
This book may not be reproduced in whole
or in part, by mimeograph or any other means,
without permission. For information address:
The Berkley Publishing Group, 200 Madison Avenue,
New York, New York 10016.

ISBN: 0-515-11386-7

A JOVE BOOK®
Jove Books are published by The Berkley Publishing Group,
200 Madison Avenue, New York, New York 10016.
JOVE and the "J" design are trademarks belonging
to Jove Publications, Inc.

PRINTED IN THE UNITED STATES OF AMERICA

10 9 8 7 6 5 4 3 2 1

He who would the daughter win,
Must with the mother first begin.

—OLD ENGLISH PROVERB

Prologue

The rim of a huge orange sun was just disappearing behind the Dorset hills when Eva Schofield's elegant brougham drew up to the door of Crestwoods, her sister's secluded country estate. Lady Schofield, eager to impart some thrilling news to her sister, hurriedly heaved her ample frame from her seat, but she could not manage to climb down from the carriage without her coachman's assistance. Once her feet were planted on terra firma, however, her impatience lessened, and she paused to gaze up with admiration at the familiar house.

While she herself was a "town mouse," she fully understood why her sister insisted on living in the country. It was lovely here. The glow of the setting sun lit the tall, many-paned windows of the manor house with a translucent, reddish glow and made the gray stones gleam with warmth. The shrubs and foliage surrounding the entrance seemed, in their spring green, to be bursting into renewed life. Even the air was different from that which one breathed in town; it was crisp and clean, and spiced with a slight whiff of the ocean. No wonder, Lady Schofield thought, that her sister did not like to leave this lovely, peaceful place for London's noise, bustle and dirt.

Lady Schofield had taken only two steps toward the doorway when it flew open and the butler emerged. He looked startled. "Lady Schofield!" he exclaimed, bowing. "We were not expecting you. I trust there's nothing wrong with Miss Cicely!"

Lady Schofield took instant umbrage. "Quite the contrary, Clemson," she snapped, frowning at him in irritation. "Not that it's your place to inquire."

"I beg your pardon, your ladyship," Clemson apologized, but without perturbation. He knew that Lady Schofield's gruff

1

manner, like a good-natured dog's bark, had no teeth.

She swept by him with her chin lifted in offended dignity, the angle of her head causing her high-crowned hat to fall forward over her forehead. "Humph! I've told my sister time and again that you don't know your place," she declared, pulling off the bonnet. "But of course she will never listen to me."

"Yes, my lady," the butler agreed blandly, hurrying up the steps after her.

Once inside the door, she thrust the enormous hat at him. "My sister is at her painting, I assume. In the library, as usual?"

"Yes, my lady. Will you wait while I announce you?"

"Nonsense! When have I ever had to be announced? I'll announce myself, if you please." She dismissed the fellow with a flip of her hand and strode off down the corridor.

Eva Schofield's younger sister, Cassandra, Lady Beringer, was standing before the library window, the last rays of the sun lighting the easel before her. At her right elbow was a small, scarred table on which were a number of pots of brushes, jars of solvents and an assortment of tubes of paint. And on a pedestal in front of her was an arrangement of fruit and crockery, evidently the subject of a still life. The artist, enveloped in a loose paint-stained smock, was dabbing away at her canvas, completely absorbed.

Lady Schofield paused in the doorway, smiling fondly at the picture her sister made as she stood silhouetted against the light, her fair hair haloed by the sun, and the planes of her face enhanced by the play of light and deep shade. It seemed to Lady Schofield that the scene itself was not unlike a painting—a Dutch masterwork, perhaps—with Maggie a chiarioscuro madonna.

Eva was greatly attached to her sister. Cassie was the closest relation Eva had left in the world, now that her beloved Schofield had passed to his reward. She and her deceased husband had not had children of their own, and being senior to her sister by eleven years, Eva lavished on Cassie (and on Cassie's daughter Cicely, too) all her motherly feelings. She and her sister even looked more like mother and daughter than sisters, Cassie being fair and youthfully slim, while Eva was dark and matronly. Only in their large, dark eyes were they at all alike.

Lady Schofield entered on tiptoe and came up behind her sister. "I like the lemon and the teapot well enough," she said, her head tilted critically, "but what's an hourglass doing standing there among them?"

Maggie whirled around. "*Eva!*" A look of delighted surprise brightened her dark eyes, but it was immediately supplanted by an expression of alarm. "Heavens, what's *amiss*? Oh, God! Is Cicely ill?"

"Of course not! You needn't look so terrified, you goose," her sister assured her. "I've not come with any bad news about your precious Cicely. In fact, I've the very best news in the world. She's made the catch of the season."

Lady Beringer sighed in relief before tossing aside her brush, wiping her hands on a paint-smeared cloth and throwing her arms round her sister's neck. "Dearest, how lovely of you to come all this way to tell me!"

The two sisters embraced warmly. Then Eva stepped back. "Heavens, Cassie, take off that dreadful smock before you cover me with smears!"

Cassie laughed and obeyed, dropping the offending garment on a chair. Then, smiling happily, she took her sister's arm. "So Cicely's made the catch of the season, eh?" she remarked as she led her sister to the door. "I'm not at all surprised. My Cicely is quite a catch herself. But you must be weary from your carriage ride. Let's go to the morning room and provide you with some good, hot tea."

"You are an unnatural mother," Lady Schofield declared as they strolled down the corridor. "One would expect you to be agog to learn the details of your daughter's triumph."

"I am agog, I assure you," Cassie laughed. "I can hardly wait to hear the news."

"Then I won't keep you in suspense. Cassie, my love, after only two months in my care, and as the result of my wise planning, my wide circle of friends and my prudent guidance, your daughter has managed to snare a veritable prize!"

This announcement coincided with their arrival at the morning room doorway. "Indeed?" Maggie inquired eagerly. "And who, may I ask, is this prize?"

Eva, grinning in triumph, stopped stock-still in the doorway and threw back her shoulders proudly. "None other than the Viscount Inglesby! What have you to say to *that*?"

"Inglesby? Inglesby?" Cassie wrinkled her brow in concentration as she stepped over the threshold and pulled the bell cord for Clemson. "I don't think I know—"

"I shouldn't be surprised if you don't, not having shown yourself in society for ages, but you should at least have *heard* of him." Lady Schofield swept into the room and deposited herself on an easy chair. "He's Jeremy Tate, scion of the Northumberland Tates. The name must mean *something* to you. Inglesby Park can't be more than fifteen miles from here. You might even have met him sometime or other in the past."

Cassie shook her head. "No, I don't think so. You know I don't go about much."

"You don't go about at all, that's the trouble. Well, that's neither here nor there. What's important is that the fellow is a charmer—polished, witty and quite handsome in a loose-limbed, lanky way. And what's more, my dear, he's a peer with two large estates and an income, they say, in the neighborhood of eighteen thousand!"

Cassie, overwhelmed by so impressive a description, sank down upon the chair opposite her sister. "I must say, that's a catch indeed. He sounds almost too good to be true."

Eva smiled with satisfaction. "Doesn't he? And to think that our Cicely managed to snare him when no other female's been able to do it in all these years."

"All these *years*?" Cassie seemed suddenly to freeze. Her breath caught in her throat, and her expression became wary. "How old is he?"

Eva's smile froze, too, and she threw her sister a suspicious look. "Thirty-eight, I believe. Why?"

Cassie turned pale as a sheet. "Why, he's almost as old as *I am*!"

"A year younger. But what has that to say to anything?"

"Cicely is only *eighteen*! My God, Eva, you can't have permitted Cicely to become entangled with an older man! Not after knowing what I—!"

"Cassie, *stop!*" Eva fixed her sister with a forbidding look. "You mustn't think such things. Lord Inglesby is not Beringer. Just because *your* experience was dreadful is no reason to believe that Cicely's will be the same."

Cassie opened her mouth to reply, but at that moment Clemson appeared in the doorway with the tea trolley. The two sisters lapsed into awkward silence while the butler poured the tea. "A cucumber sandwich, your ladyship?" he asked Lady Schofield as he handed her a cup of the steaming brew.

She shook her head, too discomposed to speak. While Clemson continued to fiddle with the tea things, Eva stared at her sister in consternation. It had not occurred to her that Cassie would make a connection in her mind between Jeremy and the overbearing Lord Beringer, her deceased husband. There was not an iota of similarity between the two men, not that Eva could see.

Eva stirred her tea absently, her mind chewing on this unexpected problem. Why was Cassie still troubled by the memories of her marriage? True, that marriage had been a nightmare. Their father had forced her, when she was only seventeen, to wed a man twenty years her senior. Carleton Beringer had turned out to be arrogant and selfish, and for a dozen years poor Cassie had suffered who-knows-what dreadful experiences. She had not been able to speak of them—not then and not now.

But it was almost a decade since Beringer died, and Cassie was still hiding herself away here in the country, still avoiding society in general and male companionship in particular, and still turning pale at the memory of the man she'd wedded. Shouldn't the memories have receded by this time?

Cassie waited until Clemson withdrew and then instantly pulled herself to her feet. "I won't have it, Eva!" She spoke with a quiet firmness that Eva knew would be hard to shake. "I *won't* have Cicely forced into a marriage like mine."

But Eva, too, could be firm. "*Forced?* Who is forcing her?" She put her cup down on the trolley with a clunk and glared up at her sister. "I care as much about your daughter as you do, my dear. And *I* won't have Cicely's life ruined because of your old memories!" She got to her feet and took her sister by her shoulders. "It's been almost a decade, my love, since Beringer's demise," she said in a gentler tone. "Isn't it time you put the past behind you?"

"How can I, when you tell me my daughter is entangling herself with a man twenty years her senior?" She shook off her sister's hold and turned away. "Twenty years," she murmured in a voice that shook. "Exactly the same difference in age as between Carleton and me!"

"That number is an unfortunate coincidence. But it has no other significance. I give you my word that there's nothing about Jeremy Tate that is *at all* like Carleton Beringer. He is as kind and generous and good-natured as Carleton was selfish and ill-natured."

Cassie blinked at her sister, nonplussed. After a moment she began to pace about the room. "I don't know, Eva," she murmured worriedly. "Even if this Jeremy is the paragon you describe, I can't put aside the feeling that the age difference is too great."

"Your daughter *loves* this man. Truly! She is barely aware that there's a difference in their ages. He is the man of her dreams, I tell you! The circumstances are not at all the same as yours. You were *coerced* into wedlock against your will, but Cicely *wishes* it more than anything. If you refuse your permission, you will break the girl's heart."

"Will I? Oh, dear!" Cassie sank down on the chair again and twisted her fingers together nervously. "Are you sure it's not a case of puppy love?"

"Give your daughter credit for a little sense! She's no longer a child. She knows what she feels." Eva leaned back in her chair, satisfied that she'd weakened Cassie's resistance. "Wait till you see them together. Cicely's eyes positively shine when they look at him."

"Very well, then," Cassie said with a surrendering sigh, "give her my blessing." But her eyes—and her heart—remained troubled.

Eva reached out and took her hands. "Don't look like that, dearest. Everything will be fine, I promise you. Wait till you meet Jeremy. You're going to *love* him. Take my word."

Chapter
~ 1 ~

At the very moment when he should have made Cicely an offer, Jeremy Tate, Viscount Inglesby, experienced a change of heart. It was a turnabout of feeling so sudden, so violent, so complete, that he was left breathless. It was not unlike the feeling one experiences when, after stealing out early on a summer morning eager for a swim, the placing of one toe in the still-icy water sends one scurrying back, shivering, to the house.

All evening long Jeremy had eagerly anticipated the moment when he and Cicely would be alone, for this was the night he intended to offer for her. But the dinner party they'd attended seemed to go on endlessly, and, as the hours passed, he'd begun to feel somewhat uneasy. He attributed the feeling to the fact that he'd never in his thirty-eight years asked a woman to wed him. Once he'd actually proposed, he told himself, he would probably feel quite normal again.

But when he and Cicely had finally said their good nights to their hostess, Lady Hallam, and had seated themselves comfortably side by side in Jeremy's phaeton, the uneasy feeling grew worse, and before he knew what was happening, he was experiencing this complete change of heart. He didn't want to wed the girl after all!

Jeremy, unused to emotional reversals, didn't know what to do. Cicely was expecting a declaration. And this was the perfect time. The night was mild, a three-quarter moon spread a silver gleam on the rooftops, and the clip-clop of the horses' hooves on the cobbles of the London streets echoed pleasantly in the night air. What made matters worse, the girl was looking up at him with a shiny-eyed expectancy. The moment was at hand. But poor Jeremy, with one toe about to dip into the

7

waters of matrimony, wanted only to go scurrying back to bachelorhood.

He looked down at Cicely's pretty, expectant face and felt his heart sink. "Cicely, I . . . I . . . ," he mumbled.

"Yes, Jeremy?" The corners of her lips curled upward, and with every confidence that his next words would be the loving declaration she was waiting for, she dropped her eyes modestly to the hands folded in her lap.

"I . . . er . . . hope you enjoyed the dinner," he said lamely.

The girl looked up at him in surprise. "You must know that I enjoyed it very much," she said, wondering if the sophisticated, mature Lord Inglesby had suddenly been taken shy. "Are you merely making conversation with me, my lord?"

"Yes, perhaps I am."

"I think you are feeling bashful," she said, smiling up at him encouragingly. "Mama does not approve of bashfulness, you know."

"No? Why not?"

"She says that modesty is a virtue, but bashfulness is pushing modesty too far."

"Your mother must be a witty woman," he murmured absently, wondering how he could *think* of hurting so sweet and charming a creature as Cicely Beringer. Yet he knew with a chilling certainty that he did *not* want to spend his life with her.

"Mama is charming," the girl was saying. "But you'll see that for yourself tonight, won't you?" She threw a quick glance up at him and then looked down again. "She's come in from Dorset especially to . . . that is, I expected . . . I *thought* you intended to come in with me and . . . er . . . meet her."

Jeremy understood Cicely's awkwardness. She was expecting him to declare himself, after which—according to proper protocol in these matters—she would have to invite him in to meet her mother. Cicely could not accept an offer from him until her widowed mother gave her approval. Since Jeremy had not yet met the reclusive Lady Beringer and thus had not had the opportunity to ask her permission to court Cicely, he was expected to do so tonight. But, judging from Cicely's warmth toward him and from the encouraging manner of her aunt, her chaperon, he had no doubt that Lady Beringer would give her approval. The woman was undoubtedly awaiting them at this very moment, willing, even eager, to give them her blessing. The attentions he'd lavished on Cicely these past few weeks had generated these expectations. And the fact that he'd asked—and received—permission to escort her to the Hallams' fete unchaperoned had been clear evidence that he'd intended to make the offer tonight. That he now found himself in this dreadfully awkward situation was entirely his own fault.

Cicely was gazing up at him, her light blue eyes shining, her heart-shaped face alight, her cheeks pink with embarrassment and her soft lips trembling nervously. The hood of her cloak had slipped from her head, revealing tousled, dark-gold hair that glowed with every gleam of light that flickered into the carriage window. She'd never looked lovelier. The girl's happy, eager expression cut his heart. Perhaps he should ignore his negative feelings and go ahead with what was expected of him. *Tell her you love her, you clod,* he told himself firmly, *and ask her to wed you! Be a man!* But he knew that a lie to her now would mean a lifetime of lies, and *that* he couldn't do, not to her or to himself. Something inside him—the attraction he'd imagined he felt toward her these past weeks—had inexplicably and suddenly died, and he could not pretend that it was still alive.

The carriage pulled up at the front door of Lady Beringer's town house. Cicely made no move. Jeremy gulped, hoping that a footman would come running out to the carriage to help the girl down, thus forcibly precluding any opportunity for discussion or explanation. But no one came. The servants had obviously been instructed to give the couple privacy. Jeremy knew he had to speak, but for the first time in all his thirty-eight years he found himself tongue-tied.

After a long moment of uncomfortable silence, Cicely tilted up her charmingly pointed chin and faced him squarely. Her eyes were suddenly fearful. "Isn't there something you wish to say to me?" she asked, her voice unusually strained and unsteady.

Jeremy could not remember ever feeling so miserable. "Cicely, I . . . I . . ."

Her cheeks paled. "It is not like you to . . . to stammer," she said, trying to smile despite her sudden awareness that her expectations were about to be dashed.

"It's because I suddenly find myself at a loss for words," he said softly, taking her hands in his. "I'm sorry . . ."

She gave a gasping intake of breath. "S-s-sorry?"

"Yes. Sorry that I have nothing to say."

"Oh?" Her chin quivered and her eyes filled. "Nothing at all?"

He shook his head, his throat too tight to permit speech.

She stared up at him, tearfully wide-eyed. "Then you don't wish to . . . to come in and m-meet Mama?"

"No, my dear. Not tonight."

She withdrew her hands from his hold, threw him one quick, tearful glance and turned away, dropping her face in her hands. After a moment she put one shaking hand out to the door handle. "Then I m-must b-bid you good n-night," she managed, her stammer filling him with painful guilt.

"Cicely . . . you shouldn't . . . mustn't blame yourself. I can't explain . . . but the fault is entirely of my . . ." His voice died in helpless inadequacy.

"Please," she begged in a small, trembling voice, "rap for your man to come down and open the carriage door."

He obeyed at once. "May I accompany you to your door?" he pleaded, putting a hand gently on her shoulder.

She shook her head. "No, p-please don't!" Her voice, caught in her throat, hovered between a sob and a gasp. She lifted the hood of her cloak so that it almost completely hid her face, but he could see that she was brushing at her cheeks with the back of her hand. When Jeremy's coachman lowered the steps and opened the door, she jumped down quickly and flew by the astonished fellow without permitting him to help her. Before Jeremy could follow her down—before he'd even found a proper phrase to say a proper good night—she'd run up the path to the house and was pounding on the door.

Jeremy watched as the fanlight above the door brightened with the light of approaching candles. Someone within was coming to the door. It opened, and the girl disappeared inside. He waited to see the light in the fanlight recede, but it did not. Her mother must have come to the door to greet them, and the girl was probably weeping in her arms right there in the entryway.

The coachman, who was also Jeremy's valet, butler and general factotum (having been the Viscount's batman in his army days), peered at Jeremy curiously. "Turned ye down, did she, me lord?"

"I wish she had." Jeremy, filled with guilt and despair (and trying not to recognize that the pain of these feelings was softened by a strong sense of relief), sighed and sagged back against the cushions. "Take me to the club, Hickham," he muttered. "I think I want to get thoroughly sozzled."

As the carriage trundled off, Jeremy turned and peered out the rear window. As if it were a penance, he kept his shamed eyes fixed on the lighted fanlight of the Schofield town house until it was absorbed by distance and darkness.

Chapter
~ 2 ~

Jeremy strode into White's, tossed his greatcoat to one of the waiters and orderd a double whiskey. "Bring it to me in the lounge," he said over his shoulder as he crossed the entryway and ran up the curved stairway.

He found his friend, Lord Lucas, slouched in an easy chair, nodding over the *Times.* Without a word of greeting, he threw himself down on the chair opposite. "I hate to admit it, Charlie," he muttered in self-disgust, "but your best friend is the worst sort of cad."

The redheaded, curly-haired, stocky Charles Percy, Lord Lucas, opened his eyes with a start. Shaking his body like a wet dog, he sat erect and blinked at his friend uncomprehendingly. "Eh? Wha' did y'say?"

"I said I'm a cad."

"*Cad?*" Lord Lucas, now fully awake, raised an eyebrow and peered with one bright blue eye at his friend. "You? A cad?" He snorted in amusement. "Well, old fellow, you'll get no argument from me."

Jeremy eyed him with rueful amusement. "What sort of friend are you? Can't you at least deny it?"

"Why should I deny it? I always suspected it."

"Suspected it?" Jeremy glared at him, too filled with self-loathing to appreciate the teasing.

At that moment the waiter appeared at his elbow. "Your whiskey, my lord."

Jeremy took the glass, put a few coins in its place and, while the waiter withdrew, threw back a hefty swig. Then he resumed glaring at his friend. "Why aren't you contradicting me, you clunch?" he demanded with boyish offense. "I've never been caddish with you, have I?"

"You've never been caddish with anyone, not that I've ever heard tell of. That's exactly why I suspected it. You're too upstanding a fellow to be believed, I've always thought." He threw his friend a grin, his eyes laughing into Jeremy's handsome face, a face that anyone could see was too open, too sensitive and kind, to belong to a cad. "Yes, so much straightforward rectitude *must* be a mask. There must be a cad lurking inside you somewhere."

But Jeremy was too perturbed to laugh at his friend's taunt. He merely sighed and stared into the glass. "Well, it turns out you're quite right."

Lord Lucas's grin died. This sort of self-flagellation was not Jeremy's style, and as far as he, Charlie Percy, was concerned, it had gone on long enough. "Nonsense, old boy, utter rot!" he declared with finality. "You couldn't be a cad if you tried."

"I was tonight," Jeremy insisted.

Charlie waited for a further explanation, but none came. Jeremy merely twisted the glass in his hand. A long silence followed. At last Charlie could bear it no longer. "So, you gudgeon, are you going to confess what caddish deed you've done, or are you going to let me die wondering?"

Jeremy threw him a sheepish glance and then dropped his eyes. "I've cried off," he said with quiet honesty. "Poor Cicely was weeping when she ran inside."

Lord Lucas's bright eyes lost whatever gleam of amusement had still remained. "What do you mean, cried off? Are you saying you offered for her? For *Cicely Beringer*? You never told me you'd made her an offer."

"I told you I intended to."

"Yes, but there's an ocean of difference between the intention and the act. Did you actually do it?"

"Well, no, that's just it. When it came to the sticking point, I . . . I couldn't go through with it."

"My dear fellow," Charlie exclaimed with a touch of impatience, "if you never actually made an offer, you can't say you cried off. There's been no agreement you can cry off *from*."

Jeremy lifted his eyes to his friend's face questioningly. "But she—and everyone else in London—expected it. Doesn't that make me almost as guilty as if I'd actually proposed?"

"Not at all. The whole purpose of courtship is to give the parties concerned a chance to think . . . to discover whether or not they suit. The only thing you're guilty of—if you ask me—is to have waited until the last minute to discover that you do not."

"It certainly was the last minute," Jeremy muttered ruefully.

"Better the minute before than the one after." Charlie leaned back in his chair and smiled with self-satisfaction. "I, for one, am not at all surprised that you backed off."

Jeremy looked over at him in astonishment. "Are you not? Why aren't you?"

Charlie shrugged. "I know you, Jeremy Tate. After resisting matrimony for all your thirty-seven years—"

"Thirty-eight," Jeremy corrected.

"Thirty-eight, then. After resisting it so determinedly despite having had hordes of females thrown at you since you came of age, I was fully convinced that it would take more than the likes of a simpering chit like Cicely Beringer to capture your affections."

"She's *not* a simpering chit," Jeremy declared angrily. "She's good-hearted and generous and sweet. And quite the prettiest little thing in all of society."

"Yes, if I remember rightly, those were your mother's exact words in describing her."

"And Mama was quite right."

"Then, if you believe that, you should have offered."

"Yes, dash it," Jeremy responded glumly, "you scored the point there."

"Mothers of bachelors," Charlie opined, "have a disconcerting way of thrusting marriageable ladies at them. They sincerely believe they know just the sorts of women who would suit their sons. They're almost always wrong."

Jeremy raised his glass. "To mothers," he toasted and downed another gulp. "Mine will probably come storming into my flat tomorrow morning and berate me soundly for failing to come up to scratch."

Charlie leaned forward. "Are you certain, Jeremy, that you

don't want to go through with it? That Cicely is not the right girl for you?"

"As certain as one can be in such matters. Why?"

"Then, if I were you, I'd leave town. The best way to resolve such problems is to rusticate for a month or so. You'll avoid your mother's wrath and the embarrassment of coming face-to-face with the girl at some fete or other. And by the time you come back, everyone will have become accustomed to the matter."

"Sounds a cowardly way to deal with it," Jeremy objected.

"If you want to be brave, by all means stay. Stay put and face your mother. Stay put and endure seeing all the gossipy females whisper behind their fans every time you enter a room. Stay put and find yourself running into Cicely at the opera or at the Pantheon Bazaar. You'll have to be very brave indeed."

Jeremy rolled his eyes heavenward and downed another gulp.

"If, however, you should decide to be cowardly," Charlie went on, touch of slyness in his voice, "and agree to rusticate as any man of sense would do, I'd go with you."

Jeremy's eyes narrowed. "You'd go with me?" he asked suspiciously. "To Inglesby Park?"

"Yes, if you'd like company."

"You *hate* rusticating. And you always claim that Inglesby Park is the dullest retreat in all of England, being ten miles from the nearest town and equally far from decent society."

"Yes, I did say that, didn't I? But it's a small sacrifice to make in the name of friendship."

"What a hum! Cut line, Charlie, and tell me the truth. Who are *you* trying to run away from?"

Charlie smiled guiltily. "There *is* a certain opera dancer who has taken it into her head that I played her false. It might be a good time for me to be far away from her."

Jeremy shook his head. "I thought as much. But are you so eager to escape that you would put up with Inglesby Park at this season, when Mama has taken most of my household staff to employ here in London? Most of the rooms are closed off. I'll only have Mr. and Mrs. Stemple and Hickham and a few of the locals to do for us."

"I don't expect to spend the month in high living. A bit of riding, an afternoon or two of shooting, evenings of quiet relaxation—that's all I need."

"Very well, then, I agree. We'll both be cowardly and run for cover."

Charlie brightened perceptibly. "Tonight?"

"Yes, why not?" Jeremy put down his glass, now almost empty, and rose from his chair. "Do you know what I think, Charlie, old fellow?"

"What?" Charlie asked, rising and clapping his friend companiably on his shoulder.

"That we're *both* cads. The pair of us."

Chapter

~ 3 ~

In the foyer of Lady Schofield's town house, Cicely was indeed weeping in her mother's arms. Cassandra Beringer, aghast, held her daughter tightly with one arm, her other hand lifting a branch of candles out of the way. "What is it, my love?" she asked softly, trying not to reveal in her voice the extent of her alarm. "What's happened?"

Cicely shuddered and clutched her mother's shoulders, too choked with sobs to speak.

Eva Schofield, who'd been hiding on the first turning of the stairs so that she might eavesdrop on the announcement of the expected good news, came running down as fast as her heavy, aging legs permitted. "Good heavens, my love," she cried, "are you ill?"

Cicely, keeping her head buried in her mother's shoulder, waved a hand to indicate that illness was not the problem.

"Then where is Jeremy? I thought he was to come in with you," the aunt persisted.

This only increased the girl's sobs. Eva and Cassie exchanged looks of worried helplessness. Eva took the candles from Cassie's hand. "Come to the sitting room," she said, leading the way. "The fire is going, and we can be cozy. We'll have tea, and after you've calmed yourself, you shall tell us what happened."

"Whatever it is, dearest," Cassie murmured with motherly tenderness, "we shall make it right. You'll see."

It took an hour of being rocked in her mother's arms on the sofa in front of the fire, and another hour of giving tearful answers to anxious questions, before Cicely was able to give the two older women an inkling of what had passed. "So you s-see," she said tremulously, rising and going to the fireplace, "there's n-nothing you can do to m-make it right."

Eva peered up at her niece from the easy chair on which she'd sunk in despair. "He merely said he had *nothing* to say?" she asked, utterly puzzled. "What can he have meant by that?"

"His m-meaning was q-quite c-clear," Cicely said, resting her head on the mantel and staring down into the flames. "He had a ch-change of . . ." Her tears began to flow again. " . . .of . . . *heart*."

"Well, if Lord Inglesby was foolish enough to have a change of heart about *you*, dearest," declared her mother, "then he is too stupid to be worthy of you." She rose and put an arm about her daughter's waist. "Come up to bed, my love. No good will come of speaking of this matter any longer. Besides, everything will look brighter in the morning."

Cassie took the girl upstairs, dismissed the abigail and readied Cicely for bed as if she were still a child. She sponged the girl's tear-stained face, brushed her hair, buttoned her into her nightdress and tucked her into bed. Then she sat smoothing the girl's forehead and murmuring affectionate endearments until Cicely drifted off into a weary sleep.

Cassie tiptoed out of the room and softly closed the door. She was not surprised to find Eva hovering about in the hallway, her brow wrinkled with anxiety. "She's asleep," she assured her sister.

The two women walked slowly down the hall toward their respective bedrooms. "I have never been so disappointed in all my life," Eva muttered, half to herself. "I always found him so very good-natured, so charming, so . . . *perfect!* How can he have turned out to be so unfeeling? I shall never forgive him . . . or myself."

"Do not take it so much to heart," Cassie said, her face a frozen mask of self-control. "I myself am not at all sorry this happened."

"What on earth are you *saying*?" Eva raised her candle and peered at her sister's face in disbelief. "Can you possibly be *glad* to see your own daughter so heartbroken?"

"Of course I'm not glad. Do you think I'm not suffering for her pain? I *bleed* for her! But she will get over it. Better that she should weep for a few weeks now than weep for a lifetime later."

"Whatever do you mean? Do you think that if Jeremy had come up to scratch he would have made her unhappy?"

"Yes, I do. I'm sure of it. I let you convince me otherwise, and see what it's brought? It's always tragic when a girl weds a man old enough to be her father."

"Are you still harping on that? What utter nonsense! The fellow would have made her an ideal husband, despite his age!"

Cassie's eyebrows rose in scornful disgust. "Ideal? You still call him *ideal*? Did I not hear you say, a mere moment ago, that he was unfeeling?"

"Yes, but only because he evidently didn't care enough for our Cicely to overcome his reluctance to enter into wedlock." Though they'd arrived at the door to Cassie's bedroom, Eva would not let her go without speaking her mind. "The man's a prize, I tell you," she declared, holding her sister's arm to keep her from going inside. "What we ought to be considering, instead of standing here arguing about his age, is how to win him back."

"Win him *back*?" Furiously, Cassie shook off her sister's hold and pulled herself up to her full height. "I'd rather die! The man had his chance and muddled it. I shall not give him another. Not ever! I'm taking my daughter home, first thing in the morning. The sooner she's far away from town, the sooner she'll start on the road to recovery. And as for you, Eva, when you come to visit, you are not to mention him, do you understand? I don't ever want to hear his name again!"

"Very well," her sister said in offense, starting off down the hall. "Let Cicely become an old maid!"

"She won't be an old maid. Not Cicely," Cassie said to her sister's departing back. "But I'll see to it that any suitor who calls on her is under twenty-five!"

Eva did not look back until she heard Cassie's door slam. Then she turned round and made a disparaging gesture in the direction of her sister's door. "Hummmph!" she muttered.

"Under twenty-five indeed! He'd not be Jeffrey's equal no matter who he is."

But it was too, too bad, she thought sadly as she continued on toward her room, that Jeremy had not come through. If he had, not only would Cicely have been happy for life, but Cassie would have been taught that a twenty-year difference in age was not always fatal to marital bliss.

Eva's disappointment was so great that she could not sleep. She tossed and turned till daybreak, a victim of her thoughts. *There must be something I can do*, her mind repeated in despair. It would be remiss of her merely to let matters stand. Cicely must not be permitted to suffer this rejection, and Cassie must be taught a lesson. But what—?

Suddenly she sat up in bed with a gasp. "Of course!" she said aloud. "His *mother*! Why didn't I think of her before?"

She lit her candle, got out of bed and pattered across the cold floor in her bare feet, to her writing desk. There she set her candle down, drew out a sheet of notepaper, picked up a quill and, without bothering to cut a new nib, dipped it into the inkwell and began to write. *My dear Lady Inglesby . . .*

Chapter
~ 4 ~

At Inglesby Park a mere two days later, Jeremy, playing a desultory game of piquet with Charles Percy, looked up from his cards to find his man Hickham making nervous hand signals in the doorway. "Blast it, Hickham," he said irritably, his mood having been considerably dampened by two days of dreadful weather, "isn't it enough that I'm imprisoned indoors in this downpour with this deucedly ill-natured fellow playing this deucedly dull game? Must I now be forced to decipher your deucedly mysterious charades? Speak up, man!"

Hickham winced helplessly and gestured with his thumb to the corridor behind him. "Your mother, me lord," he whispered with foreboding.

Jeremy leapt from his chair. "Confound it," he muttered under his breath, "she's *here*? *Already?*"

"Lady Sarah herself, right down the 'allway, lettin' 'er abigail brush off the raindrops from 'er furs," Hickham hissed conspiratorially.

Jeremy sighed. "Show her in, Hickham," he said with a helpless shrug.

Hickham nodded and left. Charlie threw a taunting grin at his friend. "Ha!" he snorted callously. "You're in for it now. Told you she'd come."

Jeremy scowled down at him. "What you told me," he corrected, "was that I'd be safe from maternal scoldings if I rusticated."

"Yes, I did, didn't I? I should've known better. Your mother ain't the sort to be put off from her aims by a few dozen miles of separation." Hearing a step in the hall, he dropped his cards on the table and lifted himself from his chair with unwonted alacrity. "This will not be a pleasant scene. I think I'll make myself scarce, if you don't mind."

"Stay right where you are, Lord Lucas!" came a stern voice from the doorway. "Since I have not the slightest doubt that my son would not have run off like a craven were it not for your urging, I have as much to say to *you* as to him."

Charles sat down. The woman in the doorway, Lady Sarah Thorpe Tate, the dowager Viscountess Inglesby, daughter of the Marquis of Rotherham and widow of the late and distinguished Horace Tate, was a tall, imposing woman who was not one to be easily disobeyed. Jeremy, despite his unease at the prospect of a tongue-lashing, glanced over at her with admiring affection. His mother was a nonpareil. Everyone from royalty to her servants held her in the highest respect. Her very appearance, as she stood poised in the doorway, gave evidence of her strength and dignity. She was almost as tall as her son and equally spare of frame, with a pronounced nose and a chin that could only be called imperious. A queenly hat decorated with curled plumes sat atop her severely coiffed gray hair, and a positively regal fur pelisse was draped over her shoulders. And to make her appearance even more formidable, her arms, covered to the elbows in long gray leather gloves, were folded across her chest in an attitude of decided disapproval. "And as for you, Jeremy," she was saying, "I shan't even wish you good afternoon, for my heart would not be in it."

"But I'll wish *you* good afternoon, Mama," Jeremy said, throwing her an affectionate grin as he crossed the room to her, "and my heart *is* in it." He planted a kiss on her cheek. "Will you take off that dreadful hat and let me give it to Hickham?"

"No. The hat is not at all dreadful. It's complete to a shade, as well it ought to be, for it cost me thirty-nine pounds."

"But you can at least take it off indoors, can't you?" her son asked, leading her in and holding out a chair for her at the card table.

"No I can't, for I'm not staying. At which news, I'm certain, you are both giving silent thanks."

"Of course you're staying," her son insisted. "You can't drive all the way down from London and then go back the same day."

"I not only can, I will." She seated herself, stiff-backed, on the edge of the chair. "I dislike this house so much I can never bear staying in it."

"Really, Mama? Why? It is considered one of the finest examples of the Palladian style."

"A much overrated style, if you ask me. Too many pediments, pillars and pilasters. And stairs everywhere. Many too many stairs! An eight-step staircase just to reach the front door!"

"I can arrange for you to have a bedroom right on this floor," her son offered. "You won't have to climb a stair."

"No, thank you. I shall be returning to London immediately. And don't be foolish enough to believe, Jemmy Tate, that you can flummery me with all this affability. It will not make me forget what I came to say."

"I didn't think it would." Jeremy pulled up a chair beside Charles and braced himself. "Very well, Mama, go ahead and say what you must."

Charles tried again to rise and get away. "But of course, ma'am," he murmured, "you'll wish me to take myself off. You will surely desire a little privacy for what promises to be an intimate mother-son conversation."

"Sit down, Charlie Percy," Lady Inglesby ordered. "You heard me say I wanted you here. Don't make me say it again."

Charlie shrugged in surrender and sat.

Lady Sarah waited in dramatic silence for a moment and then turned her eyes to her son. "I never thought I'd live to see the day, Jemmy," she said at last in a voice lowered to a dramatic contralto, "when I'd be forced to admit that my son is a cad!"

"Cad?" Jeremy echoed, exchanging a glance with Charlie.

"Cad," said his mother.

"Come now, ma'am," Charlie ventured in brave defense of his friend, "you can't be serious. Not if you're referring to the Cicely Beringer matter."

"Of course I'm referring to it. I hope there is no *other* circumstance in which my son behaved like a cad."

"He wasn't caddish in the Beringer matter either," Charlie insisted loyally. "He never made the girl an offer. Thus he can't be accused of breaking troth."

Lady Sarah raised one icy eyebrow. "Are you, the rakish and disreputable Lord Lucas, of all people, advising *me* on questions of ethical behavior?"

Charlie reddened. "No, ma'am, of course not. I wouldn't *dream* of—"

"Then don't interrupt." She looked back at her son. "It is only weasely libertines like Charlie here who fall back on the letter of the law to defend their misbehavior. A true gentleman understands that the *spirit* of the law is what counts. Everyone in London was expecting you to offer for the girl. When you didn't, you broke your troth in spirit if not in word. And that, to me, is the act of a cad."

Jeremy stared at his mother for a moment, his emotions in turmoil. He'd always thought of himself as a decent sort of fellow, until his rejection of Cicely stirred up doubts in his mind about his own rectitude. During these past two days, however, readily accepting the lighthearted excuses of his conduct offered by his libertinish friend, he'd allowed himself the luxury of self-justification. His confidence in himself as a man of basic decency had been restored. Now his mother's accusation dealt that confidence a hard blow.

His first reaction was to defend himself. "See here, Mama," he said, getting to his feet and glaring down at her, "if Cicely were a chit of my own choosing, of whom you disapproved, you would have been *happy* to have me abide by the letter rather than the spirit of the law. If you didn't like her, you'd have *encouraged* me not to offer for her, wouldn't you?"

"Perhaps I would, but the question is not to the point, since there's nothing about Cicely Beringer that I don't li—" Suddenly her eyes darkened, and she looked up at her son with a troubled frown. "What did you mean 'of my own choosing'? Are you implying that I *chose* Cicely for you?"

"Didn't you?"

Her face tightened in offense. "I introduced you, just as I've introduced you to dozens of young women in the past. I never demanded that you court any of them. Much good it would have done me if I had! It was always understood between us that whatever happened after the introduction was to be entirely up to you. In Cicely's case, I had the distinct impression that you were quite attracted to her."

Jeremy dropped his eyes guiltily. "Yes, I was," he admitted.

"Then, my dear, I can't say I understand you." Her tone became somewhat gentler, and her eyes showed deep concern. "Is it that we misjudged the girl? That one's first impression of her is false? Did she become tempestuous, or spoilt, or smug, or missish, or in some other way disappointing?"

"No," Jeremy said.

Charlie snorted. "I should say not. He described her to me just two days ago as being good-hearted, generous, sweet and—to quote his exact words—'quite the prettiest little thing in all of society.' I was so impressed I was ready to wed the chit myself."

"Be still, you clunch," Jeremy muttered. "You aren't helping."

"Then what was it?" his mother asked in confusion. "If she still has all those lovely qualities, why did you turn tail? After turning the girl's head with your attention and courting her for weeks right before everyone's eyes, why on earth did you run off without offering for her?"

Jeremy ran his hand through his dark, tousled hair. "I don't know, Mama. I can't explain it even to myself." He sat down again and faced her squarely. "It was the strangest feeling. I was on the point of asking. Word of honor. We were sitting in my carriage, and she was looking lovely and behaving with all her usual charm. And then, quite abruptly, I was struck with this . . . this *revulsion*! And I knew, with a horrifying certainty, that I didn't want to wed her after all."

"That *is* strange." Lady Inglesby studied her son intently for a moment before proceeding. "However, Jemmy, I think I can explain it. My dear, you are thirty-eight years old, and in all these years you've never come to the point with a single female. I think the revulsion you experienced is not toward Cicely but toward marriage itself."

"I don't think so," Jeremy said thoughtfully. "But even if you're right, I don't know what I'm expected to do about it."

"What you're expected to do is to force yourself to overcome the revulsion. Marry her! Once you take the plunge, it will be fine."

"Take the plunge?" Jeremy smiled ruefully. "Like diving into icy water?"

"Exactly like that. Once you've gotten over the initial shock, marriage will be quite invigorating."

"If you don't drown," Charlie muttered sotto voce.

"You're wasting your breath, Charlie Percy," her ladyship said dismissively as she rose from her chair. "Jeremy Tate is not the sort to heed the advice of a libertine. My son has always been, and will continue to be, a man of honor." That was what she'd come to say, and having said it, she glided serenely toward the door.

"And what should a man of honor do," her son asked glumly, "if he's already offended the girl in question?"

Lady Sarah paused in the doorway. "A man of honor should beg forgiveness of the scorned lady and pay his addresses again, however belatedly. Cicely's mother has taken her off to the country to recuperate from the blow. But Crestwoods, the Beringer estate, is not far from here, I understand. A note to the mother, requesting permission to renew the suit, would not be amiss. Good-bye, dear boy. I shall be awaiting further news."

She was gone. Jeremy sank down on his chair with a groan and dropped his head in his hands.

Charlie eyed him from under knit brows. "I say, old man, you're not really going to do it, are you?"

"Do it? Renew my suit?" Jeremy looked up at him, his expression gloomy with resignation. "I'm afraid I will. I don't think I'm suited to caddishness, do you?"

Charlie shrugged. "Very well, dive into the matrimonial waters. Be a man of honor if you must. But I sincerely hope you're a good swimmer."

Chapter
~ 5 ~

At Crestwoods, Cassie stood at the library window, staring out through rivulets of raindrops at the sodden garden path where Cicely was walking. The girl had insisted, for the third day in a row, on walking in the rain. Though Cassie had tried by every means she could think of—from cajolery to outright threats of confinement to her room—to keep her daughter safe and dry at home, Cicely had ignored her. Cassie had even offered to go walking with her, but Cicely wanted to be alone.

Cicely made a pathetic appearance out there in the garden, with her shoulders hunched against the rain, her head lowered, her galoe-shoes sloshing indifferently through the puddles on the paving stones and her devoted abigail, Dora, trotting closely behind her holding an umbrella over her head. But Cassie, watching her, felt a touch of irritation seeping into her feelings of motherly sympathy. She was beginning to suspect that Cicely's heart was not broken. Cicely's frequent sighs, her sad gazings into the fire, her melodramatic walks in the rain were closer to playacting than to sincere melancholy.

It was not that Cassie didn't believe her daughter was suffering some real pain. Cicely's pride had been hurt, there was no question of that. And it was indeed painful for the girl to know that she was probably the topic of disparaging gossip back in London. But Cassie had observed her beloved daughter closely these past few days, and it seemed to her that the girl was more humiliated than lovelorn. Cicely did not indicate that she felt any emptiness brought about by the absence of her "beloved"; she did not speak of missing the sight of his face or the sound of his voice; she did not dwell on the joy he'd given her that was now gone, or the tingle she would no longer feel at the touch of his hand. Instead she talked a great deal about how her friend Constance was probably taking pleasure in her defeat, how the ladies in her aunt's circle would all be asking Aunt Eva embarrassing questions, how she would never be able to enter Almack's again without dying of shame. Cicely was centered on herself rather than on her loved one, and that fact convinced Cassie that, despite Cicely's tendency to drench herself in melancholy, the girl's pride was more bruised than her heart.

As she stood at the window watching the girl, she realized there was little that she, as a mother, could do for Cicely in this matter. Her daughter had to learn for herself to over-come the effects of the blow that her first encounter with a suitor had dealt her. A mother could only stand by and offer comfort.

With a helpless sigh, she turned from the window to her easel. She would try to occupy her mind with her painting. She flipped back the long heavy braid that had fallen over her shoulder, buttoned up her smock and picked up her palette and a brush. But she discovered, to her dismay, that she was unable to concentrate. She found her mind distracted with thoughts of Lord Inglesby. What sort of fellow was he? she wondered. How could a man of his maturity desire an eighteen-year-old innocent as a lifetime companion? Of course, she realized, any man, of whatever age, might easily find Cicely irresist-ible. Cassie could forgive a man for that. After all, Cicely was very lovely, and brimming with a youthful zest that was utterly charming. But then, if he saw all that in her, why did he renege at the last moment? Had he decided, after all, that the age difference was too great?

But it was not a question to dwell on, she told herself, for she would never learn the answer. She might better spend her time working on the lemons on the canvas in front of her. The still life was beginning to take shape, but the lemons did not please her. Perhaps they should be a little plumper, she thought, beginning to dab away at them. She wanted to be able to *taste* their sour juiciness with her eyes.

She didn't realize how hard she was concentrating until she was startled by the sound of footsteps in the doorway. She looked up to find Eva pushing a bedraggled Cicely before her. "Really, Cassie," the older sister declared, "how *can* you have permitted this poor child to wander about outside in this weather?"

"Ah, Eva! So you've come," Cassie said in greeting, dropping her brush and holding out her arms. "I knew you wouldn't stay away for long."

"Never mind that," her sister snapped. "I asked a question. What sort of mother are you?"

"The sort of mother whose daughter never listens to a word she says," Cassie replied, taking no offense. "How did you persuade her to come inside?"

"I simply ordered her to," Eva said disdainfully.

"Well, you must give me lessons on how to give orders. Meanwhile, can you convince this obstinate girl to go upstairs and get into bed?"

"Oh, Mama, please," Cicely objected wanly. "I'm really quite all right."

"Please, miss," begged her rain-drenched abigail, who'd followed them in. " 'Tis dreadful wet y'are!"

"Listen to Dora if not to me, my love," Cassie said patiently. "We cannot permit you to stand about in those damp clothes."

The two sisters took Cicely's arms and dragged her with gentle firmness up the stairs. With Dora's assistance they undressed her, rubbed her hair almost dry with a heavy towel, put her in a newly pressed nightdress and tucked her into bed. "And you're to nap until dinnertime," Eva ordered as she ushered everyone out of the room.

Out in the corridor, Dora carefully piled Cicely's wet clothes over her arm. "I'll 'ave these dried an' pressed by dinnertime, ma'am," she told her mistress.

"Thank you, Dora," Cassie said, "but be sure to change out of your own wet things before you do anything else. And take time for a good hot cup of tea. You deserve it."

"Yes, m'lady." The abigail bobbed and started toward the back stairs, but stopped and turned. "Oh, Lady Schofield, I was forgettin'. Clemson said to tell ye your portmanteau's been brought up to your room."

Eva nodded and waved her off. As soon as the girl was gone, she wheeled on her sister. "It seems to me, Cassandra Beringer, that you are not sufficiently concerned with your daughter's state of mind," she scolded. "You don't seem to recognize the fact that she's had her heart broken."

"I think her heart is sufficiently resilient to mend," Cassie said dryly. "But, Eva, my love, I don't think we should encourage her to brood. You shouldn't fuss over her."

"But of *course* I should fuss over her. She's had a dreadful blow."

"Yes, I know. But perhaps it isn't as great as you think."

Eva glowered at her. "Are you suggesting that she is not suffering?"

"If her pain were really great," Cassie said thoughtfully, "she'd struggle to rid herself of it, wouldn't she? Instead, she seems to be wallowing in it. I don't think we should encourage wallowing."

Eva rolled her eyes heavenward in utter disgust. "Sometimes, Cassie, I think you haven't a heart in your breast." And she strode off down the hall to her room.

Cassie went slowly down the stairs, wondering if the worrisome turmoil in her heart—the heart that her sister said she didn't have—would ease enough to permit her to resume her work. But she was not to find out, for as she turned from the landing to the lowest flight of stairs, she saw Clemson, her butler, on his way up. "There's a man at the door, ma'am," he said, holding out a folded sheet bearing a gold seal. "He brought this note."

"For *me*?" It had been years since anyone had sent her such a missive. Right there on the stairway, she took the note from the butler's hand, her brows arched in surprise.

"The man says he was told to wait for an answer," Clemson said, watching her curiously as she broke the seal.

Inside were a few brief lines written in a neat masculine hand. Her eyes flew over the page. *7 April 1817: My Dear Lady Beringer,* she read, *I deeply regret not having taken advantage, last week in London, of the opportunity to make your acquaintance, as I was invited to do. I have no excuse for my peculiar and thoughtless behavior on that night. However, I hope you will believe that my regret is most sincere. If you and Cicely can find it in your hearts to accept this belated apology and forgive me, I would be very grateful. I would be more grateful still if you would permit me to call on you at your convenience, so that I may try to win your permission to speak to your daughter on the subject of marriage. Yours most humbly, Jeremy Tate, Viscount Inglesby.*

Cassie stared in confusion at the paper in her hand. What did this mean? Did Lord Inglesby expect to be permitted to resume his suit? What effrontery! Did the man think that he could casually blight her daughter's hopes one day and then crook his finger to beckon her back on the next? If so, he had better think again! "Bring the messenger to me, Clemson," she ordered, her eyes fixed on the insulting missive in her hand. "I'll give his lordship an answer he won't soon forget."

In a moment a stocky, half-bald, broad-shouldered fellow wearing a caped coachman's coat stood before her at the bottom of the staircase, his tall hat tucked under his arm. She was surprised at his appearance. She'd expected a footman in full livery. Lord Inglesby was a nobleman, wasn't he? And reputedly quite rich. He could afford a properly uniformed staff. For a moment she felt offended by the informality of the messenger's dress, but then she realized that if the fellow *had* been in full regalia, she would have found it pretentious. With her usual honesty, she admitted to herself that *anything* Lord Inglesby did would not find favor in her eyes. She looked the fellow over coolly. "You are Lord Inglesby's coachman, are you?" she asked.

"Yes, ma'am," the fellow said, grinning up at her. "An' his butler an' valet, too. Hickham's the name."

Well, she had to admit to herself, *that doesn't sound very pretentious, I'll grant his lordship that.* But she would not grant him anything else. "So, Hickham, Viscount Inglesby wants an answer, does he? Then I shall give you an answer. I want you, please, to memorize it and repeat it to him just as I tell you. Verbatim. Do you understand me?"

"Yes, m'lady. I knows what verbatim means. Word fer word."

"Right. Good for you. Now, then, listen carefully. You are to tell Lord Inglesby that we do *not* forgive him, that he is not welcome here, and that he is not to communicate with my daughter or me *ever again*. Not ever! Do I make myself clear?"

"Yes, ma'am, clear as glass." His grin died, and he eyed her warily, knowing that this response would not sit well with his lordship. "Ye wish me to tell 'im he ain't to call 'ere, an' he's not to send any more notes."

"Yes, but I said verbatim."

Hickham shrugged. "Verbatim, then, ye don't forgive, 'im, he ain't welcome here, an' he's not t' com-mun-i-cate wi' you nor yer daughter forever after."

"Cassie!" came a shocked cry from behind her. Eva, her face reddening in horror, came running down the stairs. "Is that the messenger from *Inglesby*? What are you *saying* to him?"

"Eva, my dear," Cassie said with restrained annoyance, "I don't think this is your concern."

"But it is *indeed* my concern!" She brushed by her sister and went down the rest of the stairs. "Listen to me, fellow. You are not to tell his lordship anything of the sort!"

"*Eva!*" Cassie cried in shocked fury.

Eva looked up at her sister over her shoulder. "I'm sorry, but I must countermand you, or you'll spoil everything!"

Cassie came down the few steps that separated them. "Must I remind you," she said in a furious undervoice, "that this is *my* message, *my* house and *my* daughter?"

"But, Cassie, dearest—!"

"Hush!" Cassie hissed. "How can we quarrel this way in front of—?"

Eva, turning her eyes from a fascinated Hickham to the goggle-eyed Clemson, flushed an even deeper red. "Yes, you're right, of course," she said, shamefaced. "But at least let's discuss this in private before you do anything more."

Cassie, despite her anger, could not bear to continue to argue in front of Lord Inglesby's man, to say nothing of her own. "Very well, Hickham," she said, trying her best to keep her voice steady, "do not deliver that message after all. Tell his lordship that I shall send him an answer shortly."

"Yes, m'lady," he said, his face impassive.

Cassie threw Eva a fulminating glance, went down the two remaining steps and started across the hall. "Mr. Hickham," she said to the coachman as she passed, "please stop in the kitchen for refreshments before you start your journey back. Clemson will show you the way. Good day to you."

With her chin high, she strode down the hall to the sitting room, her sister scurrying after her. As soon as they crossed the threshold, Eva closed the door and put her back against it. "I know my behavior was dreadful," she said, facing her sister with a desperate determination, "but—"

Cassie wheeled on her. "But me no buts! Your behavior was worse than dreadful. It was inexcusable! How *dared* you interfere with my affairs in that high-handed way?"

"I'm sorry. But I couldn't let you ruin all our plans."

"What do you mean? What plans?"

"Lady Sarah Inglesby's and mine."

Cassie stared at her, not comprehending. "Lady Sarah's—? Are you speaking of his lordship's *mother*? What has she to do with this?"

"A great deal. Perhaps you should sit down while I explain."

Cassie put a trembling hand to her forehead. "Yes, perhaps I should." She thrust Lord Inglesby's note, which was still clutched in her hand, into a pocket of her smock, dropped into an easy chair and leaned forward. "Well, go on."

"I wrote to her, you see," Eva explained, pacing. "The very night that Jeremy failed to come up to scratch. She came to see me the next day. She told me that her Jeremy had always avoided wedlock but that his attitude changed when she put Cicely in his way. She is convinced, as I am, that the fellow truly cares for our Cicely. He's just a bit marriage-shy. That's why she promised to go to see him at Inglesby Park and give him a proper dressing down. She must have done it! That message was the result."

"Just a moment." Cassie held up a hand to keep her sister from saying anything more. "Let me understand you. Are you saying that Inglesby's *mother* pushed him into pursuing 'our'

Cicely in the first place? And that now she has somehow convinced him to renew his suit?"

From the tone of horror in Cassie's voice, Eva knew she had not improved matters. "Well . . . yes," she admitted hesitantly.

Cassie rose slowly from her chair, her expression a thundercloud. "And do you imagine that I am *impressed* by this? That this recital of maneuvering and subterfuge will convince me to surrender my daughter to this man? Well, my dear sister, you have gone too far. Cicely, I beg to remind you, is not 'our' daughter, she is *mine*. And I will never hand her over to a man who not only is twenty years her senior, has a vacillating mind and is reluctant to marry, but who, at the advanced age of thirty-eight, is such a baby that he is *still under the thumb of his mama*!"

"But Cassie," objected Eva, outraged, "you are distorting everything! He isn't *at all* as you describe him. In the first place—"

"Never mind the first place, or any other place," Cassie said firmly, striding to the door. "I've heard all I care to. I shall send a note to his lordship saying exactly what you overheard me telling his man."

Eva stalked after her. "Cicely is indeed your daughter, but you are ruining her life, and I will not allow you to do it!"

Cassie paused with her hand on the doorknob and turned. "Eva," she said quietly, "you are my only sister, and I love you, but if you persist in opposing me in this matter, I shall have to ask you to leave this house."

"I intend to," Eva retorted bitterly. "First thing tomorrow. And on my way back to town, I shall stop at Inglesby Park and pay a call on his lordship. I shall advise him not to seek your permission but to take matters into his own hands and elope."

Cassie shrugged. "Do as you must. But my daughter will never be so foolish as to agree to an elopement."

"We shall see," Eva muttered as she marched off to her room.

Cassie watched her go, her brow knit. She hated quarreling. Any quarrel left her physically and mentally shaken, but exchanging bad words with her loved ones was devastating to her. All her instincts seemed to be begging her to follow Eva and make peace.

But she couldn't. She had an obligation to protect her daughter. Eva, who'd had a good marriage, couldn't know how dreadful life could be with the wrong husband. And there was nothing about Jeremy Tate and this courtship that sounded right.

She went slowly toward the stairs, her mind whirling. *What if Eva made good her threat?* she asked herself. *What if the fellow did indeed try to entice Cicely into an elopement?* Cassie had loudly declared that Cicely would never agree to it, but in her heart she wasn't at all sure. Her daughter was young, with a propensity for melodrama . . . and what was more melodramatic than an elopement?

She stopped stock-still on the stairs, a plan forming in her mind. *Yes, why not?* she asked herself. She could go to see him herself, right now, and ensure that the fellow never came into their lives again. "Clemson," she called, turning about and running down the stairs, "run to the stable and tell Boyle to ready the carriage. I want him to take me to Inglesby Park. At once!"

Chapter
~ 6 ~

Jeremy had asked Mrs. Stemple, his housekeeper-cook, to prepare a simple country dinner, which he and his guest would take informally in the morning room. Since he and Lord Lucas expected no other guests, he told her, they would not use the enormous formal dining room as they'd been doing the last few nights. "We won't even bother to dress," he explained. "So you see, Mrs. Stemple, there's no need for you to fuss. Mutton and potatoes will do."

"Mutton and potatoes indeed!" grunted Mrs. Stemple to herself as she stalked off. "Ye'll 'ave a proper meal, no matter where ye choose to eat it!"

The outcome of this discussion was that Mrs. Stemple outdid herself. When the two men sat down in their shirtsleeves at the modest morning-room table, glum and dispirited by the continuing downpour, they were presented with a meal so delectable it would have lifted the spirits even of a man about to be hanged. Thus it was that Jeremy and his friend found themselves considerably cheered. One could not feel blue-deviled when devouring succulent glazed lamb cutlets, tiny carrots "*à la hamonde*," cabbage flowers sprinkled with parmesan, and the half-dozen other dishes Mrs. Stemple had put before them. "There's nothing so delicious as a simple meal prepared by a genius cook," Jeremy remarked as he eyed the praline cake and the apple pudding with cream that were still to come. "A meal like this makes me almost forget my troubled anticipation of being leg-shackled."

"Mmmm," murmured Charlie, helping himself to a fourth cutlet, "I *have* heard it said that a condemned man will eat a hearty meal."

"It's not that I feel condemned, exactly," Jeremy said in guilty denial. "Cicely will undoubtedly make a delightful wife."

"Not if 'er mama has anythin' t'say to it," came a new voice.

Jeremy looked round to find his man standing in the doorway. "Hickham!" he exclaimed, surprised but not annoyed by this abrupt interruption of his dinner. "Back already?"

"Yes, m'lord, but the news ain't goin' t'be to yer likin'."

Charlie, who did not permit his own man such familiarity, frowned at the fellow in disapproval. "Took it upon yourself to read the lady's answer, did you?" he asked with heavy sarcasm.

"She didn't send no answer," Hickham said in quick self-defense. "She was goin' to, but Lady Schofield didn't let 'er."

"If there's no answer, why did you say I'll not like it?" Jeremy inquired, puzzled.

"Because before Lady Schofield stopped 'er, Lady Beringer *did* gi' me a message fer ye. She made me repeat it verbatim."

"Well, speak up, man. What was it?"

"I don' know if I should say," the valet-butler-coachman taunted, fully enjoying the rapt attention of the two listeners.

"And why shouldn't you say?" Charlie demanded.

"Because after Lady Beringer gi' me the message, she an' 'er sister 'ad angry words. Then she changed 'er mind an' said she'll send an answer later. So p'rhaps ye should wait fer that."

"And perhaps," Jeremy retorted, rising from his chair, "you'd like to be replaced by someone with proper manners."

"Yes, fellow, you *are* a nuisance. Speak up!" Charlie prodded. "What did her ladyship say?"

"Give it to us verbatim," Jeremy added dryly.

Hickham stepped over the threshold and drew himself up importantly. "She said she will not forgive ye, you are not welcome at her house, an' you are not to com-mun-i-cate with her or her daughter ever again," he announced with loud precision.

The words seemed to echo round the room. Jeremy stared at Hickham in speechless astonishment. There was a moment of silence while the information sank in, and then Charlie laughed. "Well, Jemmy, old fellow, that sounds to me very like a reprieve."

"A reprieve?"

"You've been rejected, refused, repulsed. You're free!"

Jeremy blinked. "Yes, I suppose I am," he said, a smile slowly lighting his face.

"Even your mother would not expect you to persist in your suit with that kind of opposition," his friend chortled.

"Yes, it does seem that I'm unhooked after all." Jeremy wiped his brow with the back of his hand in a gesture that indicated plainly his unmistakable relief.

"Unless Lady Schofield convinces 'er sister t'change 'er mind," Hickham warned.

Jeremy's smile faded. "Confound it, that's right!" He eyed his man with one eyebrow raised, half in amusement and half in chagrin. "Thank you so much, Hickham, for reminding me. But now that you've had your say, I suggest you take yourself off."

Hickham, realizing he'd pushed informality too far, promptly removed himself from the room.

Charlie studied his friend's disappointed face. "Do you think Lady Beringer'll change her mind?" he asked sympathetically.

Jeremy shrugged. "I've no idea. I never met the woman. But I do know Lady Schofield, and *she* is nothing if not persuasive. I'm afraid our celebration of my freedom will be short-lived."

"In that case, old fellow, sit down and let us enjoy the time remaining to us. Have another helping of the lamb."

Jeremy tried, but he found that his appetite had deserted him. "Dash it all, I can't even enjoy the apple pudding," he muttered.

"But you must take a piece of this praline cake," Charlie said, licking his lips. "It's the most unbelievable—"

But before he could finish, his eyes were drawn to the doorway, where Hickham seemed miraculously to have reappeared. "M'lord," hissed Hickham, "there's—"

"I thought I told you to go," Jeremy said, annoyed.

"Yes, m'lord, but her *ladyship's* come!"

"What? *Who*—?" Jeremy winced in despair. "Not my *mother* again!"

"No, m'lord. It's *her*! Lady *Beringer*!"

"Good Lord! *No!*"

"I ain't foolin'! It's her, in the flesh!"

Jeremy dropped his head in his hands. "Tell her I'm not here. Say I've gone away. Far away! *Abroad!* Tell her I've . . . died!"

"Don't be a clunch," Charlie said. "You may as well face her. You'll have to find out sooner or later what future she has in store for you."

"Yes, I suppose I must. Take her to the library, Hickham. Tell her I'll attend her there in a moment."

Hickham withdrew, and Jeremy rose reluctantly from the table. Charlie looked up at him with heartfelt sympathy. "You'd better put on a coat, old man. You don't want to greet the lady in your shirtsleeves."

"Right. I'll dash upstairs and make myself presentable. Meanwhile, you may as well stay here and finish your dinner. Wish me luck with her."

Charlie watched him go, shaking his head in concern. It didn't look well for poor Jemmy, he thought. If the lady didn't want him to pursue her daughter, she would have sent word for him to stay away. Her presence on these premises boded ill for Jeremy's future.

With a sigh, he reached for the apple pudding. He was reaching for the cream when the door opened and a woman burst in. She was wearing a rain-spattered cloak with the hood raised, so Charlie could glimpse only the lower part of a shadowed face. He could see a softly rounded chin, lips that were pressed together tensely, and—most peculiar!—a smear of yellow paint on her left cheek. "I will not be kept waiting in the library while you finish your dinner!" she said coldly. "I told your man that I require only the briefest of interviews."

"Yes, ma'am." Charlie got awkwardly to his feet, preparing to correct her mistaken identification. "But, you see, *I* am not—"

"But me no buts, my lord," she snapped. "I have only a few words to say to you, and they are these: that Cicely and I do not forgive you, that you are not welcome in my home, and that—"

"And that you will accept no further communication," Charlie finished for her. "We've already heard that."

"Have you indeed? Hickham, I take it, has confided what he was specifically asked not to reveal. I might have expected it."

"Well, you see, ma'am—"

"You needn't apologize, Lord Inglesby. I'm glad your man told you. It makes my purpose easier to accomplish."

"Your purpose?"

"Yes, to counteract any suggestion from my sister or your mother to the effect that my daughter would consider any sort of reconciliation."

"But, ma'am, if you'll be good enough to let me explain—" Charlie said, stepping forward and holding out a hand in his second attempt to identify himself.

Lady Beringer took a step backward, repulsed by what she thought was an attempt to take her hand. "You needn't explain anything to me, Lord Inglesby. I don't hold you responsible for the machinations of your mother and my sister in their attempt to encourage you to renew your pursuit of my daughter. But I do blame you for pursuing her in the first place. A man of your years should have known better than to try to attach a girl half your age."

Charlie, who had spent the past decade pursuing women far younger than himself, became instantly resentful, not only for his friend but for himself. "Attachment between the sexes, madam," he declared frostily, "is not a game of numbers. One does not ask for birthdates when one falls in love."

"I did not come here to debate ideas of love with you, my lord," she retorted, "though I quite expected that sort of defense from you. In fact"—she paused for a moment to observe him, her head slightly tilted—"you even *look* as I expected."

"Do I?" Charlie couldn't help asking the question, his curiosity being stronger than his sense of duty—duty to inform her of his true identity. "In what way do I look as you expected?"

"In your air of . . . of self-indulgence," she said.

He could feel her eyes peering at him critically. "Self-indulgence?" he echoed, offended.

"Yes, I think that an apt word. I grant you have a face and form that may appear attractive to young innocents, but the more mature eye sees deeper."

"Self-indulgence, eh?" Charlie looked down at his slightly protruding stomach ruefully. "I suppose one could describe me that way. I do overindulge in food and drink."

"And who knows what else," Lady Beringer muttered in an undervoice. "But I did not come here to discuss your appearance or your character. I only wish to warn you not to believe my sister when she comes here to urge you to arrange an elopement. My daughter will never elope. Do you understand me, my lord? You will *never* run off with her, not while there's a breath left in my body!"

"That's all very well," Charlie said, "but I think you should know that—" Here he paused, for it suddenly occurred to him that there was no good reason to inform the lady of his true identity. She was ordering the breaking off of all ties between her household and Jeremy's. Therefore, leaving matters just the way they now were was the best solution.

"What is it I should know?" she was asking.

"Nothing, ma'am." He grinned mischievously. "Nothing at all."

She looked at him suspiciously, but then gave an indifferent shrug. "Then I shall bid you good night." And with that, she swung round to go.

Her turn had been abrupt, and it caused her hood to fall back, revealing a head of long, fair hair that had been carelessly plaited in one thick braid. It flipped against her back as she marched firmly toward the door. At that moment, however, the door flew open and she came face-to-face with Jeremy.

He'd just looked up from the coat he'd been buttoning, and the sight and proximity of the woman startled him. "Oh!" he gasped, staring. The woman before him took his breath away. She had a delicately featured oval face, a rounded chin, a full mouth and a pair of magnificently dark eyes that stood out in the pale luminosity of her skin and hair. Something about that face made his chest clench.

Lady Beringer, too, was startled. The man standing before her, taller and leaner than his friend, was remarkably good-looking despite a too-large nose and a strong chin. But what was most startling to her was the expression in his face; the man had a gentleness about the mouth . . . and the kindest eyes. He seemed a strange sort of friend for the dissipated Lord Inglesby to have. On the other hand, the fellow was peering at her in a most disconcerting way that she could not like. "You are staring at me, sir," she said haughtily.

"Yes," Jeremy said, a slight smile lighting his eyes. "It's your cheek. There's a smudge of yellow paint on it."

"Oh!" Her hand flew to her cheek, which was already reddening in embarrassment. "I left my home hastily, you see. I was . . . painting lemons."

"Painting lemons?" Jeremy asked, enchanted.

"A still life," she murmured, her blush deepening. "But never mind. It's not important."

Charlie, sending indecipherable hand signals to Jeremy from behind her back, spoke up at this moment. "Lady Beringer, I'd like you to meet my friend, *Charles Percy, Lord Lucas!*"

Jeremy threw his friend a perplexed look, but his mind was too preoccupied with the woman in front of him to take notice of the misnomer. "Good God!" he exclaimed in astonished realization of who she was. "You cannot be Cicely's *mother!*"

"Yes, that's exactly who I am, as your friend Lord Inglesby can tell you."

Jeremy blinked down at her in utter confusion. "My friend Lord *Inglesby?*"

Charlie hurried round to him. "Yes, *Charlie,* old man," he said, pressing his friend's shoulder warningly. "I, *your friend Lord Inglesby,* am also surprised at Lady Beringer's youthful appearance."

"Nevertheless, gentlemen," Lady Beringer said, lifting her hood and going to the door, "since I've delivered my message, I shall bid you both good evening." And before Jeremy could think of a way to delay her, she was gone.

He stared at the door through which she'd disappeared. "What on earth did I miss?" he mumbled in confusion.

"Don't fret, old fellow," Charlie said, laughing. "Everything's gone very well. She and her daughter want nothing to do with you. You really *are* free."

"Oh, I see. She came only to tell me that, did she? But why did she call you Inglesby?"

"She stormed in here in a taking, mistook me for you, and before I could disabuse her, she informed me in unequivocal terms that she would not countenance a renewal of 'my' suit. In fact, she said quite firmly that a man of my years should have had better sense than to pursue a girl half my age."

"She did, did she?" Jeremy rubbed his chin ruefully. "But why did you feel it necessary to introduce me as you?"

"Once she became fixed in her error, I didn't want to spoil anything. What she'd said made it clear that she was freeing you of your entanglement, so what good would it have done to correct her misapprehension about our identities? She'd only have been embarrassed."

"Nevertheless, Charlie, I don't like lies. I'd have preferred to deal with her myself."

Charlie shrugged. "Well, it's too late now. Everything's settled, and all for the best, if you ask me. So let us forget all about the interruption and sit down to finish this delectable pudding."

Jeremy, suppressing an uncomfortable feeling—an emotion not unlike the discomfort one feels at suspecting one's been cheated at cards but can't prove it—sighed helplessly and sat down opposite his friend. "I wish . . ." he mumbled.

"What?" Charlie asked, reaching for the cream.

"I wish she'd stayed a bit longer."

"Good God, why?"

"I don't know, exactly," Jeremy said softly. "Except that . . . well, did you notice her hair?"

"That unkempt braid? What about it?"

"I thought it quite charming. Don't you find it fascinating to see a woman pay a call with her hair undressed and her cheek smudged with paint?"

Charlie eyed his friend with disgust. "I don't find it at all fascinating. I find it eccentric."

Jeremy gazed at the door where he'd last glimpsed the woman, his lips curved in a reminiscent smile. "Eccentric, perhaps, but also very lovely, in an unaffected way."

"*Lovely?* She's Cicely's *mother,* for heaven's sake!"

"Yes, I'm aware of that." He peered at his friend with a pitying look, but after a moment he shook his head. "Never mind. There's no point in my trying to make you see what I saw. As you said, it's too late now."

Chapter
~ 7 ~

Hickham, who was finding his master's attempt to escape matrimony vastly entertaining, had been hanging about in the corridor to eavesdrop on what passed in the morning room. From time to time, when the voices fell, he actually put his ear to the door. Thus, when Lady Beringer threw the door open and emerged, he had to jump back out of the way. "I . . . er . . . beg pardon, ma'am," he mumbled guiltily.

But her ladyship seemed not to notice him as she swept by on her way to the front door. After taking a moment to regain his composure, Hickham shook himself into action and hurried after her down the corridor. Lady Beringer, hearing his footsteps, glanced back over her shoulder. "Don't bother to see me out, Hickham," she said. "I can find my way." And before he could object, she pushed open the front door and stepped out over the threshold.

"Wait, m'lady," Hickham begged. "Le' me get an umbrella an' see ye to yer carriage."

But the lady didn't seem to hear. She stepped out onto the stone landing, lifted her face to the sky and let the rain fall on her face, as if she were a farmer giving thanks to the heavens for saving the crops. Hickham thought the gesture peculiar. He could not guess the meaning of it.

For Cassie, however, it was a gesture of triumph. *I've done it,* she said to herself proudly. *I've succeeded in accomplishing exactly what I set out to do! I acted decisively, and all on my own!*

It was not something she'd done often before in her life. She'd too frequently let others make her decisions for her. But not today! With a sigh of satisfaction, she shut her eyes and let the rain cool her heated cheeks. What difference did a few drops of rain make when she'd taken the matter of Cicely's future into her own hands and protected the girl from a lifetime of unhappiness? There was nothing, she thought with an inner smile, that Eva or the unknown Lady Sarah could do about it now. She'd told the dissipated-looking Lord Inglesby exactly where he stood. She'd handled the scene very well. All in all, she was very pleased with herself.

But Hickman, eyeing her askance, was not pleased with *himself*. He could not be a very good butler, he told himself, if he let a visitor become drenched with rain. "Please, ma'am," he begged, pulling an umbrella from an ornate china stand near the door, "wait for on'y a moment!" And he rushed out and held the umbrella over her. "I'll see ye to yer carriage, shall I, ma'am?"

"No, thank you, Hickham," she said, rejecting his offer with a kindly smile. "See there? My man is coming." And indeed her coachman, a wizened little fellow who'd been sitting stolidly on the box under an umbrella waiting for her, was at that moment leaping down to offer her his escort.

Nevertheless, Hickham followed her across the landing, holding his umbrella over her head. "Ye'll be soaked t' the skin by the time yer man climbs all eight steps," he declared.

But the lady turned to him and waved him off. "Go back inside, fellow," she ordered. "I have my cloak, but you are not dressed for this weather."

Hickham opened his mouth to object, but his words never left his tongue, for at that moment the accident occurred.

Whether it was the awkward turn the lady made when she set her foot on the top step of the granite stairway or whether she did not look down at where she was going, Hickham was not later able to say. All he knew for certain was that the sole of Lady Beringer's little half-boot skidded on the wet granite. "Watch out!" he wanted to cry out, but the cry, even if he'd been able to make it, would have been too late.

He saw her foot slip from under her. He saw her trip. He saw—in a kind of hideous slow motion, as if time itself had slowed down—the lady's body twist in a fruitless attempt to grasp at some support, but there was none within her reach.

He saw the coachman below—as frozen in time as Hickham himself—look on in horror as his mistress fell with a dreadful thump and went tumbling down the stone staircase, step by cold, wet step, until she lay in a pathetic heap at the bottom, quite unconscious.

When time started to move again, Hickham, his knees shaking with fright, ran down the stairs. Her ladyship's coachman, too, came running toward her. The coachman reached her first and knelt down beside her. "Ma'am?" he queried. "Ma'am?"

There was no movement, no response. She lay prone, one arm outstretched above her head, obscuring her face. The coachman lifted it by the wrist and tried to chafe it. "Ma'am," he whispered, white-lipped, "are ye dead?"

Hickham also knelt down. He took the limp hand from the other fellow, hoping to feel some response to his touch, but it was cold and wet and lifeless. "Please, ma'am," he begged desperately, "can ye jus' say sompin'?"

The coachman blinked at him tearfully. "Shall we try t' lift her up?"

Hickham got to his feet. "Don't move 'er!" he muttered hoarsely. "Jus' keep yer umbrella over 'er." And, heart pounding, he turned and ran back up the stairs. "'*Elp!*" he shouted, throwing open the door. "Me lord, come *quick*! I think 'er ladyship's *killed* 'erself!"

Chapter
~ 8 ~

Cassie emerged from an empty void, pushed into consciousness by a disturbing awareness of a most unpleasant, acrid smell. She tried to turn her head to avoid it, but the movement made her aware of being in great pain. She seemed to be utterly immersed in pain. It emanated from her whole body, from the soles of her feet to the top of her horridly aching head. But above and beyond the pain was this strong, sharp, almost biting smell. She had to get away from it, and with the greatest effort she lifted her hand to push it away, but something resisted the attempt. "Ugh!" she muttered in revulsion.

"She spoke!" said a strange voice.

Slowly she opened her eyes. A hand was holding a vial to her nose. "Take it away," she said, surprised at the weakness and unfamiliarity of her voice.

The hand holding the vial moved away. With a relieved breath, she looked up. She was lying on a bed, she realized, in a room she'd never seen before. Bending over her were several worried faces, none of which she recognized. They belonged to four men and a woman, all of whom were standing round her bed. One other person was present—an elderly, bespectacled gentleman, who was sitting beside her, the vial of evil-smelling liquid in his hand. The bespectacled gentleman smiled and peered into her eyes. "Can you hear me, my lady?" he asked kindly.

"Yes. But my head hurts. Dreadfully. Who are—?"

"I am Dr. Swan. Lord Inglesby sent for me when you fell."

"Fell?"

"Down the stone stairway. Don't you remember?"

"No. What . . . happened?"

A stocky, half-bald fellow leaned forward. "Yer foot slipped on the wet, m'lady, an' down ye went, hittin' all eight steps. I figured ye were done fer."

She shut her eyes in confusion. "Why does everything hurt?" she asked plaintively.

Dr. Swan lifted her right hand, which she now saw was bandaged from just above the fingers to halfway up her arm. "You've suffered many bruises, ma'am, on your legs, back and sides. What's more, your left shoulder's wrenched, we're not certain about your left hip, your right wrist's sprained, you've a blackened eye, and your head's suffered severe concussion."

"Is that all?" she said, managing a feeble smile.

"Ah! A show of wit!" the doctor said, patting her hand. "That's a good sign."

"Yes, but—" She lifted her head with real effort and quickly looked about her before dropping back upon the pillows again. "Where am I?"

"You're here, ma'am, still at Inglesby Park."

This last voice was deep and kind. She looked up at the speaker. He had a handsome face, in spite of a too-pronounced nose. But she had no recollection of ever seeing before. "Inglesby Park?" she asked.

"Yes, my lady," said Dr. Swan, peering at her with his brows suddenly knit. "Don't you remember that you'd called at Inglesby earlier this evening?"

"No. Inglesby Park? I don't . . ." She lifted her free hand to her forehead, ignoring the stab of pain in her shoulder that the movement caused. "What *is* Inglesby Park? *Where* is it?"

"In Dorset, ma'am," said the handsome man, also looking alarmed. "Not fifteen miles from your own home."

Cassie felt a sudden twinge of panic. "My own home?"

"Crestwoods, ma'am," said a wizened little fellow who'd been watching her intently, his lips pursed. "I druv ye here from Crestwoods no more'n six hours ago."

"Drove me here?"

"Yes'm. It's me, Boyle."

She gazed at the man, but had no glimmer of recognition. "Boyle, you say?" She took a deep breath, her panic growing. "Do I . . . know you?"

The man looked as if he'd burst into tears. "I been yer coachman these eighteen years!"

Her panic now became full-blown. "Then why don't I recognize you?" she cried, her eyes wide with terror. "Oh, God! Who *are* you all? And . . . and . . ." She looked from one face to another in a desperate search for an answer to the second and most important part of the question that had suddenly formed in her mind. "And . . . *who am I?*"

Chapter
~ 9 ~

In the dead of night, Boyle rode back to Crestwoods to face the unpleasant task of informing Miss Cicely that her mother had had an accident. He knew that the girl and her aunt, Lady Schofield, would not have gone to sleep while her ladyship was missing. He would undoubtedly find them pacing the floor.

He stabled the horses and wiped them down before making his way to the house. The tall grandfather's clock in the downstairs hallway was just striking three when he entered the house from the back stairs. All seemed quiet, and for a moment he thought that everyone had gone to bed. But then he saw a light emanating from a doorway down the hall. They were awake—waiting for Lady Beringer in the drawing room.

He started down the hall toward the light, but he'd not advanced half a dozen steps when Cicely heard the clop of his boots and came running toward him, her aunt at her heels. Both ladies were clad in robes that had been thrown over their nightclothes. "Where on earth have you been?" the girl demanded, anger at having been made to suffer many hours of dreadful suspense overcoming her initial sense of relief.

"Didn't Clemson tell ye?" the coachman asked, stepping back as if to get out of range.

"Clemson said he was ordered to keep mum," Lady Schofield said in disgust. "But never mind that now. Tell me, Boyle, where is your mistress? She's the one to answer our questions, not you."

Boyle took a deep breath to prepare himself for his task. But before he could bring himself to speak, Miss Cicely stiffened. "Mama hasn't gone up to bed without coming in to see us, has she?" she asked furiously. "She *wouldn't*—!"

51

"No, of course she wouldn't," her aunt declared. "Perhaps she thought we'd retired, so she went to bed herself." She waved Boyle aside and strode to the bottom of the stairway. "Cassie, where are you?" she called up the stairs. "We've been waiting down here for hours! You've a bit of explaining to do. Come down here at once!"

Boyle gave a nervous cough. "She ain't here, m'lady."

"What?" Both women stared at him aghast.

"Not here?" asked Cicely, her anger changing to terror.

"Then where *is* she?" Now it was Eva who was furious.

"Y'see, ma'am . . . there's been an accident," he began, and, turning from one to the other, he told them the details of Lady Beringer's dreadful fall.

The two faces staring at him turned pale. Cicely burst into tears. Lady Schofield sank down on the lowest step, her hands clasped at her breast. "How badly is she hurt?" she inquired quietly after a moment. "The truth now, man! No roundaboutation."

"Lots o' bruises. An' a sprained wrist. An'—" Here he threw a quick, nervous glance over at the weeping Cicely. "An' a . . . a few other things."

Cicely's head came up. "There's something worse! I know it!" she shrieked.

"Cicely, calm yourself!" her aunt ordered. "You will be of no help to your mother if you indulge in hysterics. Now, Boyle, go on. What else?"

"Her head, ma'am. Concussion, the doctor called it."

"Concussion? Isn't that something dreadful?" the girl asked fearfully.

"Hush, my dear," her aunt said. "At least there's been a doctor in attendance. Thank the Lord for that."

Cicely did not feel like thanking the Lord for anything. "I must see her!" she declared, and she flew down the hall to the entryway, where some cloaks were hanging on a rack. "Come, Boyle, take me to her at once!"

"But, Miss Cicely, it's three in the mornin'. Everyone at Inglesby Park'll be sleepin'."

She froze in the act of reaching for her cloak. "Inglesby Park?"

"Yes, miss. That's where she went."

Cicely gaped at him bewilderedly. "But . . . *why?*"

"Never mind that now," Lady Schofield said, rising. "Plenty of time to discuss the whys and wherefores later. Let's go up and get a few hours' sleep."

"I couldn't sleep!" the girl said tearfully. "Why can't we go at once?"

"Because, for one thing, we are not dressed. And for another, as Boyle said, everyone there will be abed, including your mama. The doctor would certainly have given her a sleeping draught. We must let her rest. We shall go to her first thing this morning."

"But it's almost morning already," the girl insisted. "By the time we dress and drive there, the sun will be up."

Lady Schofield, as eager as Cicely to lay eyes on her injured sister, succumbed to the girl's pressure. As soon as she nodded her acquiescence, Cicely gathered up her skirts and flew up the stairs to dress. Her aunt bit her lip as she watched the girl disappear round the turning. "The poor dear," she murmured as she started up after her.

Boyle, standing at the foot of the stairway, watched Lady Schofield's slow assent, frowning guiltily. He knew he had not said all he should. As she approached the landing, Boyle cleared his throat again. "M'lady," he muttered, looking up at her, "per'aps I should tell ye . . ." His voice petered out, and he looked down at his shoes.

Eva felt her heart contract in fear. "Tell me what? For heaven's sake, say it, man!"

"I think I ought t' warn ye. Her ladyship . . . well, when she came to, her mind . . . it was a bit . . . cloudy."

"Cloudy?"

"A' course, it might all be cleared up by the time she wakes," he mumbled, not meeting her eye.

Eva took an impatient step back down toward him. "Whatever do you mean by cloudy?"

"Foggy, like. Not thinkin' too clearly."

"What are you saying, man?" she snapped. "Naturally she wasn't thinking clearly. She'd just suffered a fall. Anyone would be a bit shaken."

Boyle knew she didn't understand. He also knew that he shouldn't let her browbeat him into agreeing with her. He squared his shoulders and looked her in the eye. "When ye see 'er," he said bravely, "she mayn't reco'nize . . . It could be she won't know who on God's earth ye are."

"Not know who we are?" Her ladyship sneered. "Don't be a fool!" With a gesture of dismissal, she turned on her heel and marched up the remaining stairs, muttering in disgust, "Not *know* us? Not know *us*? I've never heard such nonsense in all my life!"

Chapter
~ 10 ~

After the doctor left, Jeremy had sent everyone in the household to bed. He himself, however, had spent the night in the room with the sleeping Lady Beringer. For a long while he'd stood over her, staring at her face by the light of the candle he held. He was fascinated by that face. Although she was not in the first flush of youth (there were, indeed, tiny lines beginning to show at the corners of her eyes), and although her dreadful accident had left a large purple bruise round her left eye and over the cheek that still held a streak of yellow paint on it, he thought her beautiful. There was something about her—a look that combined an exquisite delicacy with a courageous strength—that moved him to the core. She reminded him of a Botticelli painting he'd once come upon that he'd stared at for hours. She had the same ropy gold hair, the same perfection of features, the same quality of ethereal loveliness. Such fragile beauty should not be made to endure the pain and suffering that this visit to his home had inflicted on her.

He continued to stare at her until the candle burned almost to the socket. Then he blew it out and sank into a chair beside her bed, determined to keep vigil.

By morning, however, he'd fallen into an uneasy sleep. Thus, when Cicely burst into the room very near hysterics, followed by her aunt and an apologetic Hickham, he was caught unprepared. "Cicely!" he muttered, blinking himself awake. "Perhaps you should wait outside until Dr. Swan—"

But Cicely caught a glimpse of her sleeping mother's bruised and battered face. *"Oh, my God!"* she cried out in horror.

Cassie heard the cry and stirred. Dr. Swan had dosed her with a strong solution of laudanum to ease her pain and

help her rest. The loud cry of anguish awakened her from
the depths of a drugged sleep. Feeling utterly thick-headed
and bewildered, she opened her eyes to find a strange young
woman bending over her, crying, "Oh, my poor mama! Your
face!"

Cassie, her head throbbing with pain and her mind clouded
in confusion, shrank away from this stranger who was trying to embrace her. "Who . . . are you?" she murmured fearfully.

"Oh, Mama! Surely you recognize me! It's Cicely!" the girl
said, tears filling her eyes.

Lady Schofield, who'd always believed that strength of
character could overcome any impediment, had little patience
for what she saw as mental weakness. "Of course you remember Cicely," she insisted, "even if you *are* a little muddled. Be
firm with yourself!"

Cassie stared at these two new strangers in complete and
terrifying confusion. "I'm sorry," she managed, edging back
against the headboard and holding her comforter up to her neck
as a shield, "but I . . . I have no . . . no recollection of . . ."

Jeremy gave his butler a glare that said without words, *How
could you have let them in without announcing them?*

Hickham responded by merely shrugging helplessly.

Meanwhile, the distraught Cicely bent over the bed and
grasped her mother's shoulders. "But you *must* know me!"
she insisted, trying to shake her mother into remembering.
"I'm your *daughter!*"

"P-please," begged the panic-stricken Cassie, "let me go!"

Jeremy pulled the girl from the bed. "Cicely, my dear,
you're frightening her," he said. "Let your aunt take you
downstairs to the morning room. The doctor should be ar-
riving shortly. After he's explained your mother's condition
and answered your questions, we can all sit down and help
you decide what to do."

During this speech Eva Schofield had been gaping at her
sister wide-eyed. For the first time since she'd had word of
the accident, it occurred to her that something truly dreadful
had happened to Cassie's mind, something that even firmness
of character could not overcome. Her heart clenched in her

breast. "Lord Inglesby is right, Cicely," she said, forcing herself to stay calm. "We must wait and speak to the doctor. Come with me downstairs." And she pulled the weeping Cicely from the room.

Hickham led them down to the morning room, where a breakfast buffet had been set. Charlie Percy was seated at the table, sipping a cup of hot coffee. He got to his feet as they entered. "Good morning, your ladyship. I am Lord Lucas. I met you and Miss Beringer several months ago in London, if you recall."

"Yes, of course we recall," Eva said testily. "Nothing has impaired *my* memory. Or Cicely's either." She dropped down upon one of the chairs and tried to calm herself. "Don't just stand there, girl," she added almost automatically. "Say your how-de-dos to Lord Lucas."

But Cicely was too overwrought to cease her weeping long enough to acknowledge his presence.

Charlie, taking no offense, made a leg to both ladies and helped the weeping girl to a chair. "I take it you've seen our patient," he said with what Eva felt was an unwarrantedly cheerful air.

His innocent remark brought on a fresh flood of tears from the young lady. "Mama looks as though she was *m-m-mauled!*" she wailed.

Charles, though he understood that the first sight of Lady Beringer's bruised face would naturally be a shock to her daughter, nevertheless could not admire such a watering pot. "You mustn't take on so, Miss Beringer," he said, going to the buffet and pouring her a cup of steaming tea. "I know matters seem appalling right now, but your mother will surely recover. Bumps and bruises, no matter how disfiguring and painful at first, do mend remarkably quickly."

"But she d-d-doesn't even re-m-m-member me!" Cicely wept.

"Doesn't she?" He exchanged a disappointed look with Hickham. "We rather hoped she'd recover her memory after a night's sleep."

Eva looked up at him in immediate alarm. "Did the doctor expect her to?" she asked worriedly.

"Dr. Swan thought it quite possible."

Eva covered her mouth to keep from crying out in her distress. Cicely, with a choked groan, dropped her head on her arms on the table. "How can I bear it to have *my own mother* not remember me?"

Charles clenched his teeth to overcome a feeling of impatience toward the girl. "It seems to me, Miss Beringer, that all this must be a great deal worse for your mother. How do you suppose *she's* feeling about being unable to recognize *you*?"

Cicely lifted her head and stared at him, her swollen mouth dropping open. "Y-Yes, of course. You're quite right." She wiped her cheeks with the back of a shaking hand. "It must be a nightmare for her. I'm a thoughtless wretch."

Charles set the teacup down at her elbow. "Yes," he said callously, eyeing her with cold dispassion, "I rather think you are."

Upstairs in the invalid's bedroom, Jeremy was attempting to console the trembling Cassie. "Please don't look like that," he said, seating himself beside her and taking her hand. "You will remember everything in time. Dr. Swan said so."

Cassie peered up at his face, which, of all the faces she'd seen looking down at her, was the one with which she was becoming most familiar. "Did he?" she asked, pulling her hand from his and grasping his lapels as if to keep herself from drowning.

Jeremy took her hands in his. "He assured me of it. In fact, he said—"

There was a tap at the door, and the doctor himself came into the room. "And how is our patient this morning?" he boomed with hearty good cheer. But then he saw her anguished face. "Oh, dear," he said, his smile fading, "what has happened here?"

Cassie shuddered and hid her face in Jeremy's shoulder.

Jeremy threw the doctor a worried look. "She's had visitors. Her family."

"And she didn't remember them?"

Jeremy shook his head.

The doctor's face fell. "Do you remember *my* name?" he asked, approaching the bed and lifting her head to look into her eyes.

"Dr. Swan, isn't it?" she offered hesitantly.

"Yes, good!"

"But I still don't remember my own name," she said. "Nor that of this kind gentleman."

"That's because I haven't told it to you," Jeremy reminded her gently.

"But I knew it before, did I not? And the names of the ladies who were just here? I must have, for one of them said she was my daughter!" She looked up at the doctor, her eyes distraught. "I've had six visitors so far and was unable to recognize a single one of them."

"Ah, but you counted them. That means you can still calculate."

"Calculate? I merely counted to six. A three-year-old *child* could—"

"Not so, ma'am. With a blow of the sort you suffered, you are lucky you can calculate at all. And not only can you calculate, but you seem to have no trouble remembering words. That's another good sign."

"Is it?" she asked doubtfully.

"Very." He loosened her grip on Jeremy's lapels, sat down in his place and, with gentle fingers, measured the size of the lump on her cranium. It was even more swollen than it had been before. "Head still hurting?" he asked.

"Like the very devil."

The doctor nodded understandingly. "Be patient, my dear. This memory lapse is temporary, I promise you, and so is your pain. I'll give you another dose of laudanum. Sleep's the best curative for concussion."

Despite his hearty optimism, Cassie's anguish was not eased. She watched him prepare the potion—mixing a glass of water with some opium powders taken from his bag— but when he offered it to her, she turned her head away. "I don't want to sleep," she said, reaching out and taking Jeremy's hand for support. "I had dreadful nightmares all night long."

Jeremy took the glass from the doctor's hand, sat down beside her and held it to her lips. "Nightmares are only dark dreams," he said gently. "Wisps of nothingness. They can't hurt you."

His voice and his nearness soothed her. She drank the concoction and sank back against the pillows. "If I didn't have this blasted headache, I'd think *this* was a nightmare," she muttered.

"So it is, in some manner," said Dr. Swan, closing up his bag. "Well, I shall be on my way. Will you come along, my lord, and see me out?"

Jeremy started to rise. Cassie, experiencing a sudden flood of terror at the thought of being left alone with her pain and her despair, raised herself from the pillow and threw her arms about Jeremy's waist. "Don't leave me," she whispered into his chest.

Jeremy could not keep himself from cradling her in his arms. He had the strangest feeling that she belonged there, tight against him. Her closeness, the softness of her, the silken touch of her hair against his cheek, her tremblingly innocent need of him, all combined to arouse in him a feeling of tenderness that was beyond what he'd ever before experienced. If it were only possible, he thought, to take on himself all her pain and her fears, he would do it. He had an overpowering yearning to keep her safe forever, to offer her his protection from all of life's hurts.

But of course he could not encourage these feelings, not in himself and not in her. He was the man whom she'd expressly instructed to stay out of her life. When her memory returned, and she learned his true identity, he would be the man she would wish never to see again.

Realizing that he must not encourage her to cling to him, he loosened her hold on him. "You will not be alone," he said, urging her gently back against the pillows and smiling reassuringly. "I'll send Mrs. Stemple in to stay with you. You'll find her a most comforting companion."

Jeremy and Dr. Swan hurried down the stairs to face Lady Beringer's family. They found the ladies sitting at the table, attended by Charles and Hickham, but in spite of the number of dishes placed before them, they had evidently not touched a bite of breakfast. Eva and Cicely jumped to their feet as the two men entered, their eyes tense and anxious. Jeremy introduced the doctor and suggested that they all sit down.

"Well, Doctor, what did you find?" Eva asked as soon as they were seated.

"I found a patient who's suffered severe trauma," the doctor said bluntly.

"Trauma?" Cicely asked. "What's that?"

Dr. Swan smiled sheepishly. "It's a word we doctors like to use to make us sound important. It simply means *wound*."

"Which severe wound are you speaking of, Doctor?" Eva inquired dryly. "Her wrist, her hip or her head?"

"I won't minimize any of them, but I'm sure it's the head wound which gives you, her family, the greatest concern. As, I admit, it does me."

"Why?" Eva wanted to know.

"Because such mnemonic impairment—the abrupt onset of derangement due to memory loss, in plain words—is very rare. I myself have never seen a case of it, although I've read of them."

"*Derangement!*" Cicely gasped. "That's a *dreadful* word!"

"Yes, I agree," the doctor said, reaching across the table and patting her hand. "But it is my understanding that such impairment is usually temporary."

"How temporary?" Cicely asked.

The doctor shrugged. "Hours . . . days . . . weeks at most."

Eva peered into his eyes intently. "Have there been cases when the . . . er . . . impairment has *not* been temporary?" she asked, searching his face for the truth.

He met her look. "To be honest, there have."

"Oh, my *God!*" Cicely wailed.

"However, I have no expectations of such a dour outcome," Dr. Swan assured her. "Your mother seems to have retained a remarkable degree of alertness and responsiveness, as well as a capacity for fairly complicated mental performances, all of which makes me quite hopeful."

"Whatever causes such a strange thing to happen?" Charlie asked curiously.

"I'm afraid we don't know much about how the brain remembers, so we cannot have a precise idea of the damage that external violence does to its mnemonic functions. I can only theorize that the blow or blows that Lady Beringer received caused a numbness in the brain that resulted in the mnemonic loss."

"What we *should* be asking," Jeremy pointed out, "is how to help her recover."

"Yes," agreed Eva. "Lord Inglesby is quite right. What can we do for her?"

"You may not like my answer to that, your ladyship," Dr. Swan said, "for I must ask you and your niece to stay away from her until she asks to see you."

"But *why?*" cried Cicely in tearful chagrin.

"Because seeing you frightens her. You both are too close to her. She understands that she ought to recognize you, and she can't. That must be a terrifying feeling. We do not wish her to become more upset than her condition has already made her. What she needs most is rest and calm." He rose from his chair and picked up his bag. "And as for the rest of you, those who go into her room, do not keep telling her who you are and expecting her to remember," he advised as he went to the door. "Answer her questions simply. Let her learn at her own pace."

After his departure, a strained silence fell upon the occupants of the room, all of them suddenly imagining how they might feel if suddenly deprived of memory. None of them had ever before considered how important memory was. The only sound in the room was the incessant reverberation of Cicely's sobs.

Upstairs in the bedroom Mrs. Stemple had not yet come to sit with Cassie, and she was frightened of being alone. Despite having drunk Dr. Swan's potion, she was too uneasy to let herself fall asleep. She did not want to dream. But neither did she want to lie awake and think, because thoughts were frightening, too. She could not create any pictures in her mind. She could not imagine herself in any place but this room, nor could she bring to mind any faces but the few she'd seen in the past twelve hours. Everything else was a vast emptiness.

She sat up and looked around her. Strangely enough, she could identify everything she saw—the bed hangings, the draperies at the windows, the little dressing table with the mirror above it . . .

Good heavens! A *mirror!* she thought with a burst of excitement. She knew perfectly well what a mirror was. She could look into it and *see* herself! If she could see herself, she'd know who she was!

She sat up and threw off the covers with her good hand. Painstakingly, ignoring the agony from her numerous bruises, she slipped down from the bed and limped across the room to the dressing table. She covered her eyes with her good hand before sitting down on the little bench. Then, taking a deep breath, she dropped her hand.

The face staring back at her was that of a not-very-young, not-very-beautiful woman. Far from beautiful, in fact, with that great purplish bruise disfiguring almost half her face. But the worst shock was that it was the face of someone she'd never seen before. A complete stranger! The unfamiliarity of that face dashed her hopes.

She pressed her fingers against the glass, trying like someone blind to touch the face of this creature she'd never before seen. "Oh, dear *God,*" she cried out in anguish, "who *are* you?"

Chapter
~ 11 ~

The doctor, already late for his next appointment, stood in Lord Inglesby's entryway fiddling impatiently with the catch of his umbrella. Hickham, who'd just handed him the ancient apparatus, was taking a perverse glee in watching the medical man struggle with the simple mechanism. He was just about to offer his assistance when he heard a sound down the hall. It was Lord Lucas, emerging somewhat stealthily from the drawing room and closing the door carefully after him. *What's afoot now?* the butler asked himself curiously.

Lord Lucas hurried down the hall. "Dr. Swan, please wait a moment," he said as he strode across the large entryway to where the doctor stood.

The doctor paused. "Yes?"

Charles glowered at Hickham, who showed no signs of taking himself off. "You may go, Hickham. I shall see the doctor out."

"Yes, m'lord, but I was about to 'elp Dr. Swan with 'is umbrella," Hickham objected.

"I'll take care of it," Charles said, taking the umbrella from the doctor's hands.

"Very well, m'lord," the frustrated Hickham said with a shrug. "I'm happy t'leave it in yer 'ands. An' ye can 'ave as many of me other duties as ye'd like as well." With that, he made a quick retreat, adding under his breath, "Per'aps ye'd like t'serve the tea fer me, too!"

"Insolent jackanapes!" Charles muttered, looked after him.

"Have *you* some indisposition you wish to inquire about, Lord Lucas?" the doctor asked impatiently, pulling his pocket watch from under his coat and consulting it. "If it should require me to examine you, I'm afraid I haven't the time—"

"No, no, not I. Fit as a fiddle, I assure you. This is a question about your patient upstairs."

"Lady Beringer?" The doctor's brow rose. "What about her?"

"It's about what you said back there in the drawing room. That we shouldn't expect her to remember who we are."

"Yes. So many faces, all new to her." The doctor sighed and shook his head. "It will be hard for her."

"I understood that," Charles said uneasily, "but what I was wondering was . . ." He paused and rubbed his chin.

Dr. Swan took another glance at his watch. "Come, man, out with it. What's troubling you?"

"A rather awkward matter, I'm afraid. It's about Jeremy's identity. Of all the people whose identity Lady Beringer will learn, Jeremy's will probably be the first."

"Yes, I expect so. He is her host, after all."

"And she will think of him as Lord Inglesby."

"Naturally."

"But you see, before her accident, I led her to believe that his name was Lord Lucas."

Dr. Swan gaped at him. "You let her think he was *you*? Whatever for?"

Charles's eyes dropped guiltily. "It was . . . er . . . a sort of joke."

The doctor frowned at him in disgust. "Seems a foolish sort of joke. Did Lord Inglesby take part in it, too?"

"Yes. But it was I who pushed him into it. It was all my fault. I take full responsibility. That's why I felt impelled to tell you about it. You see, in the next few days Lady Beringer will surely learn to know him as Lord Inglesby. But when she comes back to herself, she'll recognize him as Lord Lucas. Will that not confuse her, and complicate her recovery?"

"Hmmm. I see your point. You may very well be right. Never having had a patient with a memory dysfunction before, I'm not sure how to answer you. Perhaps the safest thing to do is to continue the masquerade."

"Do you mean . . . to keep on letting her believe that Inglesby is Lucas?"

"Yes. Then, when memory returns, she will have a sense of continuity. She can be told the truth when she's fully recovered."

"But, Doctor, suppose her memory doesn't return."

"I don't think that will happen. When her concussion heals, I believe the numbness causing the mnemonic difficulty will fade. If I am mistaken—if the dysfunction lasts beyond the healing of the trauma to her head—we will confer again. In the meantime, we should proceed on the assumption that she will recover."

"And that means we should continue to deceive her." Charles shook his head worriedly. "That may not be easy. If her illness— her dysfunction, as you call it—continues for any length of time, someone is bound to make a slip."

"That, my lord, is your problem," the doctor said curtly. "You joked yourself into it. Now it's up to you to deal with the consequences." He took the still-closed umbrella from Charles's hand and turned to go. As he stepped over the threshold, he threw a last rebuke over his shoulder. "After you dance, my good fellow," he said, snapping opening his recalcitrant umbrella with a vigorous shake, "you must pay the piper."

Chapter
~ 12 ~

Charles, chastened by the doctor's scolding, turned slowly back toward the drawing room. But halfway down the hall he came face-to-face with his friend. "Ah, Jemmy, there you are," he said in greeting. "I was just coming to find you."

Jeremy eyed him with some concern. "I noticed you slip out of the drawing room after Dr. Swan. Is something wrong?"

"Not with me, if that's what you're asking," Charles replied.

"I didn't think so. It's Lady Beringer, isn't it? Is there something in her condition—something the doctor didn't speak of—that worried you?"

"As a matter of fact there was." And Charles repeated to Jeremy the gist of his conversation with the doctor. "He expects me to see that the masquerade is carried on. Made some rebuke as he left . . . to the effect that if one makes one's bed one must lie in it, or if one makes the brew one must drink it, or some such chastisement."

Jeremy glowered. "I'd like to do more than chastise you, you clunch. I wish you'd never played that deuced trick. I shan't like having to continue the pretense at all."

"Neither shall I. We'll have to warn everyone in the household. It'll be a damned nuisance."

Jeremy noted his friend's downcast expression and was softened. "Well, we'll manage," he said with a forgiving shrug. "I'm quite aware that you only did it for my sake. But if you'd truly like to make amends, there is something you can do for me."

Charles eyed him suspiciously. "Something I shall not like, no doubt."

"It will not be unpleasant. Just go back to the drawing room

67

and play the gallant for Cicely. I must go up to Lady Beringer. I promised her I'd not leave her alone for long."

"Why can't Lady Schofield keep Cicely company?" Charles demanded. "I didn't come to the country to dance attendance on silly chits just out of the schoolroom."

"Lady Schofield has gone upstairs to lie down. This business has naturally upset her."

"Lie down? *Here,* in this house? Don't tell me you've invited the ladies to move in!"

"Yes, of course I have. They want to be near Lady Beringer. I couldn't offer them less than my hospitality."

"I suppose you couldn't," Charles sighed. "But our peace will be completely cut up."

"Can't be helped," Jeremy said flatly. "But you, Charlie, are under no obligation to remain. You may go back to London anytime you wish."

Charles glared at him. "As if I would leave you to the mercies of all these females, and one of them an invalid! What sort of rotter do you take me for?"

Jeremy smiled and clapped him on the shoulder. "I knew I could count on you. Now, go in and entertain Cicely, like the good fellow I know you to be."

"Damnation, much to my surprise I find I *am* a good fellow," Charles muttered as he went to do as he was bid. "I wish at least *one* of us was a cad."

He found Cicely standing at the drawing room window, her back to him and her head down. When she heard his footstep, she made a quick swipe at her cheek with the back of her hand and turned round. "Oh, it's you, Lord Lucas," she murmured, trying bravely to smile.

"Yes, but since I understand that you'll be staying with us for a while, you may as well call me Charlie. There's no point in formality while we're stranded here in the country."

"Thank you, Charlie. And you must call me Cicely, for I, too, prefer informality under the circumstances."

"Good. Then, Cicely, would you please sit down, for if you don't, I shall have to remain standing here like an awkward schoolboy."

She gave a pathetic little laugh, crossed the room to the sofa and sat stiffly on the edge, her hands folded in her lap. After a long moment of silence (during which Charlie, who was hardly ever at a loss for words, found himself hard-pressed to think of what to say), she seemed to steel herself—as if she were about to perform a courageous act—and spoke up. "I was wondering, Lord Lu— Charlie, if I might ask you a . . . a question."

"Yes, of course," he assured her, taking a chair opposite her. "Ask me anything at all."

"It's about Mama. I don't understand why she came here in the first place. Do you know why? She'd never met Jeremy, after all, so what could have possessed her to come and see him?"

"Didn't she tell you her purpose before she left home?"

"No. Not a word."

"I see." Charles hesitated, not at all sure he should reveal what he perhaps had no right even to know. "Why don't you ask Jeremy?"

"It would be . . . awkward."

"Why awkward?"

"Well, you see . . ." Her cheeks flamed, and she dropped her eyes in embarrassment. "You must know he . . . he jilted me."

"He did nothing of the sort," Charlie declared flatly. "He never made an offer, did he?"

"All right, then, he *almost* jilted me."

"See here my girl, if he *did* almost jilt you—and mind you, I'm not saying that I agree that he did—does that mean you can't speak to one another?"

"It means that it's . . . awkward."

Charlie looked at her in impatience. Although he had to admit that there was a certain charm in her shy blushes and a certain appeal in the way her lashes fluttered against her creamy cheeks and her full underlip quivered when she tried to hide her emotions, he was too old and jaded to have to endure her missish diffidence. "I'm certain you can overcome that awkwardness, my dear," he said, trying his best to hide his annoyance. "Jeremy is very easy to talk to."

"Not for me. Especially now, after . . ." She lowered her head and twisted her fingers nervously together. "Especially

since he so suddenly changed his mind about offering for me."
She lifted her head and fixed her eyes on his face in what Charlie felt was a completely unexpected and disconcerting directness. "You two are the best of friends, are you not?"

"I would say so, yes."

"And you confide in each other?"

"I suppose we do, to some extent. Not as I believe young ladies like to do, telling each other every passing thought. But we do exchange views."

"Views?"

"Yes . . . on politics and such."

"And on people?"

Charlie peered at her suspiciously. "People?"

"Yes. Do you tell each other how you feel about . . . well, about females?"

He gave the question a moment of honest consideration. "Yes, I think we do, on occasion," he admitted with some embarrassment.

"That's what I thought. Then you may be able to answer a question most puzzling to me." She leaned forward and studied his face curiously. "Do you know what made him change toward me?"

Charlie squirmed. How had he permitted this irritating chit to subject him to such an intimate and relentless interrogation? "If I did know," he said curtly, "you certainly don't think I would tell you, do you?"

"Why not? It would be much less painful and awkward to hear the truth from a disinterested third party than from Jeremy himself."

"That may be," Charlie declared firmly, "but I do not intend to say another word on the subject. If you want answers to these questions, you'll have to ask Jeremy, awkward or not."

Cicely sighed in defeat. "That is too bad, for I cannot possibly bring myself to ask him. Now I will never, never know."

"That, my girl, is something I cannot help."

"You could if you really wanted to," she murmured in what was unmistakably a pout.

"It is not a question of my wanting to or not!" he exploded

in exasperation. "It's a question of honor. Honoring the confidences of a friend."

"Oh, pooh!" was her response to his righteous declaration.

Her disdain was, for him, the last straw. "Very well, Cicely Beringer, if that is your attitude, I *will* say something. It is entirely my own view and has nothing whatever to do with Jeremy's." He rose from his chair and loomed over her like a threatening schoolmaster. "It is simply this: that you should have known better than to encourage a relationship with a man so much older than you. You should find yourself someone close to you in age . . . someone full of youthful vigor and wide-eyed innocence, who'd fall at your feet in awed adoration of your charms, not some confirmed old bachelor who's seen and said and done it all before."

"Good God!" exclaimed the girl, staring up at him wide-eyed. "You sound like my *mother*!" Her expression hardening, she rose from her seat and drew herself up to her full height, bringing her almost eye-to-eye with him. "Let *me* say something now, my lord. What I don't wish from you is motherly advice. Furthermore, the advice is utterly useless. I may be a wide-eyed innocent, but I know enough to realize that a person's age has little importance in matters of the heart." She gave him one last glare and strode to the door. "You should know by now, being quite old enough to 'have seen and said and done it all,' that falling in love has nothing whatever to do with numbers." And she shut the door behind her with a slam.

Charlie gaped at the door, astounded by that display of vehemence. He'd never expected, from a young chit he'd believed so naive and awkward, such a spirited display. But even more surprising was what she'd just said. Hadn't *he* said *those very words* to her mother less than twenty-four hours before? Why on earth had he, who'd long made a practice of ensnaring young ladies without paying any regard to their age, suddenly switched sides?

Chapter
~ 13 ~

For a fortnight, the manor house at Inglesby Park was a very quiet and dreary place. The two principal causes were the rain, which continued to fall with a gloomy persistance, and the patient, who spent most of this time in a stuporous, laudanum-induced sleep (for Dr. Swan insisted that sleep was the best cure for all her injuries). These were not circumstances to encourage gaiety.

During this time the number of inhabitants in the household increased by two: first, Lady Beringer's housekeeper, Mrs. Annie Upsom, who arrived from Crestwoods within hours of learning of her mistress's condition; and then Lady Schofield's abigail, who arrived from London two days later. Mrs. Upsom insisted on moving into the dressing room adjoining her ladyship's bedroom so that she might be close at hand day and night. Lady Schofield's abigail, only slightly less determined, managed to convince Lady Schofield that she was indispensable and, without a moment's hesitation, settled herself into the largest room in the maids' quarters. Though the addition of these strong-minded women to the household did not dramatically alter the hushed atmosphere, their presence did make a modest improvement. With Mrs. Upsom taking charge of the sickroom, Mrs. Stemple was able to return to the kitchen, which resulted in a decided improvement in the meals. And the abigail from London contributed what anyone could see was a marked improvement in the dressing of Lady Schofield's hair.

Jeremy, Charles and the two female guests tried to maintain a reasonably cheerful disposition. Each spent a few hours a day at Cassie's side, watching her sleep, an occupation that could in no way be considered lively or diverting. Nor were any of their other activities particularly diverting. Their days were spent in a desultory fashion, the ladies sleeping late and spending their afternoons reading or wandering about in purposeless gloom, and the gentlemen taking out horses in the mornings for brief rides despite the rain and passing their afternoons playing billiards. They all met at dinnertime (during which Charles tried to keep the flow of conversation amusing, but without much success), after which they adjourned to the drawing room and indulged in card games. But cooper loo and whist, when played for very modest stakes, could not be expected to elevate their dampened spirits. Thus the long evenings seemed very long indeed.

All of this changed abruptly one morning after the fortnight had passed. Perhaps the change was instigated by the sun, which made a royal appearance in a sky of such brilliant blue clarity it was hard to believe that just yesterday it had been completely obscured behind heavy gray clouds. Now the sun spread its rejuvenating radiance everywhere. Suddenly the spring air smelled sweet as wine, lilacs burst into lively bloom, columbine and cowslip peeped out from the edge of the woods, and all the greenery gleamed in newly washed splendor. How could mere human beings resist the warm vitality of Mother Nature at her best?

Certainly Cassie could not. From the moment Mrs. Upsom pulled back the draperies in her room and the sunshine streamed in, her condition changed. She sat up in bed, blinked in surprise at the unaccustomed cheeriness of the sunlit room and smiled. It was a purely instinctive act; she had not smiled since her fall. Mrs. Upsom, who was approaching her with a glass of the morning dose of laudanum in her hand, took a look at her mistress's face and gasped. "Oh, *ma'am*," she exclaimed in delight, "are you smiling at last?"

"Am I?" Cassie put a hand to her mouth to feel what a smile might be like. Then she pushed aside the sleeping potion firmly. "Take it away, please! I wish never to take another sip of that vile brew. I'm tired of being forever drowsy and forever thick-headed."

"But, my lady, the doctor said—"

"Never mind the doctor," Cassie declared, throwing her legs over the side of the bed. "Help me to the window, please, Mrs. Upsom. I want to see the sun. At least sunshine is something I remember."

She hobbled over to the window on Mrs. Upsom's arm, her legs dismayingly unsteady, and stared out past the sunny lawn and the shadowed home woods to where a pond, spilling its contents over a waterwheel, was sparkling in the distance. It was a lovely scene, revealing the miracle of springtime rejuvenation, and it made a rejuvenating impression on her mind. "I won't ever take a sleeping draught again," she murmured. "I must begin to face . . . to learn to live. From now on I shall rise in the mornings and dress, just as ordinary people do, and go out of this room and face the world." She threw a hesitant look at the still-not-familiar face of the woman who, she'd been told, had been her housekeeper for more than two decades. "That *is* what ordinary people do, isn't it?"

"Yes, of course, ma'am," Mrs. Upsom replied, biting her lip to keep from weeping. "You used to dress all by yourself, every day, without ever an abigail, even for church or a party, before . . . before . . ."

"Before my accident. You needn't be afraid to say the word."

"Yes, ma'am. Do you remember anything at all from before the accident, ma'am? Like how you always called me Annie?"

Cassie shook her head. "No. I'm sorry."

The housekeeper sighed. "No need to apologize, ma'am. It ain't your fault. Here, let me help you to sit down."

"No. I want to try to walk."

She started across the room, but after three steps her knees almost gave way. For the next few steps, she had to cling to Mrs. Upsom, but soon she learned how to keep her balance. In a little while she felt secure enough to take a few steps on her own. "Now, then," she said when she'd crossed the whole length of the room without holding on, "let us get me dressed."

Mrs. Upsom's face brightened. "I brought some of your clothes along from home. There's your pearl-gray muslin with the lace collar, and the lilac jaconet that always looked so sweet on you, and the green brocade with the full sleeves—"

Cassie shook her head helplessly. "I don't remember any of them. You choose."

Dressing took a great deal longer than she had expected. With her left wrist bandaged, and spasms of pain emanating from her right shoulder and hip, every motion had to be slow and careful. Even her hair had to be combed with slow, gingerly deliberation, so as not to cause pain to the still-swollen lump on her head. Eventually, however, Mrs. Upsom managed to brush out the tangles. Then she braided the long, heavy strands neatly and coiled them at the nape of Cassie's neck.

When the job was done, Cassie limped over to the mirror, which she hadn't looked into since that first day. The face looking back at her today was still that of a stranger. But now the experience was less shattering. The woman in the mirror had a pleasant enough face, Cassie thought, and the purple bruise that had seemed so disfiguring a fortnight ago had now paled to a gray shadow, except for a darker, green-and-purple remnant over the cheekbone. She did not wince at the sight, but neither could she look at that face for more than a moment. The unfamiliarity of it made her so uncomfortable that she had to look away.

"Did I hear the clock strike eleven while you were combing my hair?" she asked the woman who seemed to know her so well, and who was taking such devoted care of her. "What do ordinary people do at that hour?"

"Since you've been ill, ma'am, the ladies in this house have been staying late abed. They usually straggle down to breakfast about this time."

"Then, if you don't mind lending me your arm, let's go down and join them."

Mrs. Upsom looked frightened. "All the way downstairs?"

"Yes. All the way."

In the morning room a larger group than usual was gathered. Jeremy and Charles had ridden out early to enjoy the magnificent weather and, their appetites sharpened by the exercise, had come back eager for a meal. They found Lady Schofield already at the table with a plate of shirred eggs and pickled salmon before her, and Cicely, who'd just come down, standing at the buffet surveying the selections that Hickham was uncovering for her. "What a jolly ride we've had," Charles informed the ladies as he pulled off his riding gloves and joined Cicely at the buffet. "I declare I'm prime for either a huge late breakfast or a huge early luncheon."

"Well, there's York 'am an' buttered eggs an' salmon an' cold chicken an' toast, if it's breakfast ye choose," Hickham said, "or hot roast chicken an' greens an' river trout an' potatoes an' gooseberry tarts an' cream if ye wish to call it luncheon."

Hickham helped them to load their plates, and they joined Lady Schofield at the small morning room table to slake their appetites. Cicely took a bite of trout and found it so delicious that she turned round in her chair to tell Hickham to compliment Mrs. Stemple. But before the words left her tongue, her eye was caught by a movement in the doorway. *"Mama!"* she gasped, dropping her fork.

Cassie, standing in the doorway, suddenly found five astonished faces gaping at her. She knew she'd seen each one of them before, but there wasn't one she clearly remembered. She felt a spasm of terror and had an urge to turn and run. But she did not. For one thing, her knees were too weak. For another, she'd made herself a pledge to stand firm and face life. So, clutching the door frame with her one good hand, she forced herself to smile. "Good morning," she said bravely.

As one, they jumped up from the table, and she was immediately surrounded. "Cassie, *dearest!*" a large, formidable matron exclaimed, embracing her.

"Oh, Mama! How *well* you are looking!" cried the pretty young girl who threw her arms about her as well.

"Lady Beringer!" exclaimed the stocky man, pounding her shoulder. "You've come *down!* Oh, very deedy!"

Only the tall fellow with the kind eyes (eyes that she remembered better than anything else) stood aside. She glanced over at him questioningly. He smiled back at her with such apparent pride in her accomplishment that it warmed her heart.

"Per'aps 'er ladyship's 'ungry," Hickham suggested after the din had quieted down.

"Yes, of course she is," Lady Schofield said, drawing her to the table. "The poor thing hasn't had a proper meal in a fortnight."

A place was hurriedly made for her, and she sat down, uncomfortably aware that she was the center of all eyes. This could not be how ordinary people took their meals, she thought in dismay.

Everyone attempted to return to their breakfast, but having the hitherto somnolent patient among them was too distracting to encourage eating. "Mama," Cicely asked at last, unable to stand the suspense, "do you know me now?"

Cassie put down her fork. "You call me Mama, so you must be my daughter. But I'm afraid I don't remember you."

"Oh, Mama!" Cicely cried, crestfallen.

"Dash it, Cicely," Charles muttered in disapproval, "let her be! Remember what the doctor said."

"No, please," Cassie begged, "don't curb your tongues. I want things to be . . . ordinary."

"Ordinary?" Lady Schofield gave a disdainful snort. "How can they be ordinary when you are so completely impaired?"

"Come now, Lady Schofield," Jeremy snapped, "surely you must admire Lady Beringer's remarkable improvement today! Why not stress how far she's come, instead of dwelling on how far she still must go?"

"Thank you, sir," Cassie said, throwing him a look of heart-felt gratitude. Then she looked round the table at the others. "But to help me get on, perhaps you can teach me your names."

"But surely you've learned some of them already," Lady Schofield suggested.

"Well, there are a couple of names I've managed to learn. I know I am Lady Beringer, also called Cassie and Mama. And the woman in the doorway, watching over me so carefully, is Mrs. Upsom. And you, ma'am . . . I've just heard you called Lady Schofield."

"But, Cassie, you shouldn't call me that. I am your *sister*." She choked on the last word and had to pull a handkerchief from her sleeve to dry her tears. "You've *always* called me Eva."

Cassie reached over and patted her hand. "I'll gladly call you Eva."

Charles, realizing that they were approaching the delicate problem of identity, rose to his feet. "Since I am Lord Inglesby, your host," he said, throwing everyone a warning look to remind them of the rules that they would now have to observe, "let me make the other introductions. Next to your sister, Eva, is Cicely, your daughter. And at her right is my friend, Lord Lucas."

Jeremy rose and bowed. "A pleasure to meet you, ma'am," he said with a smile.

"Again?" Cassie said in rueful realization that they must have met before.

"Again. But it is always a pleasure to meet you," he reassured her, "no matter how often."

Hickham, from his station at the buffet, cleared his throat. "Don't ferget me, m'lord. I'm Hickham, ma'am, ready t'do yer biddin', whatever it may be."

"Thank you, Hickham," Cassie said. Then, looking at each face, she reviewed in her mind the name for each one.

Jeremy seated himself and looked about. "It seems we've forgotten to eat," he said in a tone that he hoped was pleasant and "ordinary." "Would you like a hot cup of tea, ma'am?"

Thus breakfast was resumed. It proceeded smoothly, with Cassie shyly entering into the conversation from time to time and addressing each one with the appropriate name. The mood was almost cheerful when they rose from the table at the end of the meal. Only Eva had a troubled frown. "This process of relearning seems to me most tedious and lengthy," she said to her sister as they moved into the hallway. "I think we should take you home."

Cassie paled. "Home?"

Cicely, who had preceded them, wheeled about and clapped her hands gleefully. "Yes! Oh, yes, that would be wonderful!"

"No!" The word came from Cassie's throat in a terrified whisper. She took a backward step, and bumped into someone who'd been following. She started and looked round nervously. She'd bumped into the man with the kind eyes. "I'm sorry, Lord Lucas," she mumbled.

Jeremy grasped her arm and squeezed it with emboldening support. Turning to Eva, but keeping his hand on Cassie's arm, he asked, "Why do you think it would be helpful for Lady Beringer to go home?"

"At home she will be on familiar ground, surrounded by her own things," Eva explained with finality as she headed for the stairs.

"But what if they won't *be* familiar?" Cassie asked, her knees trembling. The hand on her arm slid down until it found hers and grasped it in a strong grip, as if in response to her unspoken need. *He understands*, she thought gratefully. *Lord Lucas understands*. That grip of his hand gave her courage. "I have no recollection of what you call home," she called after Eva bravely. "The room upstairs is the only home I know."

Eva paused on the bottom stair. "Nonsense," she said firmly. "You will surely remember your own home when you see it."

"How can you think so, when I can't even remember *you*? Or my own *daughter*?"

"But, my dear, we can't remain here indefinitely, imposing on Lord Inglesby's hospitality," Eva pointed out to her. "Why, he isn't even a relation."

Jeremy, feeling Cassie's hand trembling in his, held it more tightly. "It is no imposition at all. You are, all three, welcome to stay as long as you like," he said. Then he realized he'd blundered. "I'm sure that's how Lord Inglesby feels," he added quickly. "Isn't that so, *Jeremy*?"

"Of course," Charlie said with booming sincerity, coming to the foot of the stairway and looked up at Eva. "My home is yours to use as you would your own."

Jeremy, still clutching Cassie's hand, led her to the foot of the stairs. "I know how you must feel, Lady Schofield. But I think you must let your sister become more familiar with her present surroundings before you present her with new ones."

Eva glanced down at Cicely for support, but the girl could only shake her head in confusion. With a surrendering sigh, Eva peered down at her sister. "Is that what you wish, Cassie? To remain here a bit longer?"

"Yes, please," Cassie said, breathing out in relief.

Eva shrugged and marched to the stairs. "Very well, I shall say no more for the time being," she muttered worriedly as she climbed up out of their view.

Cicely, clinging to the banister, did what she usually did when under stress—she burst into tears. Jeremy made a motion with his head, suggesting to Charlie to remove the weepy child from the vicinity.

Charlie nodded. "Come, Cicely, my dear," he said, taking her firmly by the elbow and leading her toward the front door. "It's too lovely a day to mope indoors. Come outside with me, and let me show you the apple orchard. It's all in bloom."

As soon as they were alone, Cassie looked up at her rescuer with eyes that shone. "I think I can guess what you were to me in the past, Lord Lucas," she said softly.

"Can you?" He smiled down at her indulgently. "And who do you think I was?"

She lifted his hand to her face and rubbed her bruised cheek lightly against the back of it. "My very best friend."

Chapter
~ 14 ~

Eva paced about her bedroom in a state of extreme distress. It was upsetting to be looked upon by one's own sister as a threatening stranger. *Why doesn't Cassie understand,* she asked herself, *that I want only what is best for her?*

When she'd suggested to Cassie that Crestwoods would be a better place in which to recover than this, the house of a stranger, she truly believed she was in the right. Yet Cassie had reacted as if she'd suggested taking her off to prison!

It was ironic, Eva thought, that the one person to whom Cassie seemed to cling in her memory-less state was Jeremy Tate. She appeared to be quite taken with him. If only she'd been so taken with him before, when she was in her right mind. Perhaps then she would have *assisted* Eva in mending matters between Jeremy and Cicely, instead of insisting that they never see each other again.

But they *were* seeing each other again! Eva thought in surprise. Why had this not occurred to her before? Perhaps she'd been too stunned by Cassie's accident to think clearly. But the fact was that here they were, Jeremy and Cicely, forced into each other's company every day, and she'd not until this very moment realized the advantages!

Eva sank down on her bed, her head awhirl and a little green growth of optimism budding in her chest. Perhaps some good might come from this nightmare, after all. How ironic that the accident was bringing about the very situation that Cassie, were she in her right mind, would have made every effort to prevent. But now she couldn't prevent it.

Jeremy and Cicely, together every day! Eva clapped her hands to her bosom, her heart warming at the very thought.

Such proximity was bound to rekindle the flames of their romance! A match between those two was what Eva wanted above all things. That, and Cassie's recovery, were all she needed to be perfectly happy.

Her next thought, however, withered her new-blooming optimism. It occurred to her that Cicely and Jeremy had already been together for a fortnight, and she hadn't seen a single sign of any rebirth of romance between them. Cicely hardly ever said a word to the man, and he, on his part, never showed any feelings beyond mere politeness. Proximity did not seem to have worked so far.

But that was probably Cicely's fault. Her mood had been mopish and withdrawn, certainly not a manner designed to encourage a man to resume his courtship. Not that Eva blamed the girl; she had good reason to mope. It was terribly upsetting not to be remembered by one's own mother. But now that Eva had become aware of the advantages of this situation, things would change. She would see to it herself. All she had to do was encourage Cicely to be more cheerful, to wear more fetching attire and to be a little more engaging in her manner. That would surely be enough encouragement for an eager suitor. With any luck at all, they would become properly betrothed, and with Cassie's blessing, too! Cassie was already learning what a good, kind fellow Jeremy was, and she would certainly acknowledge it when her memory returned. *And her memory will return,* Eva told herself, the bud of optimism bursting into flower in her breast. She was, for the first time since the accident, absolutely certain of that.

She went to the window, threw open the casements and took a deep breath of the fragrant spring air. She hadn't noticed before, but now she could see that it was a positively glorious day.

Eva's optimism might have suffered a decided blow if her windows had faced the opposite side of the house, for from that vantage point she would have seen Cicely strolling across the field to the orchard. Though the girl looked as pretty as her aunt could wish (for a lively breeze was tousling her hair, flapping away at her flounced skirts and bringing a bright spot of color to her cheeks), the man walking alongside her was not Jeremy, but Charles. And Cicely was laughing up at Charles in a way that would have made Eva stiffen, for it was beyond question a flirtatious giggle. And the conversation, if Eva could have heard it, would have disturbed her even more.

"You? A matchmaker?" Cicely was asking, gurgling deep in her throat in amusement.

"Why not?" Charles replied. "If the only way I can convince you that you'd truly enjoy the attentions of a young man your own age is to provide you with one myself, then I will provide one."

"And where will you find one? I don't see any in the vicinity."

"I have the perfect candidate. My nephew, Clive. In my sister's last letter, she wrote that he'd been sent down from Oxford and was doing nothing but idling about the house complaining of boredom. I shall write and tell her to send him here."

"Don't bother," Cicely said, flipping her hand in disdain and striding off ahead of her escort. "I have no interest in a youth so frivolous that he was sent down from school, and so callow that he is bored with his life."

Charles watched her walk away from him. Her long-legged stride made the flounces of her skirts dance, and the graceful swing of her arms, the sway of her slim hips and the way the long strands of her hair blew about in the breeze, all combined to create a charming picture. "Youthful femininity in motion," he muttered with reluctant admiration.

"What did you say?" she called back to him.

"I said you are striding off in the wrong direction. The orchard is over the hill that way."

She came back to him and held out her hand. "Very well, my lord. Lead the way."

The gesture was open and innocent, but as he took her hand in his, he was uncomfortably aware of holding it. Nevertheless, he kept hold until he'd led her over the rise. As soon as the orchard came in view, however, he dropped her hand. "There!" he said with a sweep of his arm. "Just as I promised—a cloud of blooms."

"It's lovely!" she exclaimed ecstatically, gazing at the view below them, where dozens of trees (whose gnarled trunks and uniquely twisted branches made a picturesque contrast to their neat alignment) were each haloed by a cloud of pink-and-white blossoms. "Let's walk under them and look up through the blossoms at the sky!"

Her skirts billowing behind her, she ran eagerly down the hill. But at the bottom, at the edge of the orchard, she paused. "Oh, confound it, the path's all mud. My slippers will be ruined if I cross."

It was quite true. A furrow of tilled soil, about six feet wide, ran along the entire edge of the orchard, and more than two weeks of steady rain had turned it into a river of mud. Charles caught up with her, looked up and down the furrow and shrugged. "Well," he said consolingly, "you've seen the orchard. We may as well go back. No need to ruin your slippers just to look up at the sky through the blossoms."

She glared at him. "You, Lord Lucas, haven't an iota of romance in you."

His eyebrows rose in offense. "Oh, haven't I?" And before she could guess what he was about, he gathered her up in his arms and, stomping through the mud in his meticulous riding boots, carried her across. "There," he laughed, setting her down. "Was that romantic enough for you?"

"Oh, Charlie!" She stared at him wide-eyed, her hands at her mouth, her cheeks flaming. "Look at your poor *boots*!"

"Good heavens, girl, what of that?" he scoffed. "Something must be sacrificed for romance. Sir Walter Raleigh muddied a whole cloak!" He reached out and took her hand. "Come. Let's get under a tree and give you your look at the sky."

But she did not budge. Though he tugged at her arm, she remained rooted to the spot, continuing to stare at him in a bemused fashion, as if she'd never seen him before.

"Cicely, what—?" he began, dropping her hand and grasping her shoulders to shake her into consciousness. But he never finished, for the next thing he knew she was in his arms, and he was kissing her soft, pliant mouth with a completely inappropriate intensity, an intensity he usually reserved for much more experienced ladies.

That intensity kept his brain prisoner for a long moment, not functioning at all, while his whole body responded to the pleasurable sensations of holding this lovely, lithe creature tightly against him. But as soon as he realized what he was doing, he let her go.

Her wide-eyed gaze had widened even more. With her lips apart, her cheeks alternating between a pallor and a flush and her breath coming in gasps, she seemed utterly astounded. Not angry, not frightened, merely astounded. He, on the other hand, felt thoroughly ashamed of himself. She was such an innocent, and he'd taken advantage of that fact, though quite unintentionally. "Cicely, I'm sorry. I didn't mean—"

But at the sound of his voice, she took a backward step, and then another, never once taking her eyes from his face. Her third step would take her right into the mud. "Cicely!" he warned, lifting his arms to catch her.

But it was the worst movement he could have made. She took two more backward steps to avoid him and sank to her ankles into the muck. "Dash it all, Cicely," he exclaimed, "your *slippers!*"

She blinked, looked down, stared, looked up at him in confusion and then down again. In a dreamlike fog she lifted her skirts from the mud and studied them in disbelief. Then she met Charles's eye. "Oh, dear," she murmured, "after all your efforts . . ." And before his shocked gaze, she began to laugh. She laughed so hard it became infectious, and he couldn't help but join in. For a moment they stood where they were, laughing uproariously. Then, still laughing, she turned, slogged her way across the muddy furrow and dashed up the hill toward home.

He soon caught up with her. "Cicely," he said, now quite serious, "please forgive me for—"

"For ruining my slippers? But that was not your doing. It was completely my own fault."

"You know I don't mean your slippers."

She dropped her eyes. "Yes, I know." She resumed her walk toward the house, but more slowly. "I suppose kissing young women is a habit with you," she said thoughtfully.

"Well, I wouldn't say I'm as bad as that," he retorted, offended.

"Was this kiss just like the others?" she asked, flicking him a glance.

"What do you mean, like the others? What others?"

"Any others. Your usual kisses. Was it . . . ordinary?"

"Really, my girl, you do ask the most irritating questions. I wouldn't describe *any* kiss as ordinary."

"Then would you describe this one as extraordinary?"

"No," he said promptly, uncomfortably aware that it was a lie. "No, I wouldn't say that, either."

"I see." She tossed back her windblown locks and strode off ahead of him without a backward look.

He did not attempt to catch up with her, but when he came round the corner of the house to the front, he saw her standing at the bottom of the stone stairway. "Were you waiting for me?" he asked, puzzled.

"Yes," she said. "I didn't answer your question."

"What question?"

"If I forgive you."

"Oh." He gave her a level look. "Well, do you?"

She studied him a moment, speculatively, her head cocked. Then, abruptly, she threw her arms about his neck and pressed her lips to his. It was a tentative sort of kiss, not quite real, and he did not permit himself to respond to it. But, though he held himself away and did not move, he felt his pulse race anyway, and a tingle ran up the entire length of his frame.

In a very brief moment she pulled away, casting him another look of sheer astonishment. Then, shaking herself as if from a dream, she smiled shyly. "Yes, I forgive you," she said and ran up the stairs.

He stood there immobile, looking after her and wondering how that young chit had succeeded in making him feel like a gawking schoolboy. *This will not do,* he told himself severely. *I'd better send for Clive. Right away!*

Chapter
~ 15 ~

Another fortnight passed. April turned into May, and still the ladies from Crestwood remained fixed at Inglesby Park. It was a much more pleasant fortnight than the first had been, for the weather was lovely and the invalid grew stronger every day. Her wrist was still bandaged, but the sling had been removed, her bruises were fading, and her cheerful determination to regain her full mental capacities infected everyone, including Dr. Swan himself, with optimism.

Jeremy, however, was beginning to feel the strain, for he found himself being forced to play two roles, both false and neither one to his liking. The first was the necessity of pretending that his name was Charles Percy, Lord Lucas. It troubled him to present himself to Cassie with a false identity, to enact a constant lie. An intimacy was developing between them, yet he couldn't bring himself to ask that she call him by his given name. The name Charles was not his; he didn't want her to grow accustomed to it. Yet every time she called him Lord Lucas, something within him shuddered. And with the lady thus forced to address him with that dreadful formality, he could not feel free to call her Cassie, or even Cassandra. Their constant *my lord*s and *my lady*s were driving him mad.

The second role he was forced to play, which he also felt was false, was that of her best friend. In that role he was her prime companion—the one in whose company she was most comfortable. They spent most of their days together. In the mornings he read the newspapers with her, filling in for her the necessary background to help her understand the current political situation; in the afternoons they took long walks when the weather was fine, or spent the time with his books in his library when it was not. Even when they were with the others in the evenings, she seemed to cling to him for support and security. It was not that he minded the companionship and closeness—quite the opposite!—but that he didn't want to be her best friend. He had something much more intimate in mind, but he did not feel free to reveal his feelings while her memory was so badly impaired.

This dilemma was very much on his mind when he sat with Charlie one night after all the ladies of the house had gone to bed. The two men were at their ease before the library fire, glasses of brandy in their hands. It had been a chilly, rainy day for May, and since they'd not gone riding or undergone any physical exertion, they were not tired enough for bed. Besides, they both had matters on their minds they wanted to share. It was Charlie who spoke first. "Women," he muttered in disgust. "Wherever they are or whatever the circumstances, they think it behooves them to flirt. It doesn't matter who the man is. Whatever man happens to be in their vicinity is fair game for their flirtations."

"What are you prattling about, Charlie?" his friend asked bluntly. "Here we are, sequestered miles from London and all female society, except of course for our guests, who are not here for any frivolous purpose. Why all this talk of flirtations?"

"That's just what I'm getting at. Even here, in the midst of all this quiet rusticity, your deuced Cicely must be constantly flickering her eyelashes and casting inviting glances and walking about with that swing of the hips—you know the sort of thing I mean—and all to attract male attention."

"Cicely? Are you saying she's been flirting with *you*?"

"Well, you needn't sound so disbelieving," Charlie said, drawing his shoulders back in offended dignity. "There have been females here and there who've found me to their liking."

"Don't be a clunch," Jeremy laughed. "I can't have been your friend for the past two decades without seeing how women throw themselves at you. Not that I'll ever understand why, of course."

Charlie retaliated by throwing a cushion at him. "It's my

red hair," he retorted, catching the cushion that Jeremy threw back at him.

Jeremy, as he took a sip of his brandy, eyed his friend curiously over the rim. "I didn't know that Cicely was susceptible to red hair."

"I don't think she is," Charlie said, growing serious. "I think all this damnable flirtation going on between us is merely a symptom of the female propensity for flirtation. And I'm the only male available, now that you're so preoccupied with her mother."

"You're being unduly modest, Charlie. Isn't it possible that the girl has developed a *tendre* for you?"

"What? Merely moments after she's been almost jilted by you?"

"Moments? It's been more than a month since—"

"What is a mere month in matters of the heart? No, no, Jemmy, old fellow. If there's any purpose at all in Cicely's attentions to me, it's to discover from me why you changed toward her."

Jeremy snorted. "If she's so eager to learn the answer to that, she could ask me, could she not?"

"One would think so. But she told me in so many words that she couldn't possibly ask you. It would be, in her words, too awkward."

"I don't think you're right about that, Charlie. She hasn't appeared to show me the least interest since she took up residence here."

"That's because you've been so preoccupied elsewhere."

Jeremy looked chastened. "Is it as obvious as that?"

"It is to me. You've completely forgotten the daughter but have gone top over tail over the mother."

"Yes, it's true. That's what has me so blue-deviled."

Charlie raised an eyebrow in surprise. "Why on earth should you be blue-deviled? Lady Beringer seems to be just as taken with you as you are with her. It's midsummer moon with you both."

"I can't be sure of that, you know."

"Why not? If you doubt it, do what you just suggested Cicely do with you. Just *ask* the lady."

Jeremy shook his head glumly. "No. No, I can't."

"Why?" Charlie snorted teasingly. "Don't tell me it would be too awkward!"

"Much worse than awkward. Without a memory, you see, Cassie's like a child in matters of the heart. Before her accident, she was a recluse. For some reason, she'd put love out of her life. And, if you remember, she'd come here to make sure I even stayed out of her *daughter's* life. One day, perhaps very soon, she'll remember it all, and may very well find me repugnant. And I *would* be repugnant if I spoke of such things to her now. It would be like taking advantage of an innocent."

Charlie stared at him for a moment, brows knit, but then he nodded in sympathy. "Yes, I know what you mean." He took a quick gulp of brandy before admitting, "I have a similar feeling of discomfort when I'm with Cicely . . . that same feeling of not wishing to take advantage of innocence."

"Are you speaking of her age? I wouldn't have such scruples about Cicely, if I were you. When I was courting her, I found her to be, in many ways, quite mature for her age. And she does seem to be drawn to older men."

"That may be because she hasn't had enough younger men around her. But I've initiated a plan to test that theory. I've sent for my nephew, Clive." He looked over at his friend with sudden embarrassment. "I thought, with so many guests in the house already, you'd not object to one more. You don't mind, do you, Jemmy?"

"Of course I don't mind," Jeremy said, tossing his friend an amused glance, "though I think it was a cowardly thing for you to do."

"Cowardly?" Charlie demanded in offense.

Jeremy took a last sip of his brandy and got to his feet. "Do you know what I think, Charlie, old fellow?" He strolled over to his friend's chair and grinned down at him. "I think you have so strong a feeling for the girl that it has you terrified." Leaving Charlie gaping at him, openmouthed, he made for the door. "Sending for Clive," he taunted before whisking himself out of the room, "is the act of a desperate man."

Chapter
~ 16 ~

Cassie, now firmly on her feet despite lingering pains from her bruised hip, took to wandering about the Inglesby manor house with the air of an explorer, as perhaps she was. She peeped into unused rooms, wandered up and down long corridors, climbed up into turrets and gazed out on the vistas below. To her it was all new, all strange, all fascinating. And the adventures of the day carried over into the night, for the places she explored during the day returned to her mind in her dreams, replacing the upsetting blankness in the background of those dreams with substantial objects—recognizable forms that had shape and color.

The house was lovely, she thought, though she had no memory of other houses with which to compare it. It seemed to her that it was lovelier than one would expect from the character of the owner. The man she believed was Jeremy Tate, Lord Inglesby, did not seem interested in the details of the house. It was Lord Lucas who shared her enthusiasm for the soft greens and golds of the Persian carpet in the library, not Inglesby. It was Lord Lucas, not Inglesby, who drew her attention to the Sheraton bench in the entry hall, with its simple lines that contrasted so dramatically with its magnificently carved back. It was Lord Lucas, not Inglesby, who took her to see the lovely round turret room atop the east wing of the house.

That room was Cassie's favorite. High above the world, it gleamed with light from the casement windows that surrounded it. From those windows one could view the beautiful grounds below in their entirety, simply by turning around. But Lord Inglesby didn't even appear to remember that the room existed. In truth, it seemed to Cassie that Lord Inglesby didn't possess an iota of the refined taste that his house exuded.

The day Lord Lucas showed her the turret room was a day that Cassie was positive would always be special in her memory, even when her old memories returned. But meanwhile, having so few, she replayed this one in her mind every day. She would go over it slowly, detail by detail, step by step, beginning with the moment when he came upon her wandering aimlessly down the second-floor corridor of the east wing. "Are you looking for something in particular, Lady Beringer?" he'd asked.

She'd jumped, and her heart had begun to pound, as it always did when she met him unexpectedly. (That heart pounding was a strange phenomenon the cause of which she often wondered about. She'd occasionally considered asking the doctor if it was a symptom of her illness. But she suspected it was something else, something she should keep secret until she understood it better, so she said nothing.) "I was just exploring," she explained to him, taking a deep breath to calm herself. "I've been all through the west wing on this floor, but I've never been in this part of the house."

"Then you haven't seen the turret room?"

"I've climbed up to the top of the west turret. And into all three others. Isn't this one the same?"

"No, it's quite different. It's larger than the others—more like a tower, I'd say—and contains more than bare stone walls with narrow openings. This is truly a room . . . my favorite room in the house, actually. But why waste words, which are always inadequate in these matters? Come, let me show it to you."

She felt suddenly shy and hung back. "Are you certain I'm not detaining you?" she asked. "Surely you have more important things to do."

"Nothing, I assure you. And if I did, I'd happily put it off. I'd much rather keep you company than do anything else."

His words filled her with an unfamiliar joy. As she followed him along the corridor and up a narrow, dark, winding stairway, the words reverberated in her mind like a strain of exquisite music.

As they climbed higher, the shadows surrounding them grew lighter and lighter until the air was as bright as day. The stairs eventually led to a small platform, and then, with one last turn, they were there, on the threshold of the most magnificent room she'd ever seen. It was a wide, circular room completely bathed in light. It seemed like part of the sky! There were hardly any furnishings to obscure the view—only a low fireplace opposite the entrance, with a desk and chair before it, and low, cushioned window seats below all the windows, marking the room's perimeter from the fireplace to the doorway in two unbroken lines. The circular effect was repeated, and enhanced, by the round carpet—all rich reds and golds—set in the center of the stone floor. It was a most unusual room, quite strange, she thought, and quite perfect.

Holding her breath, she moved to the center and turned slowly around. To the south, where the land fell away in a long, gentle slope, the view was mainly of fleecy clouds in a sea of blue, so close she felt she could put out her hand and touch them. To the east, far down below her, was the pond with its waterwheel, looking tiny, and the home woods beyond. To the north were the formal gardens, the walkways, a stretch of green fields, the orchards, and, far away, a stream flowing beneath an arched bridge. And to the west she saw a road winding over swells of land to where the spires and roofs of a distant village seemed to be rising through the mist. "Oh, my *dear*," she breathed, spreading her arms wide and whirling around, "it's a miracle!"

The dizzying turn made her totter, but he'd been standing behind her and caught her at the waist. Holding her lightly, he turned her to face him and gazed down at her with a look she could not fathom. "It's you who are the miracle," he murmured.

The words confused her. "What do you mean?" she asked.

"I'm sorry," he said, abruptly letting her go. "I don't know what I mean." He walked away to one of the windows, dropped down on one of the seats and stared out at the view.

She didn't understand his change of mood. *Would I understand him better,* she asked herself, *if I had my memory?* She felt quite inadequate in comprehending the subtleties of human relationships. Nevertheless, she tried to do what she could to recover the closeness that she'd felt a moment before. "Never mind," she said soothingly, sitting down beside him and putting a hand on his arm. "Whatever you meant, the fact remains that this room is wonderful."

He turned round to face her and forced a smile. "I'm glad you think so. It's my private place, you know, where I come when I have to wrestle with a problem or have a need to be alone. I haven't brought anyone else up here before."

She blinked at him, puzzled. "I don't understand. You sound as if you have more use of this house than Lord Inglesby."

He gaped at her for a moment, then winced and dropped his eyes. "Inglesby gives me the run of the place," he muttered, getting to his feet. "We are good friends, you see. Share and share alike."

"I see," she said. But she didn't see. The friendship between Inglesby and Lord Lucas was another human relationship she didn't understand. The friendship of the two men was obviously close and of very long standing, and although Cassie admired their attachment—their interplay, their joking, their intimacy, their affectionate understanding of each other—she couldn't quite comprehend it. The two men were so different. Lord Lucas, tall and spare, with thick, straight, unruly hair, warm, dark eyes and sensitive mouth, was invariably restrained, thoughtful and keenly aware of what others were feeling. Lord Inglesby, on the other hand, not only looked different from his friend—being broad-shouldered and stocky, with curly red hair, light, suspicious eyes and a dissipated mouth—but seemed to Cassie to be brash, overly blunt and insensitive.

Lord Lucas, apparently troubled by her silence, looked down at her worriedly. "What are you thinking about?" he asked gently.

She sighed. "There's so much I don't understand. Even ordinary things that you say to me . . . that I ought to understand. I suppose this deuced numbness in my brain—"

"No! Dash it all, it's not your fault!" He paced round the room in frustration, as if there were something he wished to explain to her but for some reason could not. "Even with your injury, your mind functions remarkably well. Beautifully, in fact."

"Does it? Truly?" She gazed up at him doubtfully. "Is that what you meant when you said I was a miracle? That my mind functions well?"

"No, I wasn't thinking of your mind at all. You'd said the view was a miracle. But to me, *you're* the miracle, you see, because . . . because . . ." He ran his fingers through his hair in a gesture of helplessness.

"Because—?" she prodded.

The answer seemed to be wrung out of him. "Because you're even more beautiful than the view." Saying the words evidently caused him great discomfort and made him begin to pace again.

"Confound it, Lord Lucas," she said, more confused than ever, "I didn't think you were the sort to tell me pretty lies."

He wheeled about. "How can you think it a lie?" He strode back across the room to her, dropped down beside her and took her chin in his hand. "Listen to me, Cassandra Beringer," he said, forcing her face up so that she had to meet his eyes, "I hadn't intended to tell you this until you'd completely recovered, but the truth is that I'd rather look at your face than at the most magnificent view in the world."

Something inside her clenched with such joy it was almost pain. "You're not making sense," she said, afraid to believe him. "I saw myself in the mirror. I'm not in the *least*—"

"Good God, Cassie, hasn't anyone ever told you—?" But, with a sudden recollection of her condition, he cut himself short. "No, blast it, even if someone had, you wouldn't remember."

Her eyes searched his face. "You can't mean what you're saying!"

"Yes, I can. And I do."

She had to believe him. His voice, his expression, everything about him was sincere. "Oh, my *dear*," she whispered, gazing up at him with shining eyes, "I'll surely remember *this*! If what you just said is truly how you see me, I'll remember those words all my days."

To her surprise, his face clouded over. "I wonder if you will," he said.

"Do you doubt it? How could I possibly forget—?"

"I'm afraid it's quite possible that, when your memory returns, all of this . . . this time we've had together in this house . . . will be erased from your mind."

Her heart contracted in her chest. "Oh, no! Can such a thing really happen?"

"I don't know. The doctor doesn't know. No one knows." He rose from the window seat and stood staring out at the darkening sky. "But you shouldn't let the prospect upset you. This time of your life—this period of recovery—is not important for you to remember."

She stared at his back in horror. "Not *important*?"

"No, it's not. It's like being in limbo for you, isn't it?"

"Limbo? I don't understand. Isn't limbo a kind of Hell? If it is, I cannot be in limbo. Sometimes, these past few days, I've felt . . . almost happy."

He shook his head. "No, I think of limbo as a kind of waiting place, where one is between worlds. In your case, it's the place where you're waiting for your real life to resume."

"My real life . . . yes." She said the words reluctantly, for she didn't want to agree with him despite the logic of his explanation. "That does seem to describe my situation. I suppose I *am* in limbo now."

He sighed deeply, and when he spoke again, his voice was low and hoarse. "That's why I haven't . . . I can't . . ."

"What *is* it?" she asked in agony, desperate to understand him. "*What* can't you?"

"Never mind. It's best we don't speak of it now."

"Why not?" She got to her feet and placed her hand on his arm. "Why can't we speak of it? I believe I can say anything at all to *you*. Why can't you speak to *me*?"

He put his hand on hers, but did not look at her. "I can't. Not yet. Before we can speak of it, you must recognize it . . . be familiar with it. You must *remember* it."

"What is this *it*?" she demanded, her heart seeming to have jumped right into her throat. "*What* must I remember?"

He looked at her then. "Love," he said.

Chapter
~ 17 ~

Lady Schofield, already dressed for dinner although she was half an hour early, walked briskly down the hallway to Cicely's room. She was eager to see what the girl had chosen to wear. While she walked, she tucked a handkerchief into the bosom of her mauve jaconet dinner gown and made a small adjustment to the diamond brooch she'd pinned to the neckline. She felt a bit festive tonight; there was something cheery about their dinners these days, now that Cassie had joined the company. Instead of the depressed gatherings they'd endured when she was still bedridden, dinnertime now had all the appearance of a party.

She stopped at Cicely's door and tapped gently. "Cicely, my love, may I come in?"

"Of course, Aunt Eva," came her niece's voice from within.

She found her niece, attired only in petticoats, sitting at her dressing table, trying to twist some strands of hair into curls. "Are you having difficulty?" she asked at once. "I can send my abigail to you. She is very clever with curls."

"Thank you, no," Cicely said, "this will do, I think." And she put down her brush and turned her face toward her aunt for approval.

Eva studied the coiffure with a critical eye. Cicely had pulled her mop of golden tresses back from her face and tied them up at the back of her head with a silk ribbon, letting the mass fall loosely down like a horse's tail. Only two strands were allowed to escape, one on each side of her face. It was these she'd been trying to curl, to small effect. Nevertheless, Eva had to admit that the girl looked lovely. "A bit too casual for my taste," she decided, "but acceptable enough, I suppose, for a country dinner."

Cicely giggled. "Am I to thank you, dearest aunt, for that high praise?" She jumped up and kissed Eva's cheek. " 'Acceptable enough,' indeed! You should say I look ravishing."

"You can scarcely expect to look ravishing when you refuse to employ a hairdresser. You're as stubborn as your mother. But never mind. I only came to see what gown you've chosen."

"The ivory crepe," Cicely said promptly. "It's right there, laid out on the bed."

Eva scowled in disapproval. "But my dear, you wore that just the other evening. Shouldn't you choose something else?"

"No, for I haven't a great number of dinner gowns with me to choose from. Besides, I like the feel of the silk against me. It clings so delectably. That's what Charlie said."

Eva's brows rose. "Charlie? Are you referring to Lord Lucas? What has he to say to anything?"

"A great deal," her niece retorted, pulling the dress over her head. "I . . . er . . . value his opinion."

"But why?" Eva demanded as Cicely's face emerged from the neck of the dress. "Lucas has never been considered an arbiter of taste, as far as I know."

"I don't care a fig about taste. I . . . well, the truth is, Aunt Eva, I like him. I like him a great deal."

"Lord *Lucas*?" Eva's eyes popped, and she sank down upon the bed with a gasp. "You can't mean you have a . . . a *tendre* for him?"

Cicely colored. "Why should I not?"

"Because you're going to have an offer from Jeremy Tate, that's why not," Eva cried, aghast.

"Stuff and nonsense. Jeremy hasn't troubled his head about me for one instant since we came here." She smoothed the gown over her shoulders and began to button the back. "I don't think he cares for me at all."

"That, my girl, is completely untrue," Eva said with a firmness she was far from feeling. This sudden interest her niece had taken in Lucas was an unexpected development she could not like. But her guiding principle had always been that one should, in all matters, act with decisiveness and firmness. Shilly-shallying never got one anywhere.

With apparently unruffled deliberation, she rose from her perch, went to stand behind her niece and calmly took over the task of buttoning. "Haven't you noticed Jeremy's attentions to your mother?" she asked. "They've been quite marked."

"Have they?" the girl asked, surprised.

"One would have to be blind not to have noticed. And can't you guess why?"

"I can't imagine."

"Because, my dear, he knows he can't win you unless he has her support. Why would he be so solicitous of her unless he was trying to win her over?"

Cicely wrinkled her brow thoughtfully. "Do you really think that's what he has in mind?"

"I'm sure of it," Eva said with absolute conviction.

"You may be right." Cicely smiled at herself in the mirror in the now-buttoned gown. "What other reason *could* he have?"

"Of course I'm right. If you behave as you ought, you'll be betrothed before you know it. And with your mother's complete approval."

"But, Aunt Eva," Cicely murmured, sinking down upon the dressing-table bench, "I'm not at all sure I *want* Jeremy now."

"Don't be foolish," her aunt snapped dismissively. "Of course you want him. What makes you think you don't?"

"The way I feel about Charlie."

"You are speaking utter nonsense," Eva declared loudly, though inside she was shaken. "What is there about that fellow—?"

"He is charming, and he makes everyone laugh, and he . . . he . . ."

Eva glowered at her. "Well, go on. He—?"

The girl put up her chin. "He kissed me."

"*Kissed* you?" Poor Eva, pushed beyond endurance, clasped her hands to her heaving bosom in agitation. "Cicely! How *could* you permit—? Have you no *morals*?"

"Perhaps I haven't," the girl said defensively. "I quite liked it."

"Did you indeed? And I suppose you permitted Jeremy to kiss you, too."

"Yes, I did, once or twice."

"Well? Didn't you like *that*?"

Cicely glanced up at her aunt worriedly. "The truth is, Aunt Eva," she admitted, "that Jeremy never kissed me . . . not *once* . . . the way Charlie did."

"That is because Jeremy is a gentleman, not a rake," her aunt declared firmly. *The best thing to do about this,* she told herself, *is to ignore it.* "Now come along. It's time for dinner."

Although thoroughly upset by this conversation, Eva did not permit her agitation to show. Decisiveness and firmness, that was all that would be needed. Therefore, before her niece crossed the threshold, she fixed an eye on the girl and spoke her final words on the subject. "If you ask me, Cicely, kissing is highly overrated. And has very little to do with marriage anyway."

Cicely mulled over those words all through dinner, though she didn't quite believe them. And she thought about the matter again when they'd all adjourned to the drawing room after dinner. She wished she could talk to someone other than her aunt about the matter . . . but whom?

Tonight the assemblage elected not to play cards. It was for Cassie's sake. Since she'd begun coming down to dinner, the playing of cards was often postponed in order to have an hour or two for reading aloud. They all knew that Cassie had no recollection of the books she'd read in her past and that she perceived that loss as a huge gap in her mind—a gap she was eager to fill. So reading had become her favorite pastime. In addition to spending several hours a day going through the books in the Inglesby library, she loved to spend her evenings listening to the others read aloud. No one seemed to mind this change of routine. It was a way to pass the time pleasantly. Eva had started by reading choice selections from Samuel Pepys's *Diary.* Then Charles, declaiming with histrionic enthusiasm, read some of the ribald adventures of Tom Jones. Next, Jeremy recited his favorite poems of Dryden. And Cicely, choking back tears, read aloud bits of the heartrending struggles of Richardson's *Pamela.* They all agreed that the readings were almost as entertaining as attending a play.

Tonight, however, Eva insisted on reading from a book of sermons. "A little moral uplift will not go amiss," she declared, tossing her niece a pointed look.

As her voice droned on, Charles became bored and quietly rose from his chair. *I need a bit of air*, he mouthed to Jeremy, who'd looked up at him questioningly. With as little noise as possible, he slipped out through the drawing room doors to the terrace.

In a little while, Cicely got up and followed him. Though Eva noticed, she made no sign. It would not do, she told herself, to draw attention to Cicely's indiscretion.

Cicely found Charles leaning on the balustrade, looking up at a bright half-moon. "Are you dreaming of some lady back in London?" she asked, coming up beside him.

"Ah, another of your impertinent questions," he said in disgust, not giving her the satisfaction of looking at her. "Why do you concern yourself with my dreaming, anyway?"

"You interest me, that's all."

"Do I?" He turned from his contemplation of the heavens and gazed at her. In the eerie light, her hair was silvered over, and her silken gown seemed drenched in liquid moonlight. She looked lovely, dangerously lovely. She gave off a glow, like a creature from some mythical kingdom of his imagination—the part of his imagination he hadn't used since childhood. But he was no child now. He was a man much too old for her. And because of that she was dangerous. He warned himself to proceed with extreme care. Nevertheless, he could not resist asking, "Why? Why do I interest you?"

"Well, for one reason, Aunt Eva says you're a rake. I don't believe I've ever met a rake."

"She says that, does she? I wonder what London gossip made her believe that."

"No London gossip. It was I."

"You?" He cocked his head and peered at her moonlit face. "What on *earth* could you have told her—?"

"I told her that you kissed me."

He winced in irritation. "Good heavens, girl, what made you do something so foolish? And did you tell her that you, brazen wench that you are, also kissed *me*?"

"No. I failed to mention that."

He snorted. "I would have wagered a monkey on that."

"It was unfair of me, I suppose. Are you angry at me?"

"I'm always angry at you," he snapped, forcing his eyes away from her. "You're a deuced annoying female."

"I suppose I am. But it's only because I know so little about life. I want to learn. There are things I ought to know."

"What things?"

"Well, for example, Aunt Eva says that kissing has nothing to do with marriage. That can't be true, can it?"

A wave of anger washed over him. *That's all she wants from me,* he told himself, *an old rake's advice!* "See here, Cicely Beringer," he growled furiously, "don't look to *me* to be your teacher. Your damnable questions make me *wild*. Most of the time I have no idea how to answer them; and when I do know, it isn't the sort of thing you should be hearing from a rake." He grabbed her by the shoulders and shook her roughly. "Why don't you do what I've told you more than once to do? Go and find yourself a nice young man and discuss these matters with him!"

Cicely thrust his hands from her shoulders in disgust. "Such a to-do about a simple question," she muttered, turning on her heel and stalking back to the doors. "I was only trying to talk about kissing. It's not as if I were asking questions about something *really* shocking, like seduction. Do you know what *I* think, my lord? I don't believe you're a rake at all. I think you're a *prude!*" And with that she flung open the drawing room doors and disappeared inside.

Charles, sighing in helpless frustration, turned back to his contemplation of the sky. "Clive, my boy," he muttered under his breath, "where are you? I need you! What the devil's keeping you?"

Chapter
~ 18 ~

For the two days following the encounter in the turret room, Cassie couldn't help but notice that her Lord Lucas was avoiding her. The memory of some of what he'd said that day continued to delight her, but there were other remarks she found troubling. These memories caused her to swing from hope to hopelessness and and back again. It was a lonely two days. She often felt like weeping, though she didn't quite understand why. Was he right not to speak to her of love? she wondered. Did she really have to remember what it was? Hadn't her instincts, if not her memory, already taught her what its nature was?

She did not have a private word with him again until they had another accidental encounter, two days later. It was in the upstairs sitting room, where she'd come to read. She'd chosen a book of poetry from the library—Wordsworth's *Lyrical Ballads*—which she'd begun reading the day before and was very much enjoying. But on this day, before settling herself on the sofa with her book, her eye fell on a painting hanging just above the sofa. She was studying it with concentration when Jeremy passed by the open door and spied her. "You're looking at a portrait of one of my . . . of Inglesby's ancestors," he said, entering the room. "A great, great aunt, I believe. Do you like it?"

"Oh, yes, in some ways," she said, throwing him a quick glance before turning her eyes back to the painting. If she concentrated on the portrait, she thought, he might not notice the palpitations that his presence had, as usual, inspired.

"In what ways, may I ask? That is no ordinary portrait, you know. It was done by Sir Peter Lely, who, I'm told, emerged after the Restoration as one of England's finest artists."

"Indeed? Yes, I can see why. Though it seems to me that the facial expression lacks depth, the composition is very fine, the colors are rich, and the brush technique beautifully rendered."

"The brush technique, eh?" He peered down at her closely. "How can you tell?"

"You can tell from the texture of the silk of her gown. See, here, how sumptuous the—" She paused, her hand freezing in its raised position. Then, lowering it slowly, she turned to him with a surprised, questioning look. "How *did* I know all that?"

He grinned at her. "You're a painter yourself, I think. The first time I saw you, you had a smear of yellow paint right there, on your cheek. I found it charming. When I asked you about it, you said you'd been painting lemons."

"Really? How odd."

"Not so very odd. You were probably working on a still life. Do you think you'd like to try to paint now?"

"Now?" She threw him an arch glance. "In my state of *limbo*?"

"Yes. Why not?"

She could see that he was quite serious. "But, my lord, I don't think I . . ."

"I doubt that the doctor would object, if that's what worries you. We can ask him, of course. And we can ask Lady Schofield if I'm right in my surmise about your being a painter." He gazed down at her, enthusiasm glowing in his eyes. "If so, we could send Hickham for your easel and paints and brushes and whatever else you might need, and we could set it all up in the turret room."

"The *turret* room?" She sank down on the sofa, for she suddenly found herself quite breathless at the prospect. "But would Lord Inglesby allow it?"

"Yes, of course he would. I . . . I'm sure of it."

"Oh, my!" She twisted her fingers together to keep them from trembling. "The light there would be perfect."

He grinned down at her. "So you realized that, did you?"

Wide-eyed in astonishment, she stared up at him. "Yes, so I did. How amazing! Perhaps I really *was* a painter."

* * *

She started painting the very next day, after Hickham brought
back the supplies he found at Crestwoods, a large number of
items that included a paint-stained smock. She put it on with
mounting excitement; the mere act of donning it made her feel
like an artist.

As she made her way up the stairs to the turret room
(with Hickham following behind with the easel, paint box
and various other strange supplies), she felt something in
the pocket of her smock. She pulled it out and glanced at
it. It was a note, dated a little more than a month earlier,
addressed to her and signed by Lord Inglesby. She glanced
over it hurriedly. It seemed to be an apology of some sort,
but she had no understanding of it and no interest in studying it now. She stuffed it back in the pocket and turned
her attention to the matter at hand—the challenge of painting.

After Hickham had set up her easel and a small table to
hold the supplies, he left her to her fate. She stared at the
blank canvas bewilderedly. How did one begin? What was
she to paint?

With a great deal of hesitation, she filled a vase with a few
spring flowers and tried to sketch their outlines on the canvas.
She didn't like the result of her first efforts, but she started to
paint anyway. It was amazing how comfortable the brushes felt
in her hand. She dabbled away for hours. It seemed a natural,
felicitous way to spend her time.

She continued to paint for several hours the next day, too,
and for several days after that. In all that time, no one came up
to disturb her. She couldn't help wondering why Lord Lucas
didn't come; he'd seemed so eager when he'd suggested this.
When he finally did come, he explained his absence. "I wanted
to let you work without the burden of being watched. I thought
visitors might make you self-conscious."

She was quick to accept his explanation. "But you needn't
have worried," she added shyly. "You have no idea how much
your presence pleases me."

When he turned to go, she begged him to come again. "I do
so enjoy the company," she said, blushing. "If you wouldn't

mind, you could read to me as I work. Now that I'm spending so many hours here, I don't have as much time to read as I'd like."

He came up often after that. When he came, it was for her the best time of the day. She loved to hear him read. He would settle on a window seat and prop up his legs or perch on the desk with his legs stretched out in front of him, and they would spend an hour or two in the company of the great poets, Shakespeare or Milton or Pope. If this was limbo, she often thought, it was the waiting room of Heaven, not Hell.

But it was not to last. Oddly, it was Shakespeare who triggered the beginning of the end of her state of limbo. Her dear Lord Lucas was reading one of the sonnets, a particularly lovely one. He was leaning on the desk, halfway across the room from her. Cassie had paused in her painting to watch him. She liked to look at his face when he was not aware of her scrutiny. She liked to study the planes of his cheek, the way his dark hair fell over his forehead and how his mouth shaped the words he was reading.

Often, she didn't listen to the words but only heard the music of his voice. Today, however, the words had captured her full attention. Completely enraptured, she was unaware that she'd put down her palette and brush. Absently she wiped her hands on a cloth that hung from the pocket of her smock and moved slowly across the room toward him.

He didn't notice her approach, for his eyes were fixed on the thin volume he held in his hands. At this moment, he was reading:

> *"Yet in these thoughts myself almost despising,*
> *Haply I think on thee—and then my state*
> *Like to the lark at break of day arising*
> *From sullen earth, sings hymns at heaven's gate;*
> *For thy sweet love remembered, such wealth brings*
> *That then I—"*

"—then I scorn to change my state with kings." It was she who finished the line for him. She said it slowly, almost dreamily, a little smile turning up her mouth.

Her voice, so close to his ear, startled him. He had not expected to see her right there in front of him. With him in this position, her head was just a bit above his own, her lips just at the level of his eyes. It seemed as natural as breathing to reach up and pull her to him.

To be held in his arms was perfectly natural to her, too. The mood of the poem had completely enveloped her. "I do so love that line," she murmured, lifting a hand to his cheek.

"Yes, I, too," he said, tightening his hold. The book fell to the floor unheeded as he drew her head down until her lips met his.

They kissed for a long moment, she so dizzy with the joy of it that she clung to him with a passionate intensity. And he, too, was carried away by it, at least for a moment. His pulse raced and his heart pounded. He'd yearned for this, dreamed of it, since that first night he'd seen her. But even now, in the midst of this heady bliss, he felt guilty for taking advantage of her innocence. And, in addition, something new was nagging at him, an alarm of some kind, a warning instinct like a bell ringing away at the back of his mind and interfering with his concentration.

Suddenly the reason for this disturbance burst upon him. He lifted his head and stared at her. "*What* did you just say?"

She gazed up at him in a dreamlike trance. "Hmmm?"

He held her off. "I'd just said, 'For thy sweet love remembered, such wealth brings.' And then you said—"

The dreamy look in her eyes died away. " 'That then I scorn to change my state with kings.' Is something amiss?"

"Didn't you tell me you'd not yet read the sonnets?" he reminded her, staring at her in shock.

"I haven't looked at them."

He dropped his hold on her and stood up, running a hand through his hair. "Don't you see? You must have *remembered* it!"

She gasped. "Good heavens! I *did*!"

He shut his eyes as if in pain. "I think, my dear, that you may be starting to recover your memory."

"Oh, dear!" She put a trembling hand to her forehead. "If I am," she said, her voice shaking, "I'm not at all sure that I'm happy about it."

He pulled her back in his arms and, praying fervently that she'd still remember this moment when her other memories returned, leaned his cheek against her hair. "Neither am I."

Chapter
~ 19 ~

Cassie went slowly to her bedroom, feeling frightened and confused. There was much she didn't understand. She didn't understand why, after that unforgettable embrace, Lord Lucas had made an unaccountably abrupt departure from the turret room. She didn't understand why she remembered the last line of the sonnet without even realizing that she was remembering it. And she didn't understand what the effect would be of other changes of memory. What would it be like to remember her past? How would her present life be changed by those memories? There was a great deal to be frightened of.

She was thankful that her bedroom was deserted. Fearfully she sat down at her dressing table and stared at herself in the mirror. Yes, just as she had feared, the face in the glass was a bit different from the one she'd seen this morning. The discoloration of her left cheek, which she knew she'd seen this morning, nevertheless surprised her. She was remembering her *other* face at last—the face she'd known before the accident! She studied it with some dismay. What had she *done* to herself these past weeks? Why had she let herself be seen looking so pale and unkempt, with that bruise disfiguring her face and her hair hanging limply down in the informal simplicity of this careless single braid? *How could I have let Lord Lucas see me like this?* she asked herself in horror.

She covered her face with her hands for a moment, to try to accustom herself to this new-old face. When she looked again, someone else was in the mirror, standing behind her. It was Mrs. Upsom, who'd been tending to her needs all these weeks. Cassie knew her perfectly well, but somehow, at this moment, her face seemed much more familiar. "*Annie!*" she gasped, jumping to her feet and whirling about. "It's my own Annie!" she cried, holding out her arms.

Mrs. Upsom, after a moment of astonishment, took her into a tearful embrace. "Oh, ma'am," she cried, "I never thought to hear you calling my name like that again!"

After a while, Cassie held her off and peered at the gray-eyed, full-cheeked face. "Oh, Annie, how could I have looked at you every day this past month and not seen that it was *you*?"

Mrs. Upsom brushed away the wetness on her cheeks. "It doesn't matter, ma'am, so long as you 'member me now."

Memories crowded in: Annie bringing up clean laundry . . . Annie in the kitchen, arguing with Cook about the dinner menu . . . Annie pinning up a hem for her. So many impressions, so many pictures crowding in on her mind. It was overwhelming. She had to sit down and shut her eyes.

Later, when she was calmer, and Annie was helping her dress for dinner, she looked over at her housekeeper with mock severity. "What on earth's been wrong with you, Annie, since you've been here? How could you have let me go downstairs with my hair like this?"

"You wouldn't let me dress it, ma'am. You didn't seem to care about it."

"Well, I care now. Let's see what we can do to make me a bit more presentable."

Nothing could have pleased Mrs. Upsom more. For the next hour she brushed her ladyship's hair to a glowing shine, twisted it into a tight curl and pinned it in a neat bun at the nape of Cassie's neck. Then she covered the bruised cheek with face powder and applied a touch of blacking to her lashes. They chose the lilac silk dinner dress, Cassie suddenly remembering that it had been one of her favorites. Then she looked at herself in the mirror. The woman looking back at her was blessedly familiar. And though she'd seen her looking better, the sight was less upsetting than it had been earlier.

She went down to dinner with nervous steps, not knowing how this strange "awakening" was going to proceed. How different would tonight's gathering be? Would she be struck with many more memories? And if she were, could she *bear* it?

Cicely, Eva and the two gentlemen were in the drawing room waiting for her, and they all gasped with delight at her improved appearance. She could see, however, that Lord Lucas was regarding her a bit nervously. *He's wondering if I've remembered anything else,* she realized. But she was too beset with new memories to be able to speak to him or relieve his mind. As she looked at each face, she was so overwhelmed with strange familiarity that she could not speak. Smiling politely, trying her best to keep from showing that anything had changed, she let her host, Lord Inglesby, lead her into the dining room.

As they took their places and settled into the routine of dining, she sat in her place and let the new sensations wash over her. She was feeling faint. A floodgate had opened in her mind, and she was drowning in memories. Opposite her sat her beloved daughter, whom she hadn't recognized for over a month. She wanted to cry out in love and agony. How could this dear child, who'd filled her life and heart for eighteen years, have disappeared from her consciousness for even a moment, much less a month? The pain was almost insupportable. And there was Eva—dear to her for a lifetime—suddenly recognizable as her sister again. She clenched her hands tightly in her lap, struggling to keep from weeping.

She turned her eyes to Lord Inglesby at the head of the table. He was contentedly eating his braised goose and carrying on a spirited argument with Eva about the wine, stoutly defending the dry white Bordeaux they were drinking, while Eva claimed that a rich red Burgundy was more appropriate for goose. Cassie, feeling a wave of dislike for him, suddenly recollected why she'd come to this house. It was to keep him from renewing his courtship of her daughter. What, she wondered, had been going on in that regard during these weeks? Had he been using this enforced association to pursue his suit? All at once the weight of her old problems and old responsibilities bore down on her. Was this the price of recovery?

Slowly, as if she'd purposely kept him for last, she turned her eyes to Lord Lucas. The sight of his lean face and unruly hair gave her heart a lift. His eyes were fixed on hers as if he had a sense of what she was going through, and, moreover, as if he were fearful that she'd changed. *Don't worry, my love,* she wanted to say to him, *you are the only one here who has not changed in my eyes.*

"If the wine were more suitable," Eva was saying to her host, "even Cicely would find the goose edible."

"No, I wouldn't, Aunt Eva," the girl put in. "I wouldn't like goose no matter what the wine."

Cassie lifted her head. "Even as a child, Cicely wouldn't touch goose," she said softly, trying to keep her voice quite ordinary. "She once had a goose for a pet, you see."

For a second or two, everyone seemed to proceed as though nothing extraordinary had been said. Then Eva gasped. The gasp stirred Cicely's consciousness. *"Mama!"* she cried, her eyes widening. "Did you *remember*—?"

"Yes, my darling," Cassie whispered, holding out a trembling hand across the table, her eyes filling with tears, "you have your mother back again."

Chapter
~ 20 ~

The three women held an ecstatic, if tearful, reunion. Later, seated in the drawing room in an easy chair, with her daughter perched on an ottoman at her feet and the others close by, Cassie tried to catch her breath. She was emotionally exhausted, but the faces around her looked too happy to permit her to bring the evening to an end. All were chattering excitedly, all were smiling, all were asking her questions about her recollections . . . all except her Lord Lucas, who stood at the window, more a watcher than a participant in the celebration.

He'd suggested to their host, a little while earlier, that the occasion required champagne, but it was not until Hickham had brought the tray and passed out the glasses that Cassie found an opportunity to speak to him privately. After the toasts, as the others merrily sipped the effervescent wine, she got up and joined him at the window. "You don't seem glad for me, my lord," she said in gentle reproof.

"You know better than that," he said bluntly.

"Then why are you not celebrating?"

"For several reasons. First, because I see in your eyes that *you're* not celebrating."

She shook her head in amazement. "It's truly remarkable how well you understand me!"

He took her hand in his. "What troubles you, my dear? You should be overjoyed."

"I am, in truth. It's only . . ." She lowered her head and sighed. "There's a benefit to being without one's memory, strange to say. When one has no past, one has no problems. There's a certain—how shall I describe it?—*lightness* in not having a past to carry on one's shoulders. Now that I remember the problems, I feel suddenly weighted down with them."

"Any problem in particular?"

"Cicely's romance with your friend is one of them." She looked over her shoulder at the man she believed to be Inglesby. "I thought I knew what to do about him before . . . but now I'm too confused to be sure."

"I see. I wish I . . ." He glanced over at his friend and then shrugged helplessly. "At least I can promise that it will all work out in time. You needn't solve all your problems at once, you know."

"Yes, I know. I told you I'm far from unhappy. But what did you mean when you said you had *several* reasons for not celebrating? What other reasons do you have?"

For a moment he seemed unwilling to answer, but after meeting her earnest gaze, he tried. "You're so rapidly going back to becoming the woman you were that I'm afraid . . ." He hesitated, dropped her hand and shook his head, reluctant to proceed.

"Afraid of what?" she prodded.

He eyed her askance, resorting to the gesture he always used when he felt helpless—running his fingers through the hair that constantly fell over his forehead. "You're so preoccupied with remembering your past that I may disappear from your mind."

To her, that possibility was ridiculous. "Oh, pooh! That could never be!"

"I fear it can. Do you remember *me* from that past?"

"Only a bit. I don't believe I knew you very well."

"You didn't know me at all. You only met me for a moment, right before your accident."

"Yes, I seem to recall that." She wrinkled her brow thoughtfully, trying to conjure up the scene. "You came into the room—the morning room, wasn't it?—just as I was leaving. You asked me about the paint smudge on my cheek."

"Yes, that's right. The entire substance of our meeting."

She heard the rasp of irony in his voice but did not understand it. "Does it matter that we were not well acquainted?"

He peered down at her intently. "I don't know. Does it?"

"Not to me."

"But you thought, when you began your recovery, that I'd been your best friend."

"I was evidently mistaken. But you are my best friend now."

He seemed disappointed by that answer. "And I'll always remain so, if that's what you wish," he said, turning away from her puzzled scrutiny.

"Of course it's what I wish." She laid her hand gently on his arm. "Did you believe I would not?"

He covered her hand with his. "I hoped—" he began.

But he was interrupted by the appearance of Hickham at the door. "My lord," the fellow said loudly, looking fixedly at each of the two men in the room, his eyes flicking from one to the other, "there's a visitor for you."

Jeremy and Charlie exchanged glances. "For me?" Charlie asked.

Hickham nodded vigorously. "Yes, m'lord. A Mr. Clive Percy." And he made a nervous gesture with his head toward the door.

"Percy?" Cassie asked, glancing up at Jeremy interestedly. "A relative of yours, Lord Lucas?"

But before Jeremy could think of an answer, and before Charlie had managed to cross the room to stop the intrusion, a young man appeared in the doorway. He was a tall, muscular, pleasant-featured young fellow about twenty-two years of age, with the ruddy complexion and confident carriage of a sportsman. His clothes also bespoke the sportsman, for his greatcoat hung carelessly open to reveal riding clothes underneath, and his boots had been chosen for rugged wear rather than appearance. He took a quick look about the room, saw Charlie bearing down on him and immediately put out his hand. "Good evening, Uncle Charles," he said with hearty good humor. "I've taken you up on your invitation, as you can see."

They shook hands, Charlie throwing Jeremy a look of desperation. "Good to see you, my boy," he mumbled, trying to shove the young man toward the door. "Come with me to the hall and let's get you out of your coat before I make you known to the ladies."

"Nonsense, the coat can wait," the boy insisted, resisting his uncle's pressure. "I must at least be permitted to thank Lord Inglesby for his hospitality." While he spoke, he made his way across the room to the window, and he was pumping Jeremy's hand before his uncle could say another word. "I say, Lord Inglesby, it was deuced kind of you to have me. I was going out of my mind with boredom hibernating at Mama's."

Charles groaned. Eva and Cicely, their faces clouding, looked over at Cassie in alarm. Jeremy, utterly speechless, let the young man shake his hand. Cassie was thoroughly confused; she wondered why no one was correcting this strange young man's mistake. "Don't you know your own uncle, young man?" she asked.

"Of course I do," Clive Percy said, looking at her with surprise. "Known him all my life."

"Then why are you calling him Lord Inglesby?"

He peered at her for a moment, his brow knitting suspiciously. "Are you making a game of me? I've known Lord Inglesby all my life as well. He's my godfather."

"But *this* man is not—" she began. Then she took note of the faces staring at her. Why, she wondered, where they all gaping at *her* so strangely when they should have been gaping at the visitor? *Unless* . . . She felt an ice-cold spasm clench her chest . . . *Unless he was speaking the truth.* But he couldn't be! She remembered Lord Lucas as well as anyone. She could even recall his face as it was *before* the accident. How could she have mistaken him?

Her eyes flew up to Jeremy's face. "Have I lost my mind *again*?" she asked pathetically.

He looked stricken. "No, no, of *course* not! Please don't think such a thing!" He threw an agonized look at Charlie. "I *knew* we should never have—!"

"Confound it, it was only meant to be a joke!" Charlie said miserably.

"The doctor thought we shouldn't tell you," Eva said, taking a step toward her, her eyes brimming with sympathy. "Not until you were fully recovered."

Cicely, as usual, started to cry.

But Cassie was staring in wide-eyed horror at Jeremy. "Then you *are* Inglesby?" she asked, her voice choked.

"Does it matter so much?" He grasped both her hands, his eyes pleading. "I'm the same, no matter what I'm called."

She didn't answer. She couldn't, for she was overwhelmed with a sense of betrayal. She pulled her hands from his, clapped them to her mouth and, throwing him one last look of reproach, ran from the room.

He stared after her, feeling more helpless than ever. "Damnation," he muttered, "what do I do now?"

Chapter
~ 21 ~

They all stood staring at the door, Charles abashed, Eva frightened, Cicely sobbing, and Jeremy white at the mouth. Young Clive, whose brash entrance had precipitated the crisis, blinked at them all in confusion. "Dash it all, what did I say?" the young fellow asked in dismay.

"Nothing," said his uncle. "It was not your fault."

"Do you think that this muddle will affect her recovery?" Eva Schofield asked in concern.

"Well, Dr. Swan did warn us—" Charlie began.

"The doctor be hanged," Jeremy snapped. "We never should have lied to her!"

"P-poor Mama!" wept Cicely.

"Must you always be a watering pot, child?" her aunt admonished. "Stop your foolish wailing! Much good tears will do for your mother."

"Hang it, your ladyship," Charlie burst out, "we know that you're alarmed, but you needn't take it out on the girl. None of this is her doing."

Cicely, unaccustomed to such defense, lifted her head and threw him a look of melting gratitude. From that moment her sobs ceased, and her tears dried on her cheeks.

That look inspired new courage in Charles's chest. "Perhaps I ought to go up to Lady Beringer and explain. This contretemps is all of my doing, after all."

"No," Jeremy said, starting for the door. "I'll go."

Lady Schofield heaved herself from the chair into which she'd been sunk. "Wait, Jeremy. I'll go with you."

As she hurried out the door, Cicely glanced once more at her protector, smiled at him wanly and followed her aunt. Her

118

voice floated back to the two who still remained: "Aunt Eva, wait for me!"

Clive, to whom none of this had made a bit of sense, nevertheless stood staring at the now-deserted doorway with a gaping mouth. "Tell me, Uncle Charlie," he asked, awestruck, "was that the chit you wrote to Mama about?"

His uncle favored him with a glower. "If it was, I certainly did not refer to the lady as a 'chit.' Her name is Miss Beringer. Cicely Beringer."

The boy grinned. "Whatever you call her, you were decidedly in the right about her. The girl's an out-and-outer if ever I saw one." He slapped his uncle vigorously on the back. "A regular out-and-outer!"

Charles tottered from the force of the boy's affection. "I'm delighted to hear it," he said tartly as he regained his balance. "Nothing is more pleasing to an old man like me than to have his opinions approved by a young upstart."

But his sarcasm went completely unnoticed. His nephew merely dropped down on a chair, stretched out his booted legs and sighed contentedly. "I'll admit to you, Uncle Charlie, that I started out on this visit only to do the pretty, you know? For your sake, because Mama said you needed me. But now, I'm sure-as-check glad I came."

Chapter
~ 22 ~

Cassie shut her bedroom door and leaned against it, breathing heavily. The past few hours had been too much to bear. The life she thought she'd lost was rushing back at her like a flood of water from a broken dam, while the life she'd been clinging to for the last month was crashing down in ruins all about her. She was drowning and being battered, both at the same time.

They would all be coming up to see her, she knew that. To make explanations, apologies, promises. But she didn't want to listen. She had to be alone for a while, to think, to try to sort out this confusion of old memories, new impressions and turbulent feelings, to make some sense of it all, to find some peace. But she'd foolishly revealed her inner frenzy by running out of the room in that dramatic fashion, so the others were bound to come up and show their concern. In fact, she could already hear footsteps down the corridor. If there were only a way to lock them all out . . .

As if in answer to a prayer, Mrs. Upsom emerged from the dressing room at that moment. "Is the celebration over already, ma'am?" she asked cheerfully. But then she saw her mistress's face and clutched her chest in alarm. "Oh, my poor heart! What's *happened* to you?"

"Annie! My dear, you're just the person I need. Go outside, quickly! If anyone wants to see me, tell them I've gone to bed. If they insist, assure them that I'm quite well but very tired. I'll see them all tomorrow." She gave the woman a quick embrace and thrust her out the door. "Please, Annie," she begged before shutting the door on her, "be firm!"

Evidently Annie *was* firm, for despite some low-voiced exchanges out in the corridor, no one knocked at the door.

Cassie sighed in relief when the footsteps retreated. Still too upset to go to bed, however, she blew out her candle and perched on the window seat. Annie peeped in, but seeing that the room was dark, she too retreated. All became silent. Now at last, Cassie was alone.

She stared out the window at the night sky. The moon was playing hide-and-seek with the clouds, but Cassie did not really see it. She was too concerned with the tumult of her feelings. If she were honest with herself, she would admit that this inner turbulence was caused more by learning Lord Inglesby's true identity than by anything else she'd discovered in this day of shattering discoveries. He was not Lord Lucas. He was Jeremy Tate, Viscount Inglesby. Why was that discovery more shattering than the others? It made no sense. What difference did the name make? As he himself had pointed out, he was still the same man, whatever his name. Why did she feel so *betrayed*?

To find the answer, she had to ask herself why this matter was of such concern to her. Why, in fact, was his every word, every look, every facial expression so significant to her happiness? But she knew the answer to that question. She loved him. She'd known it for weeks. She hadn't let herself confront that feeling because he'd said she had to *remember* love first. Well, she remembered now, for all the good it did. She remembered that she'd never experienced love before. Yes, she knew what mother love was. And familial love. But the love between a man and a woman was new to her. Her experience as a wife had been so unpleasant that she'd made up her mind to avoid marriage—and thus love—forever. She might never have permitted herself to fall in love with Lucas—no, Inglesby!—if her memory had not failed her.

But it *had* failed her, and she loved him now. It was too late to use her old memories as a shield.

But she loved *him,* not his name. Why had the discovery of his real name come as such a blow? Was it because she loved him, and he'd lied to her?

No, there was something more to it. There was an explanation for the lie, she knew that. She wasn't sure what the explanation was, but she was sure Charles Percy was responsible, not her Jeremy. ("Jeremy," she murmured, aloud. It was a beautiful, melodious name. It suited him.) So what was there about the name that was so disturbing?

She had to search that newly restored memory for the answer. She knew she'd not seen him before the night of the accident, but she *had* heard the name. Where? How? In what connection? She remembered she'd come to this house to see him, but why?

Suddenly her mind made the connection. Good God! It wasn't the red-headed, stocky, rakish Charles Percy who had courted Cicely—it was her *Jeremy*! It was Lord Inglesby from whom Cicely had wanted an offer!

Her heart sank in her chest like a stone. The man she loved had wanted to marry her daughter! She'd opposed the idea from the first, but now that she knew him—how fine, how kind, how perfectly suitable he was!—she could not in good conscience stand in Cicely's way. Yet she felt ill at the thought of it . . . ill of jealousy . . . jealousy of her own daughter!

But wait, she thought. If memory served (though it had served her ill for a long time), Jeremy had not come up to scratch. Or had he? It was all so confusing. Had he wanted to make an offer to Cicely or hadn't he? Why were the details so blastedly vague?

As if in answer to the question, a memory flashed into her mind. A recent memory. She was climbing up the stairs to the turret room, with Hickham behind her carrying the easel. She was wearing her old smock, and she found a note in the pocket. An apology of some sort, from *him*! She hadn't bothered to read it, believing it to have been written by the man she now knew was Lord Lucas. But she wanted very much to read it now. She *needed* to read it. It must still be in the pocket of the smock, she realized. But the smock was hanging on the easel in the turret room.

Without a moment's hesitation, she leapt up from the window seat and, with shaking hands, felt for the tinder box and candle on her night table. She would go up to get the note right now, this moment. She could not bear to wait till morning.

The candlelight threw huge, frightening shadows on the stone walls of the winding stairs as she made her way up.

The familiar passageway was not at all familiar without daylight streaming down. And when she stepped over the threshold into the glass-enclosed room, she found it not quite dark but faintly frosted with an eerie light that made her gasp. Yet, though she shivered in fright, there was something beautiful about the room at night. The hide-and-seek moon was completely covered by a cloud at this moment, but the hiding place was made immediately apparent by the cloud's silvered edge. It was that rim of silver that gave the room its unearthly glow.

She set her candle down on her worktable and went to the nearest window. *Poor moon,* she thought, gazing out at the luminescent sky, *you're too conspicuous a creature to hide away successfully.*

With a sigh, she turned back to the task at hand. She pulled the note from the pocket of the smock, unfolded it and spread it on the table near the candle. Her eyes raced over the words. It was the last sentence that smote her heart. She had to say the words aloud to convince herself that they were true: *"I would be more grateful still if you would permit me to call on you at your convenience, so that I may try to win your permission to speak to your daughter on the subject of marriage. Yours most humbly, Jere—"*

"Jeremy Tate, Viscount Inglesby," came his voice from somewhere behind her. "Yes, I wrote those words."

Cassie stiffened in shock. Too startled to move, she could only gasp.

"I'd never have asked to speak to the daughter," he said from the shadows, "if I'd ever had a glimpse of the mother."

She whirled about. "You!" Her heart pounding, she peered into the gloom where she could just barely discern his outline. "Good God, you made my heart stop beating!"

He materialized from out of the darkness, looking gaunt and ghostly as he moved toward her in the eerie light. "I didn't mean to frighten you, my dear, but I didn't know how to make my presence known without doing so."

"You needn't have waited until you overheard me," she said furiously, hoping that this flash of anger would have a calming effect on her racing pulse.

He grinned down at her fondly. "How could I have guessed, little idiot, that you'd *speak*?"

She dropped her eyes. "What are you doing here at all, at this ungodly hour?"

"I told you I come here when I'm troubled. I often do so, even at ungodly hours. I might also point out, Cassie, my dear, that it's an ungodly hour for letter reading, too."

She picked the letter up and crushed it in her hand. She wished she didn't have to speak of it. But she had no choice. It was a matter she had to face.

With a show of spirit, she looked up and met his gaze. "Why do you choose to call me Cassie now, when there should be a strict formality between us, after you called me Lady Beringer all these weeks when I yearned for the informality of my given name."

"It *is* ironic, I admit. I didn't call you Cassie then because I couldn't bear to have you call me Charles. But why, ma'am, should there be strict formality between us now?"

"You know perfectly well why." She tossed the crushed letter on the table, the symbol of what stood between them. "You are my daughter's suitor. You must treat me with the dignity one accords one's prospective mother-in-law."

"I *was* your daughter's suitor. But you must know I cannot be that any longer."

"Nonsense. Of course you can. And this time round I shall give you both my heartfelt blessing."

He gasped her shoulders with angry cruelty. "Don't be a fool. You can't pretend that nothing has happened between us."

"There *is* nothing between us. Nothing but . . . but friendship. You said it yourself, this very evening."

"If I said that, it was a lie."

She twisted in his grasp but couldn't free herself. "It seems I've had little else but lies from you."

His grip tightened. "Damn it, Cassie, I love you! And that's no lie!"

The words burned into her, making her wince in pain. But after a moment she made herself look up to meet his fiery eyes. "But I don't love you," she said.

"Now, *that* is a lie," he declared, "and, with your leave or without it, I'll prove it to you."

Before she could guess what he was about, he pulled her to him and kissed her, hard. It was an act of belligerence, defiant and angry. It was not like him. Not like the kind, generous, unselfish man she knew. Nor was the kiss at all like the gentle, loving, dream-drenched kiss he'd given her before. This kiss was demanding, and passionately arrogant. If she could have freed her arm, she would have slapped his face. And yet something inside her, something over which she had no control, responded to it. She felt a flush of heat, a spasm of desire, a powerful yearning just to surrender to the demands of his arms and mouth. *Good God*, she thought, *has he kissed others this way? Cicely?*

The thought of Cicely gave her strength. She wrenched herself from his hold and backed away. "No," she gasped, "no! This proves nothing but your arrogance."

"Arrogance?" He glared at her scornfully. "Because I know what I see in your face? Do you think me a green boy, or a blasted coxcomb who flatters himself that he finds adoration wherever he sets his eye? I felt your tremors in my embrace. How can you pretend that you feel nothing?"

"Whatever I feel for you was won from me by trickery. By the trick of a memory dysfunction. By the trick of a much-needed friendship. By the trick of a false name." She dashed away the tears that had sprung unbidden from her eyes. "By the trickery of this room, and the moonlight and the force of your attack."

His jaw, his hands, every muscle in his body stiffened in chagrin. "I intended no attack—!"

She held up a hand to stop him. "I don't blame you for it. We are both victims of these damnable circumstances." She moved on trembling legs to the window seat and dropped down on it, fixing her eyes on the scudding, gilt-edged clouds. "You said once that you would not speak to me of love until I remembered it," she reminded him, her voice now soft and forgiving. "That was kind. So very kind. But, you see, the only love I remember is the love I feel for Cicely. It has been—and will always be—the guiding force of my life. I cannot become her rival. The very thought is repugnant."

The finality of her words struck him like a blow. He was silent for a long time. "What is it you expect of me, then?" he asked at last.

"Only that you do what you asked to do in your letter. Offer for Cicely."

"Only that?" He laughed bitterly. "A small task indeed." He strode over to her and sat down beside her. "How can you ask it, Cassie, knowing that it's you I wish to wed?"

His words made her heart clench like a fist, but she forced herself to speak in a detached tone that would not reflect her inner agony. "It is not a serious desire, my dear," she assured him.

"That is something you cannot know," he retorted.

She stared at him in the dim light, at the lines of his face, the lock of hair that always fell over his forehead, his strong chin and the shapely mouth that, so few moments ago, had stirred up an agony of passion in her breast simply by touching hers. But she could not let herself dwell on these things. Nor could she permit him to do it. "It's merely calf-love, the kind boys feel for an older woman," she insisted. "You'll soon get over it."

"You know that's humbug," he said dully.

She heard the despair of defeat in his voice. "But you'll do it? Renew your offer to my daughter?"

He nodded glumly. "If you wish it."

"I do. More than anything."

They sat for a moment in miserable silence, not looking at each other. Then he expelled a deep breath. "You will give me a fortnight or so to . . . to collect myself, won't you, before I pursue my courtship?"

"Yes, of course, if you think it necessary."

"Quite necessary, I assure you."

She rose and went to the table for her candle. "You'll see," she said with a confidence she did not feel as she made for the doorway. "You'll forget all this. Forgetting is quite easy, I promise you. It's remembering that's hard."

"Right," he said dryly. "All I need is a memory dysfunction. Perhaps I should go outside and take a fall down the stairs."

She showed no reaction to the riposte. But at the threshold she paused. "Good night, my lord," she said, taking a lingering look at his form silhouetted against the eerie light.

"Damn it," he said furiously, getting up and striding across the room to her, "at least call me by my name this once."

The candle wobbled in her hand. "Good night, Jeremy," she whispered.

He gave her no return of her good night. Instead, he grasped her shoulders once more, lifted her up and kissed her mouth. Her candle fell to the floor, where it continued to burn unheeded. She struggled in his hold, whimpering, but he merely held her tighter. Only when they were both bereft of breath did he let her go. "There," he said coldly, setting her on her feet, restoring her candle to her hand and making off down the dark stairs. "Let's see how easily you can forget that."

Chapter
~ 23 ~

There was no trace of a cloud in the sky the next morning, but Cicely, still depressed about the ending of the celebration the night before, was not cheered by the glorious day. She came down to breakfast heavy-eyed and glum. No one was in the morning room but Hickham and the new arrival, Mr. Clive Percy. The young man, very dashing in his riding clothes, was at the buffet, helping himself to a thick slice of ham. When Cicely wandered in, trailing yards of the sheer dimity flounces of her morning robe and a cloud of sighs, Clive's face immediately brightened. "Ah, Miss Beringer! Good morning! I was hoping you'd be the first."

"Were you indeed?" she responded uninterestedly. "And why is that?"

"I wanted to ask you to go riding with me."

"Thank you," she said, taking a place at the table and reaching for the teapot, "but I'm in no mood to go gallivanting this morning."

"Why not? Firstly, a sport like riding cannot be called gallivanting. Secondly, it's a marvelous day, exactly right for outdoor exercise. And thirdly, you'll have your choice from among the very best horses. The Inglesby stables are the best in the county."

She snorted. "I don't need you to tell me that. I've been here more than a month."

"But there's something you may not know, and that is that I—if I do say so as shouldn't—am the perfect riding partner for a young lady. I know horses, and I can choose one that will be both spirited and gentle enough for your safety."

"Oh, you can, can you? You're quite a conceited young man, aren't you?"

"No. Only confident."

She gave him a long look, ripe with disdain. "And what makes you think I can't choose my own horse?"

He placed his loaded plate on the table, threw his leg over the chair beside her with youthful energy and dropped down upon it. "Because you ladies don't take the time and trouble to study the animals. You're too busy filling your heads with trumpery things—frills and furbelows and suchlike nonsense."

"Is that so?" She rose to her feet with the proud hauteur of an avenging goddess. "I'll have you know, Mr. Clive Whatever-your-name, that women are often better riders than men. I myself have been riding since I was six, and will take second to no man in my knowledge of horseflesh. And if you don't believe me, I'll choose my own horse and outrace you without so much as turning a hair!"

He grinned up at her. "You will, eh? Now?"

She stalked to the door. "As soon as I can change."

"That's the spirit," he said, chuckling, and turned his attention to his breakfast.

On the stairs, she came face-to-face with Charles, who was on his way down. "Good morning, my dear," he greeted cheerfully. "Where are you going in such a hurry?"

"I'm off to ride with your obnoxious nephew," she said, brushing by him. But after taking three steps, she stopped in her tracks. "Oh, I say! That's not . . . he's not—! *Charles!*"

He looked up at her over his shoulder. "Yes?" he asked innocently.

"That's not . . . It can't be . . . the young man you've chosen to . . . to *court* me!"

The scorn in her voice made him stiffen in defense. "Why not?" he demanded. "He's handsome, is he not? And charming? And bursting with youth and vigor?"

She frowned down at him. "Yes, I suppose he's all of those things."

"Well, then?"

She threw him a pitying look before turning on her heel

and marching on up the stairs. "Charles Percy," she said as she disappeared from his view, "you *are* a fool."

She had donned her riding habit and just sat down at her dressing table to put up her hair when there was a tap at the door. "If you think I will explain myself any further, Lord Lucas," she said to the closed door, "you much mistake me. You're quite old enough to decipher my meaning for yourself."

"This is not Lord Lucas, my love," came a voice from outside. "It's your mother."

"Mama!" the girl cried, flying to the door. "Come in!"

They embraced warmly on the threshold, and then Cicely drew her mother into the room and shut the door. She studied her mother's face closely. "Are you well, dearest? The ado last night didn't too greatly overset you, did it?"

"I'm quite recovered. But I seem to be interrupting you. Are you going to ride?"

"Yes. I promised to race with Lord Lucas's overbearing nephew. I was about to put up my hair."

"Let me do it," Cassie said, urging the girl to the dressing table. "I think I can still remember how."

"Oh, Mama," the girl sighed, meeting her mother's eyes in the glass, "how very lovely it is to have you back."

Cassie smiled at her and picked up the brush. "I remember doing this when you were little. There was a red ribbon you always insisted on wearing. You would not give it up until it had frayed so badly it was nothing but string."

"But you didn't come in to reminisce about red ribbons, did you? What is it, Mama?"

Cassie twisted Cicely's silky hair into a tight bun, but with the ends hanging loosely down in short ringlets, in a style that would look charming beneath her cocky little riding hat. "So you're enjoying this stay here at Inglesby Park, are you?" she asked, beginning to pin the bun up.

"I am lately . . . since you started to heal," the girl admitted. "Why?"

"Are you enjoying it so much that you wish to remain much longer?"

Cicely, surprised by the question, turned round on the seat, causing the half-pinned bun to tumble down. "Remain? Why?" Then her eyes widened in delight. "Oh, my dearest, do you mean you're ready to go *home*?"

"More than ready," Cassie admitted. "I'm positively *eager*."

"Oh, Mama!" The girl threw her arms about her mother's waist and hugged her tightly. "If it means that you're well again, and that we shall be as we used to be, there's nothing I'd like better than to go home."

Cassie held her close for a long moment. Then she stepped back, turned her daughter to face the mirror and reached for the hairpins. "But we can speak of this later," she said, pinning up the bun again. "Meanwhile, we must finish your hair. It won't do to keep Lord Lucas's overbearing nephew waiting."

Chapter
~ 24 ~

Once the idea of departure was accepted by both Cicely and Eva, Cassie did not take long to put it into execution. By the next morning the carriage their host offered them for their transport home was loaded with their luggage, and by nine the three ladies were dressed and ready for travel.

Mrs. Upsom and Eva's abigail were already seated in the phaeton when Eva, Cicely and Cassie came downstairs. The small household staff had lined up in the entryway to say good-bye. Mrs. Stemple wept unashamedly. Hickham boldly stepped forward and actually shook Cassie's hand. "Best of luck to ye, m'lady," he said gruffly, and blew his nose into a large handkerchief. After he recovered, he added, "I 'ope ye'll come back soon."

Jeremy, Charles and Clive were pacing about outside, near the carriage. But they stopped in their tracks when the ladies emerged, and they watched, motionless, as the three of them descended the stairs.

It was an almost silent little group that milled about at the side of the carriage. Jeremy was the first to act. He kissed Eva's hand and handed her up. Then Cicely turned to Charles. "I hope you'll come to Crest—" she began, holding out her hand to him.

But the brash young nephew stepped between them and took her hand for himself. "I hear that Crestwoods is only fifteen miles distant," he said with his charming grin. "You can wager I'll call on you tomorrow." And before she could turn back to Charles, Clive was lifting her up on the steps.

If Charles was frustrated by this usurpation of his opportunity to say his farewells, he gave no sign of it. "Good-bye,

Cicely, my dear," he said to her over the boy's shoulder. "All the best."

Meanwhile, Jeremy turned to Cassie, his jaw set and his mouth stiff. "There's no need for good-byes," he said with stern dispassion. "We've already said them."

"Yes, we have." Nevertheless she put out her hand. "But I haven't said my thanks," she said, unable to keep a slight tremor from her voice.

"No need for that, either." But he took her hand and held it for a moment before he wrenched his eyes from hers and handed her up.

Hickham, who'd followed the ladies down, shut the carriage door and jumped up on the box, having insisted that he and no other would act as coachman. He flicked his whip at the horses, and the vehicle moved briskly down the drive. Inside, mother and daughter turned on their seats to take a last look out the rear window, each one hoping that the other would not see her tears. Cicely's heart jumped as she saw Charles lift an arm in a long farewell wave. For Cassie there was no such comfort. Jeremy was already gone.

Chapter
~ 25 ~

In spite of everything, the return to Crestwoods turned out to be a joyful occasion. Clemson, who'd received word the night before that his mistress was returning, had filled the entryway, the drawing room and all the bedrooms with bowls full of May flowers—jonquils and larkspur and bright pink dianthus. Cook prepared a festive welcoming dinner of two full courses, each one boasting more than a dozen dishes. (Not one of the three returning ladies admitted aloud that her cooking was less inspiring, even on this special evening, than any one of Mrs. Stemple's most simple meals.) Every housemaid and footman beamed at them. There was no question that everyone was glad that Lady Beringer and family were home again.

Cassie herself was overwhelmed with emotion, although she couldn't quite decide what the emotion was. She walked from room to room, letting her eyes drink in every familiar object—the chairs in the dining room, the escritoire in the study, the painting of her grandfather that hung over the drawing room fireplace, the still life of a violin and candle—a work of her own—that hung in her bedroom. Seeing it all again had a poignancy that no one who'd not experienced memory loss could possibly imagine. Not so long ago, she hadn't been able to bring any of this to mind. Now she was actually here, moving among these precious pieces of her life; she could see them, touch them, *remember* them. It was all so blessedly *familiar*. She was home!

But what made the emotion ambiguous was that now she had a memory of another home, one that she'd grown to love as much as this one. In it was a bedroom that looked out on a pond with a waterwheel, and a room in a turret with the most amazing light.

As she climbed into her own bed that night, however, she told herself she must not think too much about that other house. She was delighted to be in her own bed, to feel the familiar carving of the bedpost under her fingers, to slide into the worn grooves of the mattress that fitted her body so well, to pull her own old goose-down counterpane up to her neck and breathe in its funny, musty, deliciously familiar smell. It was true joy to be home again. Dwelling on what she could *not* have would only bring pain and poison her joy in what she had.

Life quickly settled into the old, comfortable routine. Cassie busied herself with the details of housekeeping, with gardening, with taking walks with her sister and her daughter, and with her painting. Eva talked daily about returning to London, but with the weather so pleasant, she didn't go. Life here was too deliciously lazy to give up.

The only change in their lives was the frequent presence of Clive Percy. It seemed to Cassie that he called almost every other day. He was obviously courting Cicely. They rode together, played cards together, took walks together and generally seemed to enjoy each other's company in spite of the fact that they quarreled and taunted each other constantly. Cassie often wondered, as she watched them tossing a ball or cavorting on the lawn, if something more than friendship was developing between them, but after a while she decided that they were more like brother and sister than lovers. Cicely clearly did not take Clive seriously.

Besides, when Cicely thought no one was watching her, her face took on a sad, yearning expression that could only be called lovelorn. She would scarcely be lovelorn for someone who was constantly underfoot, Cassie reasoned. Cassie firmly believed she knew what brought that expression of longing to her daughter's face: the girl was missing Jeremy. But the fortnight of delay that Jeremy had asked for was quickly passing. Cicely's heartache would soon end. *Don't worry, my love,* Cassie told her daughter in heartfelt, unspoken messages, *he'll be here soon. Just give him a little time.*

Matters took an unexpected turn one afternoon when, after one of their vigorous rides, Clive and Cicely came clumping into the house in their riding boots and made their noisy way down the hall to the library. They found Cassie at her easel, working diligently on her *Still Life with Lemons*, and Eva contentedly engaged in needlework. "I've just stopped in to say my adieux," the boy said from the doorway, taking off his riding cap and tucking it under his arm.

Eva looked up from her embroidery frame. "Won't you stay to tea?" she asked in surprise.

"Not today."

"He has to get back to the Park to see to his packing," Cicely explained, idly striking her riding crop against her boots, her eyes lowered.

"Packing?" Eva asked curiously.

Clive nodded. "This good-bye is my last, I'm afraid, ma'am. We're going back to London tomorrow."

Cassie's brush dropped to the floor. "*We?*" she asked.

"Yes. When Uncle Charles suggested it, I didn't object." The boy threw a lugubrious glance at Cicely. "After all, there's little incentive for me to stay. I've been rejected by this stubborn daughter of yours three times."

"I should be returning to London myself," Eva remarked, returning to her sewing. "The season is already in full swing." *I wish I could take Cicely with me,* she added to herself. *Especially if Jeremy will be there.* She had not yet given up hope of the match that was still dear to her heart.

"I hope you all have a pleasant journey," Cassie murmured absently as she picked up her brush. Her brain was in a turmoil. Was Jeremy included in that "we"? *How can he be going off to London when he's promised to come here?* she asked herself.

Meanwhile, Cicely had taken Clive's arm. "I'll see him out," she said, pulling him firmly away from the library doorway and down the hall.

"I hope you realize, Miss Beringer," Clive said as they neared the front door, "that I leave you a broken man."

"Oh, pooh! You know perfectly well that we're nothing more than good chums."

"Only because you won't permit me to be more to you."

"What humbug. You don't want more than a riding companion any more than I do."

He snorted. "So you say."

"Let's not go over this again," she said dismissively. "I want to speak to you about something else entirely." She dropped her eyes and tapped her riding crop nervously against her boots. "Did your uncle send any message for me?"

"No. Were you expecting one?"

"I thought . . . at least a good-bye . . ."

"Of course he sent his best to all of you. I didn't think you meant something as innocuous as all that."

Her eyes flew up to his face. "Were those his exact words? 'Send my best to all of them'?"

Clive shrugged indifferently. "More or less. What does it matter?"

Somehow the riding crop snapped in two in her hand. "You're right," she said, biting her lower lip. "It doesn't matter at all."

Later, after she'd seen him off, she wandered listlessly back to the library and dropped down upon the sofa. "So that's that," she said moodily.

Eva raised her brows. "Heavens, child, has the boy's departure upset you?"

"No, Aunt Eva. Nothing's upset me."

Cassie wiped her hands and crossed the room to her. "You do seem depressed, my love," she murmured, sitting down beside her. "I know it's hard to lose a friend."

Cicely nodded. "It will be very quiet here, I suppose, without Clive's boisterous company."

"If that's how you feel," Eva said, plying her needle with unduly close attention, " you shouldn't have rejected his three offers."

"Just because I may miss him as a riding companion, Aunt," the girl retorted, "doesn't mean I want him as a husband. Besides, he's too boyish for wedlock. All he wants to do is race his horses and go with his chums to sporting events."

"That's just how I suspected you felt about him," her mother said with a small smile.

Eva, too, was smiling in relief. "But that still leaves you without a companion," she pointed out, as if the idea had just struck her, "and with very little to occupy you. You ought to come with me to London."

The very word electrified Cicely. "To *London*?" she echoed, sitting up straight.

"Don't be foolish," Cassie said at once. "She can't go off to London now."

"No, of course I can't," the girl agreed. "I wouldn't dream of leaving you alone."

"It's not that. It's not that at all." Cassie peered at her daughter in awkward helplessness. "It's just that . . . in a few days . . ." But she couldn't go on. It would ruin everything if she indicated in any way that she knew Jeremy was coming to renew his offer.

"What, Mama? In a few days, what?"

"Nothing. Only that in a few days the . . . the early roses will be blooming."

Eva cast her a look of utter disgust. "As if Cicely cares for that!" she exclaimed.

Cassie twisted her fingers in her lap, her mind whirling. She did not know if Jeremy himself was off to London. But he couldn't be! He'd promised to call on Cicely in a fortnight. That fortnight had almost passed. He would not break his word; she was sure of that. He'd be here any day now!

On the other hand, she had the impression from Clive's words that Jeremy *was* going to London with the other two. If so, why? He was not the sort to run away from an obligation. Perhaps he believed that Cicely would return to London for the season, and he could resume his courtship there. Of *course*! That *must* be it! It was the only sensible answer. How much more comfortable it would be for Jeremy if he could pursue Cicely far away from the watchful eye of his prospective mother-in-law! "You're right, Eva, of course," she said, looking up and nodding decisively. "I don't know what I was thinking of. Cicely *must* go to London with you. It will be the very best thing for her."

"How can you *say* that, Mama?" Cicely jumped to her feet and glared down at her mother like an accusing barrister. "Do you think I would go off to pursue my own pleasures and leave you alone, after all you've been through?"

"But, dearest, I'm completely well again. And I like being alone."

"No, I won't hear of it." Cicely turned her back on her mother and stomped across the room to underline her determination.

"Really, Cicely, you are being as stubborn as Clive said you were. Don't you *want* to go to London for the season? There's so much more to interest you in town than here."

"That may be, but I can't possibly, in good conscience—"

Cassie rose, followed her daughter across the room and slipped her arm about her waist. "Will it ease your conscience if I promise to come to London myself in a few weeks?"

Cicely turned about slowly, her eyes lighting with hope. "Would you, Mama? Word of honor?"

"You have my word. A month at most."

"Oh, Mama!" She wrapped her arms about her mother in an ecstatic embrace. "I *do* want to go to London just now. But only if you're sure you'll be all right without me."

Cassie patted her cheek reassuringly. "Don't worry about me, my love. I'll be just fine."

Chapter
~ 26 ~

Cassie did not miss Eva and Cicely very much. At least, not for the first two days. It was good to be alone for a while. She needed solitude. She needed to be free of the strain of smiling and being cheerful. She needed privacy, so that she might weep and feel sorry for herself a little. But most of all, she needed to concentrate on making plans for the future, and it was good not to have the distraction of company.

The plans she had to make concerned Cicely's happiness, not her own. Cassie was convinced that she would soon be receiving word that her daughter was betrothed. When that word came, she would have to face her prospective son-in-law. She wanted no hint of her past association with Jeremy to interfere in any way with her daughter's marriage. Although she knew she would never forget (barring another tumble down a stone stairway) what Jeremy had been to her, it was essential that he forget her. He had to begin thinking of her as a mother-in-law instead of as a woman he once thought he loved.

But how was she to make him see her as a mother-in-law? She tried to remember her own mother-in-law. The dowager Lady Beringer had been a decent sort, much kinder than her son, but of course quite old. Like many of the elderly women in London social circles, she'd always dressed in dark dresses with long, lacy sleeves, had kept her hair tightly bound in a chignon pinned to the back of her head, and always covered her hair with a white widow's cap. She'd worn the cap all day, everywhere she went, even outdoors, under her bonnets or hidden beneath the turbans she donned for dinner parties. And there were other appurtenances that added to the

impression of advancing age: Lady Beringer had walked with
a cane and kept a pair of silver-rimmed spectacles perched on
her nose. Cassie, remembering her fondly, realized now that
her appearance had been eminently suitable for her mother-
in-law role.

The trouble was that Cassie's mother-in-law had been, at
that time, more than thirty years older than Cassie was now.
But Cassie could certainly adjust her appearance to give a
similar effect. She could borrow one of Annie's white caps,
and she could wear it over tightly restrained hair. And though
she hadn't any dark lace gowns or turbans, she could certainly have some made. She even had a pair of magnifying
spectacles stored away somewhere that she'd once used when
she was learning to paint miniatures. She would, this very
day, set about looking for them. With these accoutrements,
she might be able to become a very proper mother-in-law
indeed.

With this scheme in mind, she became more relaxed. She
had her first good night's sleep since the night Jeremy had
surprised her in the turret room. And the following morning,
knowing she had no responsibilities at all for the day, she
luxuriated in bed for two full hours past her usual time of
rising. She was still abed—though awake—when Annie bus-
tled in. "I hate to disturb you, my lady," the housekeeper said
breathlessly, as if she'd run up the stairs, "but he's downstairs,
askin' for Miss Cicely!"

"He?" Cassie sat up with a shudder, having a premonition
of trouble. "Not—?"

"Lord Inglesby, yes'm. And he's furious that he wasn't told
she's gone to London. He told Mr. Clemson that he'd not
budge till he gives you a piece of his mind."

"Then he *didn't* go to London, after all." Under those circumstances, she could see why he was out of temper. It must
have seemed to him that, while he'd kept his part of the bar-
gain, she'd not kept hers. She threw off her covers and slid
out of bed, her mind racing over possibilites. "I don't suppose," she murmured speculatively, "that Clemson could convince him to go away. He could suggest that his lordship call
again . . . at some other time."

"I don't think so, ma'am. His lordship told Mr. Clemson to tell me to get you downstairs if I had to pull you by the hair from bed and push you out in your nightshift!" She gave her mistress a shrug that was half-alarmed and half-amused. "I don't expect he really meant it, do you? But neither do I expect that he'd agree to depart the premises."

Cassie sighed. She would have to see him, that much was obvious. In nervous haste, she ran barefoot to the mirror and peered into it. Everything was wrong about her appearance this morning. Just when she wanted to look peaked and haggish, she was looking well. With her hair hanging in tousled profusion about her face and her cheeks rosy from sleep, she looked almost youthful. This was not the mother-in-law-ish face she wanted to present to him. Something had to be done.

She immediately began to dress her hair. As she pinned it into a topknot, she glanced at the hovering Annie. "Annie, I know you'll think this strange," she said hurriedly, "but don't ask questions now. Please, my dear, let me borrow your dress. It's a dark gray, not black, but it will have to do. Oh, and your cap, too. The cap is perfect."

A few minutes later, dressed and capped, she peered at herself in the mirror, but what she saw did not yet convey the impression she wanted. Desperately she began to rummage through her dressing-table drawers. "Help me, Annie," she begged. "See if you can find my magnifying spectacles. They must be here somewhere."

Annie turned them up a moment later. Cassie put them on and returned to the mirror. But she couldn't see properly through them. She lowered them on her nose and looked over them. There! she thought in considerable relief. That was a bit more like the old biddy she wanted to be.

Leaving a gaping, half-dressed Annie behind in her room, she started down the hall to the stairs. She had to take off the spectacles in order to navigate the stairs, but just outside the drawing room, where Jeremy was waiting, she put them on again. "Good morning, your lordship," she said cheerily as she stepped briskly over the threshold. She took a step forward with hand outstretched, tripped over the carpet and fell right into his arms.

This clumsy entrance might have been amusing, but he was too furious to be amused. He set her on her feet, stormed over to the door to shut it so that the staff would not be privy to his scold and began to lace into her at once. "After extracting a promise from me to offer for your daughter, ma'am," he began icily, "it seems to me you might have kept her on hand so that I might—"

By this time he'd turned back to face her. At the sight of her, words failed him. She was standing in the middle of the room, watching him warily. She looked different, somehow, from the woman he remembered. He stared, wondering for a moment what the difference was. She was wearing a dowdy garment much too large for her, with a white mobcap covering her hair, and she was peering at him over the silliest-looking pair of square, silver-rimmed spectacles he'd ever seen. It was those spectacles, of course, that were the cause of his befuddlement! They couldn't be real. They were too thick, too ill-fitting. And she'd never worn eyeglasses before, not once in all the time he'd known her. Was it some sort of jest she was playing on him?

Yet she looked utterly adorable, he thought, with those ridiculous glasses on her nose. How could he possibly remain angry with her while she stood there peering at him in that irresistibly appealing way? All the pent-up anger—anger that had been stoked throughout this past fortnight, during which he'd had to prepare himself to make an offer he had no wish to make, that had burst into a blaze when he discovered Cicely was gone and that had intensified to a hot flame in the more than half an hour he'd been kept pacing the floor waiting for her to put in an appearace—was immediately smothered, dissipated, gone. Worse, a hiccuping laugh gurgled up from his throat.

She drew herself up in offense. "Are you laughing at me, my lord?"

The grin he'd been trying to hold back broke out and lit his face. "Can you actually see through those spectacles, ma'am?"

"Would I be wearing them otherwise?" she snapped. "What's wrong with them?"

"Nothing at all. I find them charming. You look like . . . like . . ."

"A dowager? A crone? A grandam?"

"No, not at all. You look . . . scholarly. Like a schoolmistress."

"A forbidding old hag of a schoolmistress?" she asked hopefully.

"More like a schoolmistress to whom all the little boys send drawings of hearts with arrows piercing them."

"Oh, *Jemmy*," she breathed, "what a very sweet thing to say!" She was so touched she didn't realize she'd called him by the nickname people used for him only in moments of intimacy. His affectionate words had made her throat contract. They were little arrows, piercing her heart.

But her disguise had not worked. She took off the glasses and pocketed them, sighing in defeat. "I was hoping to look like a . . . a . . ."

"Yes?" he urged, amused and curious.

She glanced at him ruefully. "Like a mother-in-law."

He blinked for a moment and then burst into a guffaw. Laughing, he fell down upon the sofa, where he rocked with laughter until the tears came. "A mother-in-law?" he roared, and laughed some more.

She stood there watching him until he'd wiped his cheeks and caught his breath. "It's not a matter for amusement, you know," she said worriedly.

"Isn't it?" He stood up and confronted her, his expression turning serious. "But, my darling idiot, don't you see? This proves how impossible, how ridiculously impossible this situation is. Did you really believe I would stop loving you if you dressed like a mother-in-law? Don't you know that I would find you adorable even if you dressed up like . . . like Hickham?"

"Then tell me what to do!" she cried in real agony.

"Isn't it obvious? Give up this silly game. This ridiculous pretense. Marry me, and let Cicely find someone else to wed."

"No. I can't! I won't!" She took a turn around the room, her determination strengthening with every step. Then she wheeled round to face him. "Dash it, Jeremy," she exclaimed, "you gave me your word."

He stared into her face and saw in it the end of all his hopes. Something in his chest cracked with pain, the pain of realizing that she didn't really love him. He'd wrestled for two weeks with this problem, but only now was he facing up to it: she couldn't truly love him if she was willing to give him up forever, to sacrifice him on the altar of mother love. Well, he would do as she asked, but he'd not forgive her for it. "Yes, I did," he said, tight-lipped. "I gave my word. And I'll honor it. My mother raised her son to honor his word at all costs. I suppose I'll learn to live with it."

"Live with it?"

"I will have to take a vow, will I not? To love and to honor and to forsake all others? How can I do it when I know that you're somewhere close by?"

"Then I'll go away. I should have thought of that before. After the wedding, I'll go abroad, for an extended stay. Yes, that's it! I'll go to Italy and rent a villa and . . . and paint. I'll see Rome. And Paris. And by the time I come back, you and Cicely . . . you'll have lived together intimately . . . you'll have a child . . . you'll have forgotten—"

"Stop! I don't want to hear any more. We'll both do what we must." He got up and strode to the door.

It was not until he'd put his hand on the knob that he remembered why he'd demanded to see her. "By the way, why on earth did you send Cicely to London?" he asked, his earlier fury coming back to him. "Didn't you think I'd keep my promise?"

"I had no doubt you would." She flashed him a wry smile. "I knew you were the sort whose mother raised him to honor his word."

He did not smile back. "Then why didn't you keep her here?"

"I thought you'd find it easier to court her there."

He nodded glumly. "Yes, I suppose I shall. Well, then, it's good-bye, ma'am. I'm off to London to keep my blasted promise."

"Thank you, Jeremy," she said with quiet misery. "I wish with all my heart that you'll be happy."

"I'll try to make the best of it," he muttered as he threw open the door and strode off down the corridor, "but I'd be a happier man if my mother had raised a cad."

Chapter
~ 27 ~

Cicely did not find London much to her liking. It was almost a week since she'd moved into her aunt's town house, and Charles Percy, Lord Lucas, had not yet called on her. She knew he was aware of her presence, for she'd wormed the information from Clive, who'd already visited her four times. She'd quizzed him on the subject during their very first meeting. "Do you stay with your uncle?" she asked in a not-very-subtle attempt to bring up the subject of Lord Lucas.

"No, I have rooms on Upper Seymour Street," Clive responded with irritating indifference, "but I'm only a step away from him. His place is on the other side of Portman Square."

"I know where he lives," she said impatiently. "So you are only a step away? That means, I suppose, that you often dine with him."

"Dine with him?" He looked at her as if she were touched in her upper works. "Why would I dine with him?"

"Why would you not?"

"I don't care to dine with elderly relations," the idiotic fellow replied. "Nothing is more of a bore than that. Though I did see him at the boxing match the other night. Looked trim as a trencher in a green cord coat. Weston cut it, I'd give odds. Up to the mark, my uncle Charles, I'll give him that. Looked neat as wax."

"For an elderly relation," Cicely retorted. She glared at the boy in frustration, wondering how to get the information she wanted without giving herself away. "I hope the 'elderly relation' was well."

"Ripping," Clive said blandly. "By the way, I told him I was coming to see you tonight, and he sent his best."

His best! Cicely had had to be content with that meager message. But ever since, she'd lived in eager anticipation of a visit from Charles. He knew she was in town. He *had* to call, she thought, if only out of mere politeness. She jumped every time she heard the door knocker. But it was never he.

As the days passed and her discouragement grew, Cicely became despondent. Clive noticed it. Even Aunt Eva noticed it. And Aunt Eva would not let her beloved niece wallow in despond. "Let's go to the opera tonight," she suggested with sunny enthusiasm. "It is *Cosi Fan Tutte,* with that wonderful new soprano, Madame Pesta. A performance of *Cosi* is bound to cheer you. We'll let Clive escort us."

Cicely, who knew that falling into the dismals would do her no good, tried to feel festive. She put on her loveliest gown—it was a Saxony green, of the very softest lawn, and with a wide satin sash that tied in the back with an enormous bow. She permitted Eva's abigail to dress her hair *à la grecque,* a style requiring a great number of curls to frame the face, with the rest of the hair pulled back and tied in place with spangled ribbons. She even wore the strand of pearls that her mother had given her on her last birthday, that she usually saved for the most special occasions.

Clive, resplendent in his black evening coat, satin breeches and high, starched shirtpoints, gaped at her when she came down the stairs. "You are a *vision!*" he exclaimed. "Every fellow in the theater will envy me."

"You *do* look well, my love," Eva said complacently, pleased that her plan seemed to be working. "But come along, or we shall be late."

They were not at all late. There was plenty of time, after their arrival at the King's Theater, to mill about the lobby. Eva turned right and left, greeting friends and exchanging gossip, the feathers of her turban bobbing. Clive, too, saw a number of chaps of his acquaintance and took a good deal of swaggering enjoyment in introducing Cicely to them. But Cicely did not see a familiar face, especially the one she wanted to see. Not until the gong sounded the first-act warning. Then, making her way up the crowded stairway to the box, she thought she caught a glimpse of him.

She turned out to be right, for immediately after taking her seat, she glanced into the adjoining box, and there he was! The box seemed crowded with people, five or six at least. He was holding the chair for a woman in a dark red gown with a shockingly low décolletage. The woman was lushly beautiful, with black hair, dark lashes framing green eyes, and a truly magnificent figure. Cicely felt her insides clench with jealousy.

As soon as he'd seated the woman, Charles glanced up and saw her. "Cicely!" he exclaimed, his eyes lighting with delight. (Yes, she was certain, when she reviewed the events of the evening later, that "delight" was the proper word for his expression.) But his expression immediately changed to one of embarrassment. He glanced uneasily at the woman he'd help seat and, seeing that she'd turned away to chat with one of the other women in the group, made his way through the press of people to the edge of the box. Eva and Clive now saw him, too. "Why, it's Lord Lucas," Eva exclaimed warmly.

"Lady Schofield, good evening," Charles murmured with a polite bow. "And Miss Beringer. How do you do? I'd heard from Clive that you're in town for the season. I hope all is well at Crestwoods."

But Eva, who by this time had taken a good look at the company he was with, lost her smile and warmth. "Very well, thank you, my lord," she said shortly.

His face flushing, Charles patted his nephew's shoulder. "I hope, ladies, that you are finding yourself in good hands," he said, giving Cicely a small but meaningful smile.

Does this man think Clive and I are courting? Cicely asked herself in irritation. *And does he believe he deserves the credit for it?* "Yes, Clive is an excellent escort," she said, putting up her chin.

"I'm glad to hear it. I do hope you enjoy the music. I understand Madame Pesta has great vocal power and range."

Eva, to Cicely's surprise and chagrin, snapped open her fan and, waving it vigorously, coldly turned her face to the stage. "So I hear," she said dismissively.

If Charles was offended, he did not show it. He merely made a bow to both ladies, nodded to Clive and turned back to his friends.

Cicely, heartbroken by this worse-than-formal exchange, took her seat in a daze. Eva was annoyed by him, that much was clear, but Cicely didn't understand why. Nor did she understand why Charles hadn't introduced them, if not to his friends, then at least to the woman he was escorting. All during the first act, and the second, too, she surreptitiously cast her eye over to the next box. The woman with Charles looked luxuriously at her ease, one arm over the back of Charles's chair, one leg extended. Every few moments she lifted her fan to cover her mouth while she whispered something to him. Sometimes he laughed at whatever she'd said. There was undoubtedly some sort of intimacy between them. Cicely felt her fingers clench. She'd never before felt like a cat, but at this moment she had a startlingly feline urge to scratch the woman's eyes out.

During the second interval, Eva went out to greet a friend, and Clive excused himself to hobnob with some cronies who were milling about in great spirits down in the pit. Cicely, alone in the box, was startled by the touch of a hand on her shoulder. With a little cry, she looked up. It was Charles. "Oh!" she said, her pulse racing.

"I just stopped in to tell you how perfectly charming you look," he said, smiling down at her in the way he used to at Inglesby Park.

"Thank you," she said, blushing. "That's because you've never seen me in evening clothes." Emboldened by the happy awareness that he'd sought her out, she looked him over brazenly. "I've never before seen you quite so elegantly attired, either. Clive is right when he says you are up to the mark."

"He says that, does he? I must remember to thank him. It's not often a young whippersnapper has a kind word for an old man's appearance."

"If you're so old," she taunted, "you must be tired of standing there. Won't you sit down?"

"I suppose we have a few minutes before the others return," he said, taking the chair beside her.

"Speaking of the others," Cicely ventured boldly, "why didn't you introduce us to the lady with you?"

His cheerful, friendly expression changed at once. "Never mind why," he said curtly. He shook his head at her in avuncular disapproval. "Will you never learn to stop asking outrageous questions?"

"How can I stop if I don't know they're outrageous?" she asked reasonably. "Though, since I've already made you angry, I may as well go ahead and ask a question I *know* is outrageous. Is that lady . . . Are you . . . ? Confound it, I'll just say it without roundaboutation. Do you love her?"

He jumped to his feet, red-faced, and glared down at her. "That does it, Cicely Beringer! As usual, you've put me completely out of frame. This tête-à-tête is at an end. I shall bid you good evening. I hope you enjoy the rest of the opera. You've certainly succeeded in ensuring that *I* will *not*."

"I'm glad of that, at least," she muttered to his retreating back.

But for the rest of the evening, though she watched the next box as assiduously as possible, she could see nothing in his demeanor toward his companion that showed any lack of enjoyment.

When Clive brought the ladies home, Cicely lingered at the doorway after her aunt had gone inside. "Clive," she said nervously, "I want to ask you a question which you may find outrageous. But even if it is, I want you to promise to answer it."

He snorted. "I know your outrageous questions, my girl. I won't make any such promise."

"Will you at least try not to be shocked? And not to be prudish in your answer? I'm not a little innocent babe, you know."

"You do seem a little innocent in that gown," he said, grinning at her fondly.

"Do I?" She looked down at herself in disgust. "Perhaps that's why—! Dash it, I should have worn something red. With a real décolletage."

"I don't know what you're prattling about. You look as pretty as the prettiest girl at the opera. Prettier. I'd even kiss you, if I thought I wouldn't get my face slapped for my pains."

"Yes, but if I looked less innocent, perhaps you'd feel *compelled* to kiss me, slap or no."

"That's a challenge if I ever heard one," he said, and he reached out to embrace her.

She held him off with a not-so-innocent display of skill. "Don't be a clunch. You know we don't care for each other in that way. Do you want to hear my question or don't you?"

He sighed in defeat. "Go on and ask."

"It's about your uncle. Why didn't he introduce us to the lady he was with?"

"You *are* an innocent," the young man declared. "Couldn't you tell what sort she was?"

"What do you mean? What sort?"

"The *wrong* sort, you goosecap. That was Mrs. Moreslow. The rather notorious Mrs. Moreslow. I've heard the fellows call her Mrs. Not Moreslow."

"I don't understand," she said, her brows knit.

He laughed, gave her a peck on the cheek and started down the walk. "Because, my little innocent," he threw over his shoulder, "the woman is known to be *fast*."

Cicely went to bed that night with much to think about. She was not surprised, after all, to learn that her Charlie associated with fast women. She'd known from the first that he was a rake. That fact had never disturbed her; rakes could be reformed. But she had to win him first, and that was evidently going to be harder than she'd expected. He was adamantly clinging to the difference in their ages as the barrier to what she was certain was a mutual attraction. She hadn't figured out how she might overcome that barrier . . . until now. But now she had a clue.

She smiled to herself as she blew out her candle and settled into her bed. "Very well, my lord," she whispered into her pillow, "if it's a fast woman you want, a fast one you shall have."

Chapter
~ 28 ~

Jeremy arrived at the Inglesby house in Dover Street quite late at night and thus was surprised to learn from Beecks, his mother's elderly butler, that his mother had not yet retired for the night. Lady Sarah, who occupied the London house most of the year (having taken an eccentric dislike to all the other Inglesby residences), had fallen asleep in a winged chair in the downstairs sitting room, her feet up on an ottoman and a book open on her lap. "She don't like it if I wake her," Beecks confided. "She usually rouses herself before midnight an' goes on up, but she's spent the night in that chair more'n once."

"Let's try not to wake her, at least until I've made it to up to my bed," Jeremy whispered. "I'd rather not have to face her until morning."

But Hickham, who hated coming to the London house (it being the only place where he had no other role in the household than valet to his lordship, and thus had to take second place to Beecks in the staff hierarchy), let out his dissatisfaction by making a considerable racket with Jeremy's baggage. He even dropped a portmanteau with a great clatter. "Damnation, Hickham, must you make such a bustle?" Jeremy hissed from the stairs. But it was too late. The noise had reached all the way down the hall, where her ladyship awoke with a start. "Who's there?" she cried out.

"Only me, Mama." Jeremy, after throwing his valet a glare, poked his head in the sitting room doorway. "Sorry I didn't have time to let you know I was coming."

"What rubbish! As if you have to notify me when you want to stay in your own house. Come in, Jemmy, my love, and let me take a look at you. It's good to have you home."

Jeremy, shrugging with the aplomb of a good-natured loser, crossed the room, bent over her and kissed her cheek. Mother and son surveyed each other for a moment, each one with a smile of approval. "You are remarkable, Mama," Jeremy said in admiration. "How can you manage to look dignified even when being awakened from a nap?"

"I was *not* napping. I do not nap. But never mind me, you makebate. It's you I wish to speak about." She withdrew her legs from the ottoman and motioned for him to sit on it. "I'm quite put out with you, you know. I heard, only yesterday, that Cicely Beringer is back in town, still not—"

"Still not betrothed," her son finished for her. "Yes, I'm well aware of that. But don't get on your high ropes, Mama. I've come to town for the express purpose of rectifying that situation."

"Have you really? I'm relieved to hear it. But I can't imagine why it's taken you so long to get to the point. It's been more than a month since I called on you at the Park. Why didn't you do something about Cicely at once?"

Jeremy ran his hand through his hair, wondering just how much his mother should be told. "I tried," he said with studied casualness, "but her mother objected."

"Objected? To *you*?"

Jeremy had to smile at her motherly indignation. "Not everyone thinks as highly of me as you do, Mama. Besides, you must remember that I'm twenty years the girl's senior, which fact hardly qualifies me as an ideal suitor."

"Nonsense. There isn't a mother in all of England who wouldn't want to snatch you for her marriageable daughter, no matter what the daughter's age."

"There was one. Lady Beringer informed me quite bluntly that she didn't want me anywhere near her daughter."

"Oh, she did, did she? Well, then, my love, she shan't have you. As far as I'm concerned, that releases you from any obligation in that direction."

He smiled sardonically. "Good of you, my dear, but you are not the only party concerned. In any case, let me hasten to assure you that Lady Beringer has changed her mind since then. In fact, she is now quite enthusiastic about my becoming her son-in-law."

Something in his tone caught her ear. "You don't say," she murmured, eyeing him closely. "How did this delightful change come about?"

"Very simply. The woman took a tumble down the outside stairs—the very ones you so dislike—and injured her head. She had to recuperate in my house, during which time she came to appreciate my finer qualities. You certainly can't find fault with that, can you?" He got to his feet, placed a quick good-night peck on her cheek and went swiftly to the door, congratulating himself on having given her all the salient points with admirable brevity and without revealing the tiniest hint of the heartbreak underlying the outward details.

But his mother did not let this smug feeling last beyond the few seconds it took him to reach the doorway. "You may scurry off to bed if you like, my love," she said, "but you don't fool me for one moment. There's more to this tale than you've seen fit to tell me."

He stopped, leaned his head against the door frame in weary resignation and sighed. "I knew this should have been kept till tomorrow. What did I say to make you believe—?"

"Do you think I don't know despair when I see it in my son's eyes? But never mind, I shan't keep you now. I'll dig out the missing pieces sooner or later, will-you nill-you. Good night, my dear, and sleep well."

Chapter
~ 29 ~

Jeremy had dressed with care for this occasion; it was not every evening one went out to make an offer of marriage. And even though it felt more like offering his head on the chopping block, he was nevertheless eager to make a proper appearance. He'd put on his light gray camlet breeches, he'd let Hickham have his way with the folds of his neckcloth (which Hickham considered a great honor and by which he was much cheered), and he'd topped it all off with a satin waistcoat, whose embroidered fleur-de-lis design was nothing if not discreet, and one of his finest blue coats.

He'd hoped to escape the house without having to endure another interview with his mother (she'd already wormed enough of the story out of him to suspect that it was the mother, not the daughter, who'd captured her son's heart), but he found her waiting at the bottom of the stairs. She looked so troubled he could not feel annoyed. "How do I look?" he asked with forced good spirits.

"You needn't go through with this, Jemmy," she said worriedly. "It can't be worth sacrificing all hopes of future happiness just to honor your word."

"Wasn't it you who said to me, not over a month ago, that once I 'take the plunge into wedlock,' everything will be fine?"

"Perhaps I did. But that was before I suspected—"

"Suspected what?"

"That you'd lost your heart to another."

"You deduced that, did you?"

"It did not take the mind of a genius. There's a certain look in your eyes every time the name of Cassie Beringer is mentioned."

"I'll get over it. And meanwhile, it will help if you put it out of your mind, Mama. I have no hopes in that direction. And since there's little to be gained in dwelling on an impossibility, I shall try to find happiness where there is at least *some* slight possibility of achieving it."

His mother gave him a brave smile as he took his leave, but her heart was not eased. She'd put together the meager bits and pieces of the story, and she knew now that if she hadn't interfered by going to Inglesby Park that day and telling him what she believed he ought to do, her son might never have found himself in such a coil. How dreadful, she thought in guilty misery, that mothers, while meaning well, so often barge into their children's lives and bring ruin.

Jeremy had sent word that he would call, so both Lady Schofield and Cicely were expecting him. Eva was almost beside herself with excitement. That her favorite candidate for her niece's hand, her dearest Jeremy, was still interested in pursuing her niece was almost too wonderful to believe. She tried her best to present a calm appearance, but the tremors of her fingers and knees were a good indication of the turmoil within.

Cicely, on the other hand, was strangely placid. She knew that her aunt believed that Jeremy was coming to make an offer, but she herself rejected that possibility. He hadn't come up to snuff the first time because he realized he didn't love her. And nothing had occurred, not one thing in all the weeks since, to cause him to change his mind. They'd been in the same house for a month or more and barely passed the time of day. No, she told herself, there had to be another reason.

He arrived right on time, looking resplendent in his town garb and bearing an armload of flowers, which he presented with admirable élan to his hostess. Eva, blushing and breathless, led him to the drawing room, where Cicely sat waiting. Using the flowers he'd so conveniently provided as her excuse to leave them alone, she trotted off, babbling about finding "a proper vase and some water for these beautiful blooms."

Cicely welcomed him with warmth and made room for him beside her on the sofa. "My, but you look splendid, Jeremy," she said in greeting, surprised that she'd lost the shyness she used to feel in his presence. "Have you just come to town?"

He decided to plunge right in. "Yes, just yesterday. And with the express purpose of coming to see you."

Her brows rose in sincere surprise. "Really? Why is that?"

"Need you ask? Surely you remember that, a mere six weeks ago, you were sitting beside me in a carriage—looking, I recall, almost as lovely as you do now—and we were engaged in an important conversation which I suddenly cut short."

"Yes, of course I remember. But—"

"I want to pick up the threads of that conversation now, if I may."

"You can't mean it!" She gaped at him in shock. "Are you saying you want to *offer* for me?"

"I don't blame you for your astonishment. I've been a slowtop beyond all reason. But I'm determined to make up to you for the delay by hurrying you into wedlock with all haste and spending the rest of my life making you as happy as I can."

"Jeremy! I don't believe a *word* of this! You don't love me. You never have."

It was his turn to be astonished. He'd never expected so frank an outburst from this hitherto shy young miss. "What makes you think that?" he asked in discomfort.

"Why should I not think it? I lived in your manor house for weeks without receiving so much as a glance from you."

"Come now, Cicely, that's not true. The situation was not conducive to—" He ran his fingers nervously through his hair. "After all, your mother's illness—"

"I'm not blaming you, Jeremy, not at all! You were a godsend to Mama, and I shall always be grateful. But you cannot pretend to have given me a single thought in all that time. Why, any stranger who might have happened in would have believed you were more taken with *Mama* than with me."

He stared at her in a kind of panic, his innards knotting in tension. How could he counter her clear-eyed honesty with no more ammunition than this deplorable deceit he'd sworn to foist on her? "Dash it, Cicely," he exclaimed in desperation,

"I was distracted, I admit. But I've had time since then to . . . to think. If I neglected you, I'm truly sorry." He reached out and took her hands in his. "Please believe me, my dear. It shall never happen again, I give you my word."

"I don't *want* your word for that, Jeremy. I don't understand why you're making these promises."

"Because I want you to wed me. It's as simple as that."

"But have you noticed, my dear," she pointed out gently, "that there's one thing you haven't said? You haven't said that you love me."

He gulped. "What else can I *mean* when I ask you to be my wife?"

"I don't know. But I know it isn't love." She wriggled her hands from his hold. "I've learned a bit about love since you first courted me, you see. That's why I must decline your very overwhelming offer."

"Decline it?" He was startled, astounded, horrified. The one thing he hadn't expected was to be declined. How had he managed to botch this affair so badly? Cassie would never understand. Or forgive him. "Cicely, my dear, are you sure?" he asked lamely. "Sometimes young ladies like to be coaxed—"

"I don't need to be coaxed. I'm quite sure." She stood up and looked down at him, her eyes misty with girlish regret. "I'm truly sorry."

He rose and took her hands again. "I don't wish to discomfit you any more than I already have, my dear," he said softly, "but I must ask this. Are you sure you're not declining my offer because I was foolish enough to hurt you before? As a kind of—forgive me for sounding like a coxcomb, but I so sincerely wish to win you that I must try every avenue—as an instinctive need for . . . revenge?"

"No, truly, that's not the reason," she assured him. "I think I would have thrown my arms about your neck and said yes in spite of everything, if something else hadn't happened to me since that day in the carriage."

"What happened to you?"

She dropped her eyes. "I fell in love," she said. "Madly."

"Good God!" He gaped at her in bewilderment. She was full of surprises this evening. How could Cassie have sent him on this wild-goose chase without a word of warning? No, she wouldn't have sent him if she'd known. "But your mother didn't say— Dash it, girl, why haven't you told her?"

Cicely blinked at him. "How do you know I haven't?"

He winced. He'd put his foot in it this time. How was he to answer without botching up this interview even more? "Because I went to her before coming here, to get her permission," he improvised.

"Did you? How very thoughtful, Jeremy! Really. I'm quite touched."

"But that's no answer. How is it she doesn't know?"

"Because I haven't told her. Because she would not approve. He . . . the man in question . . . is even older than you."

"I see." He took a deep breath and tried to make sense of all this. "Older than I, eh?"

"Yes, but only by a bit."

"Then what's the predicament?"

"Mama does not believe that there should be large age discrepancies between husbands and wives. There was a twenty-year disparity between her and my father, you see, and I believe the marriage was not a happy one. My aunt Eva has hinted to me that the man had a monstrous temper and mistreated my mother."

He felt the blood rush from his face. "I had no idea—!"

"That's why she's such a recluse. I think she dreads the idea of marrying again."

Jeremy stood rooted to the spot, trying to digest this information. Poor, lovely Cassie. How he yearned to prove to her that he was different, that he could never hurt her, that he would only love and protect her, that he would spend his life making her happy. He wondered how much Cassie's past accounted for her reluctance to marry him. It was ironic to think that he'd refrained from declaring himself until she could "remember love," yet the only love she was able to remember was one she ought to forget.

But he could not stand here before Cicely like a gaping fool. She'd rejected him quite unequivocally. There was nothing for it now but to take his leave of her. He started to the door. "But, Cicely," he felt impelled to add before departing, "perhaps you should tell your mother of your feelings. She may have had a change of heart about the age question. After all, she gave her blessing to me."

"That's so, isn't it? She did!" Thoughtfully she took his arm in a friendly way and walked with him toward the door. "But there's no point in my doing so until the deuced man in question realizes that he loves me."

He stopped in his tracks. "Do you mean, silly child, that this fellow has not had the good sense to declare himself? He must be a fool, and therefore you should give him up directly."

She giggled. "He'll declare himself soon enough. I have a plan to entrap him."

They paused on the threshold. "Seriously, my dear," he asked, "are you certain I can't make you change your mind?"

"Yes, quite certain. In spite of being thoroughly aware that you're the very nicest man in the world."

"Yes, of course I am. That's why you're so madly in love with someone else. Very well, I'll bid you good night. I hope everything comes about as you wish it."

"You *are* the very nicest man in the world, you know," she called after him. "I wish you'd offer for Mama. You did get on so well together at the Park. Everyone noticed it. But I suppose you think her too old for you."

Jeremy threw her a quick glance. "Much too old," he said.

Chapter
~ 30 ~

Jeremy knew his mother would be waiting. He didn't even try to avoid her. After pouring himself a brandy from a bottle in the drawing room, he went directly to the sitting room, where she was pretending to be busy with her embroidery frame. Wordlessly, he dropped into an armchair opposite her, lifted the glass and stared into the amber liquor as if he could discover in it the answer to the riddle of life.

His mother studied his face for a moment, but could read nothing in it. "Well?" she demanded. "Am I to wish you happy?"

"I thought you were so adept at reading my eyes that I didn't need to tell you anything."

"Jackanapes! Tell me!"

His took a swig of his drink. "She rejected me."

Lady Sarah's mouth dropped open. "I don't believe it."

"Of course you don't. How could anyone reject your son? Then you will surely not believe that she's in love with someone else. Madly."

"Is she, indeed? The girl must be a fool."

He glowered at her. "She's every bit as charming and lovely as she was when you chose her for me. More so, in fact."

"Are you now saying that you're sorry you've lost her?"

"No, of course not. The truth is, I'm a great deal relieved."

"Naturally. Now you can go and offer for the mother." The words were scarcely off her tongue when she clapped her hands to her mouth. "No! You must erase those words from your mind. I made myself a vow that I would not ever again interfere in your life."

He smiled wryly. "Can it be? No, no, that's quite beyond the realm of possibility. Never again to interfere? It goes beyond all motherly instincts."

"Nevertheless, I shall try. So don't pay any mind to what I said about offering for Lady Beringer."

"I won't. Not only because I have for many years been capable of taking my own advice, but because I'd already decided that to offer for her would be a useless exercise."

"Why?

"I don't think she'll have me either."

Lady Sarah opened her mouth to object, but then closed it again. It was very difficult to refrain from giving advice, but she sincerely wished to mend her ways. Nevertheless, was there any harm in merely encouraging him to discuss the matter? She sewed a few stitches while she reviewed in her mind what she might safely say. "Really, Jemmy, I don't understand you," she said last. "I had the distinct impression that there was a strong attraction between you and Cassandra Beringer."

He smiled at her noticeable—and noticeably unsuccessful—struggle to keep from meddling. "Yes, Mama, but evidently not strong enough on Cassie's part to compete with mother love. You, my dear, are living proof that mother love is stronger than any other emotion. Cassie's feeling for me is much too mild to overcome that."

"But there is no longer any mother love to compete with, is there?" she asked, throwing all her vows to the wind in her desire to see the pain gone from her son's eyes. "You did as she asked; you offered for the daughter. You can't be blamed if the girl refused you."

"Cassie will blame me. She will say I didn't try hard enough. And she'd be right. I made a mull of the business."

"Oh, come now, Jemmy, this is too much self-blame! The girl's heart was elsewhere. So how could the 'mull' be of your making?"

"I couldn't bring myself to say the crucial words."

"What crucial words?"

" 'I love you'. They come easily to the tongue, don't they? But I couldn't say them."

"Would it have made a difference if you had?"

"Probably not. But Cassie will not believe it."

"You can't be sure, can you? Why don't you drive to Dorset in the morning and ask—?"

He gave a snort of laughter. "Really, Mama, for someone who's promised never again to interfere, you are certainly making a great many suggestions."

"Oh, dear, I am." She glanced over at him guiltily. "I seem to be a hopeless case. You must do what you think best, of course."

"What I think, Mama," he said, rising, draining the last of his drink and making for the door, "is that I've had enough rejection for a lifetime. I shall never offer for another female. Your son will be a staid old bachelor. I know that disappoints you, but you'll get used to it in time. One gets used to everything . . . in time."

Chapter
~ *31* ~

Cicely was well aware that her mother, her aunt and everyone else would judge her harshly if they knew what she was planning. It was a decidedly shocking plan. Repugnant, even. It required her to lie, to trick and to cheat. But she could think of no other way to combat Charles's adamant resistance. Why, the man had never called on her, not even after the encounter at the opera. Not once!

It was obvious that something drastic had to be done, and, in the words of Macbeth when he was planning *his* evil deed, *"If it were done when 'tis done, then 'twere well it were done quickly."* So she set her plan in action.

First, she had to lay the groundwork. That required a promise from Clive to make himself available the following day to take her for a long ride. This she accomplished with little trouble. Next she had to free herself from the watchful eye of her aunt. That would be a harder task. She set about it the next morning. "Aunt Eva," she said casually at breakfast, "I think I'd like to make a quick trip home to see Mama."

Eva looked up from her teacup. "Why? Is anything amiss?"

"No, of course not. I just want to make certain she's well. I've not had a letter in several days."

"I had a letter just this Tuesday. Everything is fine."

"She always says everything is fine. I'd rather pop in and see for myself. It will only be overnight."

"Very well, dearest, if you think we should." Eva pulled her appointment diary from her pocket and consulted it. "We can go next Monday."

Cicely, knowing her aunt, was prepared for this. "I'd rather not wait. Why not today?"

"We are invited to the Murchisons' dinner tonight. I've already accepted."

"Then you must go, of course. But you needn't have me with you. It is only your friends, with not a single young gentleman or lady my age in the assemblage. I'd much rather go home and see Mama."

"But how can you go without my escort?" her aunt demanded. "And, if I'm to have the carriage, what would you use for transport?"

Cicely made a great pretense of considering the matter. "Perhaps I can prevail upon Clive to take me," she said as if she'd just had a wonderful idea. "We could probably take his phaeton. We could leave early this afternoon and be at Crestwoods by sundown."

Eva looked over at her niece dubiously. "Just you and Clive?"

"Heavens, Aunt Eva, why not? He's quite reliable, and you know perfectly well that he treats me like a sister. You'd let me go with a brother to escort me, wouldn't you?"

"Well, I suppose . . ."

Cicely didn't wait for another word. "Oh, *thank* you, dearest!" she exclaimed, flying round the table and kissing her aunt's cheek. "You are the best aunt in the world!"

The next step was the hardest of all—the letter to Charles. She worked on it for two hours, tearing up and burning three drafts before she was satisfied. The fourth version she folded and sealed. Then she sought out her aunt's second footman. "Martin," she whispered, giving him the note and a gold sovereign, "you must deliver this note to Lord Lucas in person. And it must be handed to him before seven tonight, but after five. You'll find him either at his rooms on Portman Square or at White's Club. Is that clear? You must place it *in his hand*, and it must be between five and seven tonight. And Martin, please don't fail me!"

By three that afternoon, sitting beside Clive on the driver's seat of his dashing high-perch phaeton, Cicely was so nervous and frightened she almost wished she hadn't embarked on this enterprise. But there was no turning back now; the note was out of her hands.

"I don't mind taking you for a drive," Clive said, "but I don't see why you insisted that we take this road. We're going due west, and the sun is in my eyes."

"I may as well tell you now, Clive. This is not just a drive. You're taking me home."

He gaped at her. "Home? To Crestwoods? Why on earth?"

"I want to see Mama."

"But that's three hours from here! We won't be back till . . . till well past midnight!"

"We could stay the night at Crestwoods, couldn't we?"

"Yes, I suppose we could. But, good God, Cicely, you could have asked me properly. Why didn't you?"

She shrugged. "I was afraid you'd refuse me."

"And so I might!" he snapped. "What if I'd had an engagement tonight?"

"Well, do you?"

"No, but—"

"Then I don't see why you're raising such a dust. Do you *mind* taking me home?"

He glared at her. "Well, I mind being tricked into it."

"Then you can turn back. Go on, turn back. We're only a short way from town. You'll only have wasted an hour or so."

"No, I'll take you," he growled. "But you've a strange way of treating a fellow."

"I'm sorry," she murmured. "I'll make it up to you someday."

He sulked for the next hour, but his normal good spirits reasserted themselves after that, and to Cicely's relief, he actually whistled to himself as they tooled along.

When they gone about halfway to home, just past the town of Swallowfield, Cicely began to watch for a particular inn she knew could not be far distant. As soon as she spotted its thatched roof, she began to moan. "Oh, dear me," she said in a weak voice, "I suddenly don't feel very well."

Clive cast her a look of alarm. "What is it?"

"I don't know. I feel . . . faint . . ."

"Faint? Oh, good Lord!"

She wavered on the seat. "I think I'm . . . going to . . . swoon!"

"Cicely, no! Don't do that. I wouldn't know what to do! Please, *please,* don't swoon!"

She put a trembling hand over her face. "Water . . . " she croaked.

"Look, there's an inn just ahead!" He whipped up the horses, getting to his feet to do it, like a charioteer of old. "See it? The sign there says the White Falcon. You'll have your water in a trice. Hold on, old girl, there's a dear!"

She peeped at him through her fingers, smiling behind her hand. She felt very pleased with her performance. Things were going exactly as planned.

Chapter
~ 32 ~

It was just growing dark in London, a time when most of the members of the ton were gathering at various distinguished homes for festive dinners, for late May was the very height of the social season. But in the Inglesby town house no one was preparing for a gala evening. Lady Sarah was standing in her front hall sniffing into her handkerchief, while all around her the servants were bustling about carrying Jeremy's baggage out to his carriage.

Jeremy came down the stairs pulling on his driving gloves. Seeing her in tears took him by surprise. "Come, come, Mama," he said affectionately, patting her shoulder, "it's not like you to turn on the waterworks just because I'm taking off for the Park."

She dabbed at her eyes. "I shall never understand you. Why won't you stay for a while? You have friends here! There are all sorts of fetes and galas to attend—the opera, the theater, your club! Why do you want to rusticate now, when there's no one of any consequence anywhere near the country house?"

"Don't fret about me, Mama. I like it there. Charlie has promised to come for a long stay. And if you come out for a visit now and then, that will be all the consequential company I'll need."

His mother shook her head sadly. "I don't think it at all salubrious for you to cut yourself from society. I have a writing table full of invitations, all of which include you. You could have a rousing good time if only you'd stay."

He cocked an amused brow at her. "Are you matchmaking again, Mama? I thought you'd given up—"

He was interrupted by a pounding on the door. Hickham, who was about to carry out a portmanteau, opened it at once. Charles came bursting in. He was in evening clothes, but his top hat and neckerchief were both askew, and he was so out of temper that his face was darkly flushed. "Ah, Jemmy, you're still here!" he said in relief, taking his friend in an excitable embrace. "Thank the Lord I caught you in time. Here!" He thrust a crushed paper into Jeremy's hand. "Read this, and tell me what you make of it."

Jeremy took a quick look at the missive. Lady Sarah, meanwhile, not accustomed to being ignored, fixed a disapproving eye on the visitor. "Do I not deserve a how-de-do, you rudesby?"

"I'm sorry, Lady Sarah, but my mind's not on trivialities right now."

Jeremy looked up. "I think, Mama, that I may not be leaving for the Park just yet, so there's no reason now to wait about to see me off."

"Indeed?" She looked with raised brows from one gentleman to the other. "Very well, I shall leave you, then. I know when I'm *de trop*." She started up the stairs with unhurried dignity. "Please inform me when you *are* ready to make your departure."

"Well?" Charles asked anxiously as soon as her ladyship had disappeared. "What do you think?"

"I don't know what to think. Let me read it again." He carried the paper closer to a branch of candles burning on a side table and went through it once more. "*Dear Charles*," the letter said, "*When you Read this I shall be Embarking on an Adventure completely Inspired by You. I shall be at the White Falcon, an Inn just beyond Swallowfield, engaged in a Tryst with your Nephew Clive Percy. The reason I write to tell You of it is because You, in a sense, Brought this about, having—in your Desire to push me into a Connection with a Man close to my own Age—been the one who Brought us Together. Even at the Opera you indicated your Approval of my Continuing Connection with him. I have no Intention of Wedding him, of course, having my Heart set on Another, but I thought you might be Pleased that your Efforts to bring Clive and Me Together have*"

Not been for Naught. I Trust you will not Reveal what I have told you to my Aunt or any Member of my Family, for they would Not Understand, not being as Worldly as You are. In Gratitude and Affection, I remain Most Sincerely Yours, Cicely Beringer."

"What I think," Jeremy said, shaking his head over it, "is that this is the silliest letter I've ever read."

"I quite agree with you," Charles said in disgust. "Having a tryst with one man while her heart's set on another! Did you ever hear of anything so ridiculous? And thinking I'm worldly enough to *approve* of this nonsense! What sort of rotter does she think I *am*?" He took a turn about the hall to vent his spleen, and then he threw Jeremy a worried glance. "But what do suppose she means by all of this, eh? Do you think she truly intends to . . . to do what she says?"

"Engage in a tryst, you mean? I haven't the least idea. I know less than nothing about the minds of young females. But I suspect she had a reason for warning you of it."

"Because she's so clearly given away her whereabouts, you mean?"

"Yes, exactly. She means you to prevent her."

"But it makes no sense. Why would she embark on such an escapade if she wants to be prevented?"

"I don't know. But she ought to be stopped if she's serious about this. If anyone should learn of it, the girl would find herself in a devil of a fix."

"I should say she would!" Charles began to pace about again, biting his lip. "I suppose there's nothing for it but for us to go out to this inn in Swallowfield and stop her."

"*Us?* What have *I* to do with this? It's you she wrote to."

"Yes, but if I went alone, it would be like admitting that I have some responsibility for this. And after all, your connection with the chit is as strong as mine."

"Is it?" Jeremy gazed at his friend with a look of amused speculation. "I have the strangest notion . . ."

"What? What are you thinking?"

"Never mind." Jeremy clapped his friend on the shoulder and gave him a wide grin. "Very well, Charlie, I'll go with you. I have a feeling it will be an entertaining adventure."

"And *I* have a feeling we're engaged in a wild goose chase. I don't know why you're grinning in that fatuous way, except that you think this is some sort of joke. And you're probably right. When we get to that inn, there won't be a soul there."

Chapter
~ 33 ~

Clive Percy, sportsman and bon vivant, was having one of the worst nights of his life. He'd started the day in his customary good spirits, anticipating a pleasant little afternoon riding in Hyde Park with Cicely and then an evening of high-stake billiards with his friends at Warkworth's (the club he preferred because the wagering there was more intense than at the other clubs). Instead, here he was, captive to a sick girl in a dingy, low-ceilinged, dormered room in the attic of a dull little inn located in a place at the back of beyond.

Cicely had fainted away when they arrived at the inn that afternoon. He was terrified by her swoon; he had no notion of what to do for her. The innkeeper's wife had brought her round by holding a bottle of sal volatile under her nose, but then the girl said she felt too weak to go on.

"Shall I get you a doctor?" Clive had offered worriedly. "There must be one in the vicinity."

"No, no," she'd said a bit hysterically. "All I need is a little rest. An hour, no more." She'd then turned to the woman, who was still holding her. "You do have a bedroom I may bespeak for a while, don't you?"

"Aye, we do, but on'y one. We don't 'ave many trav'lers," the innkeeper's wife said. She and Clive helped Cicely upstairs. Then the woman eased her onto the bed, unbuttoned the top of her dress, put a cold cloth on her forehead, and shooed Clive from the room. He'd had to spend the next few hours pacing about downstairs, clumping from the taproom to the little private parlor and back again, with nothing better to drink than a thin home brew, nothing better to eat than overcooked mutton and nothing better to do than shuffle a deck of shabby playing cards. And without anyone troubling to tell him anything about the patient upstairs except that she was still resting.

Finally, about eight in the evening, Cicely had sent for him. He'd had to bring his head down to get in the low doorway. She was lying on the bed, propped up against the pillows. She looked very pretty, he thought, and not at all ill. But when he asked how she did, she lowered her eyes and shook her head. "Just another hour or two," she said in a small, plaintive voice. "I'm sure I'll feel strong enough to go on after that." She smiled up at him and motioned to the side of the bed. "Sit down here, Clive, and keep me company."

Clive, an offspring of a robust family, was unaccustomed to illness and very uncomfortable in the presence of invalids. He sat down very gingerly. "What on earth's wrong with you, Cicely?" he asked. "You seem well enough to me."

"I don't really know," she murmured. "It's my head. I get a bit dizzy if I get up."

"Then let me go for a doctor."

"No," she insisted. "I don't want a strange doctor."

"Please, Cicely, it doesn't seem right for me just to sit here and do nothing. I can saddle one of my horses and ride for your mother."

"I tell you I'll be better in just a bit. Just stay here with me and hold my hand."

He looked around uncomfortably. "But we're alone . . . in a bedroom . . ."

A giggle escaped her. "If it's my reputation that's worrying you, just leave the door open."

So here he was, sitting beside her as she'd asked, holding her hand, searching desperately in his mind for pleasantries to say and wondering how he'd gotten himself into this fix.

There was no question that Cicely was behaving strangely. Every few minutes she asked the time. Eight-fifteen. Eight-thirty. Eight fifty-five. When she asked again, he became annoyed. "Why do you keep asking for the time?" he demanded impatiently.

"No reason," she murmured, looking troubled. "I thought that by this time . . ."

"Yes?"

Her eyes fell from his. "I thought . . . I'd be feeling better."

They sat in silence after that. A few minutes later, he noticed that she'd fallen asleep. He stared at her face, wondering what he ought to do. He didn't know how to take care of a sick young lady. And the innkeeper's wife, though helpful at first, had not made an appearance since the evening patrons had come crowding into the taproom. What would happen if Cicely worsened? She hadn't wanted him to ride for her mother, but she was now fast asleep. If he went on horseback, he could get to Crestwoods in an hour and have Lady Beringer back here before midnight. And perhaps even before Cicely woke up. Carefully he released her hand and laid it gently on the coverlet. Then, as stealthily as a thief, he tiptoed from the room.

It was more than two hours later when something—a sound in the doorway, perhaps—caused Cicely to awaken. She blinked in the dimness, for now it was dark outside, and the only light in the room came from a candle at her bedside that had burned low. It took her a moment to remember where she was. *Heavens*, she said to herself, *I shouldn't have let myself fall asleep. What if he—?* And then she realized someone was standing in the doorway. Her heart leapt up into her throat. "Charlie!" she gasped. "You *came!*"

"Yes, we did," he muttered in disgust. "Jeremy and I. The question is why?"

"To save me, of course," she said with a satisfied smile, lying back against the pillows in a pose she hoped was lascivious. "What did you think?"

"That's what I thought I was doing—what your idiotic letter led us to believe. But there seems to be no one here to save you *from.*"

"What?" She looked round the room in bewilderment. "Where is Clive?"

"I have no idea. Jeremy is downstairs trying to locate him. What sort of peculiar assignation is this, Cicely? How can you have an assignation if one of the lovers is absent?"

"But he was right here—!"

"Was he? Are you telling the truth? Or is this simply a child-ish prank of some sort, as I suspected?"

Cicely sat up in bed, nonplussed. "I don't know what's become of Clive, and I don't care if you believe me or not. But if you thought it was a prank, why did you bother to come?"

"I'm dashed if I know. If I'd had a grain of sense I would have thrown your deuced letter in the fire and gone to Lady Holland's, as I'd engaged to do. It was to be a gala of galas. I had every expectation of playing whist tonight with Prinny himself!"

"I'm sorry. Forgive me," she said, pouting. "I didn't know I'd be wheedling you out of a game of whist."

"So it *was* a wheedle after all!" With a groan of disgust, he stomped in and dropped, exhausted, upon the room's one chair. "You, Cicely Beringer, are the most irritating little trouble-maker I've ever encountered. Not only did you make a com-plete fool of me and cut up my evening, but you caused us to go chasing all over the countryside for more than three hours. The blasted inn doesn't have a night lantern, and we kept passing it by without seeing it. I went almost wild, I can tell you, agonizing over the possibility that we'd be too late to keep you from ruin! And now it's almost midnight, this deuced inn has no other rooms, and we have no place to sleep. I could wring your neck!"

In all that diatribe, Cicely heard one thing that lifted her spirit right out of the doldrums. "Wh-what did you say?"

"I said I'd like to wring—"

"No. About being almost wild."

"He *was* wild," came Jeremy's voice from the doorway. "A father could not have been more agitated or more determined to save his daughter from seduction. What were you thinking of, Cicely, to run off with Clive in this madcap fashion?"

"Good evening, Jeremy," she mumbled, shamefaced. "I didn't expect *you* to be drawn into this. But if you believe that I'm telling the truth about Clive, then I'm glad you came."

"I never doubted that he was here. The question is, where has he gone? The only clue I've managed to uncover comes from an ostler, who saw him saddle one of his horses and ride off."

Charles leapt from the chair. "Do you mean there actually *was* a . . . a seduction? When I get my hands on that boy, I'll horsewhip him within an inch of his life!"

"Take a damper, Charlie," Jeremy said mildly. "Just because Clive was here doesn't mean anything untoward took place. *Did* it, Cicely?"

"Of course not," Cicely said.

Charlie threw up his hands. "Then what was the *point*—?"

"Yes, Cicely," Jeremy said, sitting down on the edge of her bed and taking her hand. "I think it's time you told this poor fellow just what the point is."

A flush rose from her neck all the way up to her forehead. "You guessed?"

"It was not difficult. You'd given me too many clues. A man you loved madly, just a wee bit my senior, whom you had a plan to entrap—"

"Be still, you clunch!" the girl cried, clapping her hand over Jeremy's mouth. "I want him to figure it all out for himself."

"Whom are you speaking of?" asked the bewildered Charlie. "I demand to know what is going on here! See here, Jemmy, if you knew something about this blasted rigmarole that I don't, why didn't you tell me?"

"Because I couldn't determine the purpose of this little scheme, and I didn't want to do or say anything to spoil it until I knew just what this goosecap had in mind."

"It should be perfectly obvious by now," Cicely said, looking at Charlie hopefully.

He glowered at her. "Nothing is at all obvious. Except perhaps that you contrived an assignation just to get us here."

"Not *us*, you gudgeon," Jeremy laughed. "*You*."

"Me?" He rose from his chair, an arrested expression on his face. "You arranged all this just to have *me* come and rescue you?"

"Yes," she said, "but I didn't expect—"

"She didn't expect you to be such a deuced slow-top," Jeremy said, getting up and going to the door.

Charles stood gaping down at her. "You don't mean that *I'm* the fellow . . . the one in your letter . . . ?"

She lifted herself to her knees and threw her arms around his neck. "Oh, Charlie, my love, you *are* a slow-top!"

He peered at her suspiciously for another moment, but as soon as he permitted himself to believe what her eyes were telling him, he was not slow to gather her in his arms and kiss her with all the passion that complete astonishment would permit. "But you can't love me," he whispered when he let her go. "I'm old enough to be your father."

"I've loved you ever since the day you kissed me in the orchard," she whispered back.

"Madly," Jeremy added, beaming at them from his post in the doorway.

They ignored him. "A few months ago, when Jeremy was courting me," Cicely pointed out, "you didn't tell *him* he was too old for me, did you?"

"That's right," Jeremy agreed. "You didn't."

"So there!" Cicely said in triumph.

Charles, overwhelmed, could only kiss her again. "Jemmy, old man," he said after a moment, lifting his head but not taking his eyes from the girl's face, "I would like to tell this outrageous child that I love her to distraction, but I would prefer to do it without an audience. Would you mind making yourself scarce?"

"Very well, I'll go," his friend said, bending down and backing out from under the low door frame into the dark corridor, "but I must remind you that this is a bedroom in a secluded inn—a location ideally suited for an assignation. So if you're not downstairs in five minutes, Charles Percy, I shall come storming up to rescue the girl from *you!*"

Chapter
~ 34 ~

Later, when the starry-eyed couple came down to join Jeremy in the inn's tiny private parlor and announced their betrothal, Jeremy insisted that the weary innkeeper bring them the best wine the establishment had in its cellars. A celebration was called for, and a celebration they would have.

"I fear we ain't goin' t'get any sleep tonight," the innkeeper complained to his wife as he crossed the kitchen on his way to the cellar.

The woman looked up from the cutting board, where she was slicing thick pieces of bread to accompany a platter of cold meats and cheeses. "It'll be worth it," she said happily. "The tall gent gave me six yellowboys!"

Thus the three celebrants gathered round the small table and toasted the upcoming nuptials with a wine that Charles declared was not half bad.

"I'd enjoy it more," Jeremy remarked, "if I knew what had become of Clive."

"He wouldn't have gone back to London and left me," Cicely mused, biting into a piece of cheese hungrily. "Not Clive."

"If he's so blasted reliable, why did he agree to a tryst in the first place?" her betrothed demanded.

"Because he had no idea it *was* a tryst, silly," the girl explained. "I pretended to be ill, you see, and he—"

But a commotion at the outer door stilled her tongue. Their heads turned toward the corridor, Jeremy starting out of his chair. But before he could get to his feet, he discovered that a small crowd had materialized in the doorway: Clive, Cassie's housekeeper Mrs. Upsom, and Cassie herself, looking every

179

inch a distraught mother. Her face was pale and drawn, her posture tense and her clothes disheveled. Her hair was hanging down her back in one thick, carelessly plaited braid (just the way Jeremy loved it), and she'd hurriedly tossed a shawl over her painting smock. Her appearance smote Jeremy's heart. He wanted nothing more than to take her in his arms and soothe her.

But her eyes barely took note of him as she looked round quickly. At the sight of her daughter, however, her whole face brightened. "Cicely!" she cried, holding out her arms. "You're *eating!*"

"Well, you see, I was famished," Cicely said sheepishly as she ran across the room and flung herself into her mother's embrace.

"But that means . . ." Cassie held her off and studied her face intently. " . . . you're all *well.*"

Clive, standing in the doorway and surveying the scene, began to suspect that he'd been the victim of a hoax. "Dash it, Cicely," he muttered, ogling his uncle and Jeremy suspiciously, "what's going on here? I'd wager a monkey you weren't ill at all!"

Cicely broke from her mother's hold and faced him. "I'm sorry, Clive. I tricked you. But I didn't dream you'd go so far as to ride all the way to Crestwoods for Mama."

"Are you saying you were *not* ill?" Cassie asked. "Oh, what a relief! I was terrified. I even brought Annie to help in the sickroom. Clive had me believing you were at death's door."

"Well, she *swooned,*" the boy cried in self-defense. "I saw it. She actually swooned!"

"No, I didn't," Cicely confessed. "Not really."

"But dearest, why?" her bewildered mother asked.

Jeremy came forward and took Cassie's elbow. "Why don't we all sit down and have some refreshments? And while we do, Cicely can explain everything."

"Must I?" the girl asked, blushing. "Wouldn't it be enough just to announce the outcome?"

"Outcome?" Cassie asked.

"Oh, Mama, I'm bursting to tell you—" Cicely threw her arms round her mother's neck. "I'm betrothed!"

Cassie gaped at her daughter for one frozen moment before turning right around to Jeremy. Her eyes sparkled in tearful gratitude. "Oh, my dear!" she said, putting a hand on his arm. "I'm so glad!"

Jeremy was startled. It hadn't occurred to him until this moment that no one had informed her of his unsuccessful suit. "I think you've made an error, ma'am," he said gently. "It's Charles who deserves the congratulations."

"Charles?" Her eyes widened in shock, and her hand fell from Jeremy's arm. She took a step backward, her whole demeanor expressing her astonishment and disappointment.

"Yes, I'm the lucky man," Charles said, too delighted by the events of the evening to take offense. "Come, sit down, ma'am, do, and let Cicely tell you the whole. It's a very romantic story, I promise you."

Cassie sank into the chair that Charles held for her, and all the others gathered round, even Annie. There was a merry babble of voices as Cicely told her tale with assistance from Charles, questions from Clive and exclamations of delight from the housekeeper. Only Cassie, tight-lipped and pale, and Jeremy, watching her face with intense attention, were silent.

When the tale was told, Cassie rose and wrapped her shawl tightly round her shoulders. She looked down at her daughter with a strained smile. "Cicely, my love, you know without my saying it that I wish you happy. We shall speak of this again, but meanwhile, you must excuse me. It's very late, and I'm very weary." She leaned down and planted a kiss on her daughter's cheek before turning to the door. "Clive, my dear," she added before departing, "if you'd be good enough to see me home, I'd be most grateful. I'll leave Annie to chaperon Cicely on the trip back to her aunt's."

"Of course, your ladyship," the lad said. "My pleasure, I assure you." He cast a glance at Cicely—who looked as if she'd been doused with cold water—before following Cassie out.

Jeremy sat motionless as he watched her go, trying to straighten out his confused thoughts. Then he shook himself out of his lethargy, jumped to his feet and hurried out of the room. As he left, he heard Charles speak consolingly to his betrothed. "Don't look so stricken, my love," the happy man said with buoyant confidence. "I'll bring her round. Your mother'll be very fond of me before I'm through, take my word."

Clive was just about to help Cassie up the carriage steps when Jeremy came out to the courtyard. "Wait a moment, please," he said, coming up behind her and grasping an arm. "I must speak to you."

She shook his hand off. "I have nothing whatever to say to you, my lord," she said icily. "Step out of my way, if you please, and let Clive hand me up."

"Clive," his lordship said quietly, "leave us for a moment."

"The boy will stay right where he is!" Cassie said furiously.

"Clive," Jeremy said in a voice neither of them had heard before, "*go inside!*"

The poor fellow succumbed at once. "I'll be right back," he said to Cassie lamely as he scurried off.

Cassie turned her back on Jeremy, seething in helpless fury. "Well, since you've prevented my departure, say what you have to say."

"Damnation, ma'am, what's wrong with you?" he demanded. "I know you've always believed that Charles is a rake, but he's a very fine fellow, really. One of the finest. And they do say, you know, that a reformed rake makes the very best husband. You should be overjoyed. You've just learned that your daughter, rather than lying prostrate at death's door, is perfectly healthy and has won her heart's desire."

Cassie wheeled round. "*Her* heart's desire? Don't take me for a fool! It's *your* desire, that you've somehow convinced her is hers. Not willing to offer for her yourself, you manipulated your friend into *doing it for you.*"

"Good God," he exclaimed in utter stupefaction, "is that what you think?" He ran his fingers through his hair, momentarily deprived of speech.

"It's what anyone would think who knew our situation."

"You can't really believe what you're saying!"

"Oh, yes, I believe it. And I'll never forgive you for it."

He wanted to slap her! How could she even think such things of him? he wondered. But then something in him softened. Perhaps she didn't deserve his anger. After all, no one had told her about his offer. "But Cassie, you don't know the whole," he pleaded in desperate urgency, fearing that her lack of trust would kill whatever was left between them. "I *did* offer for her. She refused me."

"Don't make matters worse with lies," she said scornfully. "She would *never* have refused you."

Enraged, he took hold of her shoulders, his grasp purposely cruel. "Do you really think I'd lie to you? Damnation, woman, look at me! Is that the sort of man I am in your eyes? A lying, manipulating cheat? And I was fool enough to think you loved me. It finally occurs to me that I never really knew you. I don't think you're capable of love. Perhaps not even mother love. If you truly loved Cicely, you'd see how she really feels, not as you think she ought to feel." He thrust her away in disgust and strode back toward the inn. "Clive, you may come out now and take this woman out of my sight!"

Chapter
~ 35 ~

Eva was not completely surprised by Cicely's news; she hadn't forgotten that the girl had developed a *tendre* for Charles when they'd stayed at Inglesby Park. Of course, now that the matter had become an actual betrothal, she immediately made some discreet inquiries about the fellow, and learned from her friends much that gladdened her heart. The Percys were an old, honorable family, and Charles's title brought with it several large holdings and an income in the neighborhood of twenty thousand. With such an income, the fellow could be forgiven his libertinish tendencies, which, after all, one had to expect when a man was single, idle and rich. *"You should feel nothing but delight,"* she wrote to her sister, *"for in addition to his wealth and name, the fellow has a great deal of charm, and, moreover, everyone knows that there is no better husband in the world than a reformed rake."*

Cassie wrote back that since Cicely's letters were so full of enthusiasm, she could not but accept the situation and give her blessing. She also thanked Eva from the bottom of her heart for offering to take care of the details of the wedding breakfast, which the bridegroom insisted had to take place no later than mid-June. Eva could not have been more pleased to do it. She loved planning fetes and galas, and this one for Cicely was especially dear to her heart.

At her daughter's insistence, Cassie arrived in London a fortnight before the wedding. Cicely was right to insist, for there was a great deal to do. She warned her mother in advance that not only did Cassie have to approve her daughter's gown, order one for herself, go over the guest list with Eva, and visit an assortment of glovemakers, shoemakers and milliners, but she would be expected to engage in a round of parties and dinners and other prenuptial celebrations. For Cassie, who'd not come to town in many years, it was enough to have her quaking in her boots.

On the second day of her stay, Cassie received her first caller. It was her son-in-law-to-be, who breezed into Eva's drawing room in riding clothes, his crop tucked under his arm, and demanded that she get her hat at once. Before she could voice an objection, he'd pulled her out of the house, thrust her up on the seat of a small, dangerously high-perch phaeton and set off for a spin round Hyde Park. "This carriage is Clive's," he said after he'd maneuvered it into a place in the line of carriages making similar afternoon spins. "I wouldn't own a silly little contraption like this."

"Then why did you borrow it?" Cassie asked. "Surely you have carriages of your own you could have used."

"Not one as small as this." He turned and looked at her frankly. "I wanted us in close quarters, and this is as close as we can properly get."

"But why?"

"So that we might have an intimate talk. You see, Cassie—may I call you that? I somehow don't think it would be comfortable to call you Mother."

She gave a reluctant laugh. "Yes, I suppose you may as well."

"Thank you. You see, Cassie, I'm well aware that you don't like me. Your evaluation of me that very first night at Inglesby Park is seared in my memory. You called me self-indulgent."

"But that was when I thought you were Inglesby."

"Did you like me any better when you learned I was Lucas?"

"No," she admitted. "I suppose not."

"That's why I had to speak to you. I don't know exactly what you mean by self-indulgence, and I suppose I *have* indulged myself over the years. I never had to go hungry, after all. I don't deny I enjoy the luxuries my place in life affords me. But I've never cheated anyone, or treated anyone unfairly, even the ladies who from time to time have lived under my protection. And I did acquit myself with honor in the Peninsular campaign."

"I didn't know you served in the army," she murmured, glancing up at his face.

"I don't mean to make too much of it. Serving in the army is a family tradition. I only did what was expected."

"But with honor."

"Yes. It isn't modest for me to speak of it, but if you'd like to hear the details, you could ask Jeremy. We served together, you know, and were both decorated, though he more than I."

"I didn't know," she said in a low voice.

"But of course that's neither here nor there. The point is that I love your daughter very much, much more than I ever thought I could love anyone, and you can be sure I'll never do anything to hurt her. It would hurt her, however, if she believed you did not approve of the match."

"I gave my blessing, did I not?"

"Yes, but not quite with enthusiasm."

"Perhaps it's not possible for me to look on marriage with enthusiasm. My own was not . . . ideal. But I will say this, Lord Lucas—"

"Charlie."

"Charlie. I like you better for having spoken to me like this."

"Well," he said cheerily, flicking his crop at the horses, "at least it's a start."

She was remembering that conversation a couple of evenings later while sitting with Eva on the sidelines of a ballroom. The ball was hosted by Eva's friends, Lord and Lady Murchison. It was a large affair, with more than one hundred guests. There were two rows of chairs edging the dance floor to accommodate those who were not dancing. A goodly number of dowagers and widows occupied those chairs. Eva sat in the first row, chatting happily with friends, but Cassie had taken a place in the vacant second row, where the light from the chandeliers was less bright and where there was no one seated nearby who might force her to make polite, meaningless conversation. She didn't wish to chat, for she wanted to watch her daughter waltzing with Charles. It was a pleasure to see them dance together. Cassie was recalling how sincere Charles had sounded when he spoke of his love for Cicely. He certainly seemed at this moment like a man in love, for he kept his eyes fixed on her face as he whirled her round the floor. Cassie's heart warmed with motherly satisfaction as she watched.

But that warmth was to be short-lived. At that moment her eye was caught by a face so familiar that her heart stopped beating. It was Jeremy, waltzing by with a lovely young lady in a spangled white gown. Jeremy, dancing the waltz! She'd never envisioned him dancing. It was a sight that delighted her eyes and tore her heart.

Clenching her hands, she ordered herself to be calm and not let his presence affect her. She had warned herself, when she was preparing to come to London, that she might run into him. She'd eased her qualms by assuring herself that such meetings would not present undue difficulties. After all, she and Jeremy were no longer on speaking terms. If they were ever to come face-to-face, all she'd need to do would be to return his bow and move off.

Reminding herself of that, she regained her equilibrium and permitted herself to watch him dance. It was a sight of him with which she was totally unfamiliar. He looked remarkably handsome in his evening clothes, his shirtpoints stiff and modestly high, his pristine neckerchief intricately folded and his silk breeches perfectly fitted to his shapely legs. And his execution of the steps of the waltz, too, won her admiration. He was smooth and graceful, well schooled in these social amenities that she knew nothing of. Perhaps it was just as well that nothing had come of their . . . their little moment of attachment. She could never have kept up with him.

When, a few seconds later, the dance ended and he was escorting his partner from the floor, he passed someone he knew—a dignified lady wearing a jeweled, feathered turban atop a head of elegantly coiffed gray hair and seated half a dozen chairs down from Cassie in the first row—and he smiled and nodded to her. Then, as he looked up, his eyes fell on Cassie. His face stiffened; she could see that. But it was so small a change of expression that she was sure no one else would detect it. But the woman to whom he'd nodded did detect it. She immediately turned her head, lifted her lorgnette

and stared at Cassie with such intensity that Cassie blushed and
looked away. But Jeremy did not look at her again. He turned
back to his companion and walked on.

When next Cassie glanced up, she saw the lady in the
jeweled turban whispering to her neighbor and pointing at
Cassie. The neighbor whispered a response, and the turbaned
lady stared at her again. This time Cassie lifted her chin and
coldly looked away. That stare was rude if ever one was.

Before she knew it, however, the lady was standing right
at her elbow. "Good evening, Lady Beringer," she said in a
deep, mellow voice. "You *are* Lady Beringer, are you not?
Cassandra Beringer?"

"Yes, I am," Cassie answered stiffly.

"I know you must find me abominably rude. And my son,
I'm certain, would kick up the devil of a dust if he knew I'd
accosted you in this way—"

"Your son?" Cassie felt her knees begin to tremble.

"Yes. Oh, dear, haven't I introduced myself? I'm Jeremy's
mother, Sarah Tate."

"Oh! H-how do you do, your ladyship," Cassie stuttered in
confusion.

"I know I shouldn't be doing this . . . introducing myself to
you in this unorthodox way, and striking up a conversation
with you, especially after I'd *sworn* to myself that I would
never, never interfere again! But he's spoken of you so often,
you see, and when I saw . . ." She gave a helpless shrug. "To
see you here, sitting all alone like this . . . You can understand,
I'm sure, that I couldn't resist the opportunity to meet you."

"Well, yes, of course, I quite see . . . I mean, won't you
please sit down, ma'am?"

"May I?" Lady Sarah took the nearest chair and turned it
so that they could be face-to-face. "It's very good of you to
indulge an old woman this way," she murmured, studying
Cassie with discomfiting intensity.

"Not at all. I've often wished to become acquainted with
Lord Inglesby's mother."

"Truly? May I ask why?"

Cassie, attracted by the woman's directness, opened up to
her for the first time. "I don't know if your son told you, but

I spent a month at Inglesby Park recently, recovering from an accident, and I often came across your books in the library. I saw the little notes you wrote in the margins. Often my feelings about the readings were similar to yours. It seemed to me we might have . . ." Here her courage failed her. Perhaps she'd assumed too much and gone too far.

"Tastes in common?" the older woman supplied. "I shouldn't be at all surprised." She tilted her head and studied Cassie's face again. "You do not look quite as I expected. I knew you would be beautiful, but I hadn't expected the . . . the softness."

"Softness?"

"Yes. I thought that a woman so determinedly protective of her daughter would look a little harder at the edges."

"Is that how Jeremy described me?" Cassie asked, unable to keep the hurt from her voice. "Hard at the edges?"

"No, no. He never described you at all. He is not at all forthcoming about his private feelings. Everything I know about him I had to learn either by indirection or by bludgeoning him for information, insisting that it's my motherly right to know." She sighed. "It's not easy to be a mother, as you no doubt have learned."

"No, it's not," Cassie agreed.

Lady Sarah leaned back in her chair and smiled. "I was quite ready to hate you on sight, you know. As I would hate anyone who'd hurt him as you did. But I find myself quite drawn to you. Isn't that astonishing?"

"Did he tell you I'd hurt him?"

"No, of course he didn't. He didn't have to. But you do not seem the sort who would callously cause pain to another."

"Thank you for that," Cassie said, lowering her eyes. "I'm afraid that, between your son and me, there was pain inflicted on both sides."

"I am sorry for that." She suddenly leaned forward and took Cassie's hand. "He would boil me in oil if he heard me," she said, "but I must ask. Do you love my son?"

"Oh, Lady Sarah," Cassie said, wincing, "please don't ask me that!"

"Very well, I withdraw the question. I shouldn't have asked. I know I mustn't interfere. I shall leave you, then, before we become the subject of gossip for keeping our heads together for so long. But if ever you wish to speak to me, about my son or anything else, please call on me." She stood up and smiled down at Cassie with real warmth. "In fact, do come to tea. You'd be welcome at any time. Good night, my dear."

Chapter
~ 36 ~

Cicely was having a fitting of her wedding gown. Eva's French modiste, Madame Brenet, was pinning it up in the upstairs sitting room. Cassie, who'd not yet had a look at it, went upstairs to see. As she stepped over the threshold, the first sight to meet her eyes was Cicely standing on a box in the center of the room, the sunlight pouring in the window from behind her, outlining her hair. Tall and youthfully slim, the girl looked breathtakingly lovely in a tamboured muslin gown with a band of seed pearls fitted tightly just under the breast. The very sight of her gave her mother a twinge of pride. "Oh, my dear," she sighed, "you are a vision."

Cicely giggled. "You sound just like Clive. That's what he always says."

"And why shouldn't he? You're as pretty as a picture whatever you wear." She sat down on the window seat and watched as the the seamstress set about pinning up the hem. "You've done a beautiful job, madame," she said to the seamstress.

"Thank you, my lady," the woman said, throwing her a smile.

"Speaking of Clive," Cassie remarked to her daughter, "I'm surprised the boy is taking your forthcoming nuptials with such good grace."

"You mustn't think Clive is heartbroken about my marrying Charles. He isn't in the least discomposed. He doesn't care for me above half, not in that way."

"Since when have you become so expert in these matters, my love? You can't be sure about Clive. Boys like Clive don't wear their hearts on their sleeves. They think it manly to hide their pain underneath."

"Pain? *Clive?*" She threw back her head and laughed. "Don't be a gudgeon, Mama. He's just been offered membership in the Four-in-Hand Club, and he's happy as a lark. You may take my word on it."

"I won't take your word," Cassie retorted. "I have at *least* as much knowledge on the subject of love as you, no matter how knowing you've become in the last few weeks."

"Turn about a bit, miss, please," said the seamstress from her seat on the floor, her mouth full of pins.

Cicely turned. "Really, Mama, you've always overestimated the interest that men take in me. I suppose that's something mothers do. But the truth is that nobody's ever really loved me but Charles."

"Turn around, miss, again," the modiste ordered.

Cicely turned again. "Even Jeremy," she said, half to herself. "When he came to offer, he said everything he ought but the words 'I love you'."

"What?" Cassie felt her whole body stiffen. "*What* did you say?"

"I didn't mind, really. It was sweet that he did it. Offered, I mean. But I knew he didn't feel about me as Charles did. I suppose he thought he ought to offer, having disappointed me that time before. But I could sense his heart wasn't in it. It's strange, isn't it, Mama, how one can sense when a man truly loves one?"

"Turn around again, please, miss," the modiste said.

Cassie swallowed hard. She could not have heard correctly. "Are you saying that Jeremy *offered* for you?" she asked, her voice shaking.

"Yes, didn't Aunt Eva tell you?"

"No one told me. When did he do it?"

"I don't remember exactly. A day or two before I ran off to Swallowfield. Why?"

"Once more, please," the modiste put in.

Cassie looked down at the seamstress with half-blind eyes. "Would you mind taking a bit of rest, madame? You could use some refreshment, couldn't you? Why don't you go downstairs and ask the butler for a cup of tea?"

"Yes, ma'am," the seamstress said, looking at her curiously

before whisking herself out. "Of course, ma'am. Thank you."

Cicely was looking at her strangely, too. "Why did you send madame away, Mama? Is something amiss?"

Cassie put a trembling hand to her forehead. "Please, my love, this is very important. Sit down and tell me about everything. And very slowly, because my head is spinning."

"Tell you about what, Mama?"

Cassie looked at the girl as if she'd suddenly lost her wits. "About what you were just saying! About Jeremy making an offer."

Cicely blinked at her. "There's nothing important about that."

"There is to me."

"I don't see why. That entire business with Jeremy was a stage of my girlhood, without any permanent significance. But if you really must hear about his offer, I'll tell you what I remember."

"Yes, I really must hear. Everything."

Cicely shrugged. "There's not very much to tell. Jeremy called just after teatime, with an enormous armful of blooms for Aunt Eva. And then he sat down beside me, took my hand and said he'd like to resume where we'd left off in the courtship before. And I said I couldn't believe he was serious, and he assured me he was, and I said I was very flattered but I had to refuse, and after a bit more backing and filling, he left. Oh, yes, I remember one thing more. I said he ought to offer for you, but he said you were too old."

Cassie, brushing aside the insult as too insignificant when compared to the primary information, merely gaped at her. "I don't understand, you *refused* him?"

"Yes, of course I did. Why are you so astonished?"

"But how could you refuse him? He's everything you wanted in a husband. Isn't that what you told me, time and time again?"

"Yes, but that was before."

"Before? Before what?"

"Before Charlie, of course."

Cassie could not accept what her daughter was trying to tell her. Her own preconceptions, her own preferences, her own desires loomed so large they blocked her mind. "Do you honestly expect me to believe that, given the choice, you'd *prefer* Charles Percy to Jeremy?" she asked in disbelief.

Cicely's patience came to an end. "Good heavens, Mama," she exploded, "haven't you been *listening*? Can't you hear anything I've been saying? I *love* Charlie. I wish I could make you see. He charms me and excites me and inspires me and attracts me . . . and also irks me and infuriates me . . . and— Oh, I don't know! It's just that in every possible way he touches my heart. I've never felt this way toward anyone before. Not any of the gentlemen who called after my comeout. Not Clive. Not Jeremy. Not anyone."

The truth burst on Cassie at last, a lightning bolt of comprehension. "Oh, my dear," she murmured, awestruck. "Is that what you've been trying to say to me? You're right! I *haven't* been listening to you. I had no *idea* you felt this way!" Dazed, she stumbled across the room to the window and stared out at the little walled garden behind the house. "I don't believe I've been really listening to *anyone*."

Cicely came up behind her and put an arm about her shoulder. "I'm glad, Mama, that you finally understand. *Now* will you be happy—completely happy—that I'm going to wed Charles?"

Cassie looked over her shoulder at her daughter's blissful face and wanted to weep for sheer joy. The terrible ache—the ache that she'd carried in her chest for weeks and weeks—dissolved away like a lump of salt in boiling water. The whole world was suddenly brighter, cleaner, lovelier.

She put a hand lovingly on her daughter's cheek. "Happier than you'll ever know," she said.

Chapter
~ 37 ~

She couldn't eat or sleep. She couldn't think. Her own daughter was about to be married, and she couldn't concentrate on the wedding plans. She was, to put it bluntly, in a state.

She knew exactly what she had to do to settle her mind, but she didn't know how to do it. A properly reared female, even one of a certain age, could not call on a gentleman, throw herself into his arms, tell him she was sorry and request that he please ask her again to marry him.

Of course she *could* call on his mother. She'd been invited to do so, after all. But the very thought of it put her in a quake. What if she were drinking tea with Lady Sarah and Jeremy happened to come into the room? She would be overwhelmed with embarrassment. The only thing to do was to call when she was certain he would not be at home. But how was she to tell when that would be?

In finding the answer to that question, she was unwittingly aided by her delightful son-in-law-to-be, who happened to remark, when he called at the house to escort Cicely to the Pantheon Bazaar, that he would bring Cicely back by three because he'd promised to meet Jeremy at White's at four.

That is why Cassie, knowing that Jeremy would be safely ensconsed at his club on St. James Street, stepped down from a hired hack at the corner of Dover Street promptly at four that afternoon. She adjusted her dashing new straw bonnet on her carefully coiffed hair, shook out the skirts of her stylish new walking dress—an extravagant concoction of rose-colored cambric—and marched bravely up to the door of the Inglesby town house.

She was admitted by an aged butler who took her name and disappeared down a shadowy corridor for what seemed a very long time. When he reappeared, she saw Lady Sarah herself hurrying down the hall after him. "My dear Lady Beringer!" she exclaimed, holding out her hand. "I'm delighted that you've seen fit to call on me. And looking so splendid, too! Beecks, bring us some tea in the sitting room. Come this way, my dear. That's the drawing room, there to your right, but the sitting room is much more cozy."

This warm reception did much to ease Cassie's tension. She followed her hostess into a modest-sized room in which two wing chairs faced a large fireplace. On the wall over the mantel was a painting of a strong-looking young woman seated on a chair with one leg outstretched and a small boy standing at her elbow. Cassie, recognizing him at once from the lock of dark hair falling over his forehead, stared at the painting in fascination. "Oh, what a fine piece of work!" she exclaimed.

"Yes, we think so. I'm so glad you like it. I'd heard that you yourself are a painter."

"I only dabble," Cassie said, unable to take her eyes from the portrait. "This striking woman is you, isn't it? And that's Jeremy, of course. One can see in that face the beginnings of the man he would become."

"Yes, that's quite true," Lady Sarah agreed proudly. "But do sit down, my dear. Speaking of Jeremy, I'm sorry to tell you that you just missed him. He left only a moment before you arrived."

"I'm glad he's not at home," Cassie said, perching on the edge of a chair and looking over at Lady Sarah nervously. "I've come to see you."

"For a special reason, or just to pay a social call?"

"For a very special reason. Special to me, at any rate. I would like your help, but I . . ." She hesitated, suddenly afraid to go on.

"But, my dear, there's no need to look at me like a frightened rabbit," Lady Sarah said with a kindly smile. "There's nothing I'd like better than to help you. In any way I can."

"Yes, but . . . you told me the other evening that you'd vowed not ever to interfere in your son's life."

Lady Sarah's eyes lit up. "Ah! Then this has something to do with Jeremy?"

"It has everything to do with Jeremy."

"And is it something that will make him happy?"

Cassie looked down at the fingers she was twisting in her lap. "I'm not certain, your ladyship. I hope so."

"If there's even the slightest chance that it will, then I want nothing more than to interfere. My vow be hanged!"

"Oh, Lady Sarah," Cassie exclaimed, a freshet of hope welling up inside her, "do you mean it?"

"Of course I do. Now that I think it over, I'm not sure my vow was wise. After all, what are mothers for but to interfere?" She leaned toward Cassie, her face alight with eager curiosity. "Tell me quickly, before Beecks comes along with the tea tray and interrupts us, just what you wish me to do."

Cassie took a deep breath. "Very well, ma'am. It's a simple request really. I'd like you to convince Jeremy to come and call on me. He won't want to do it, for he's furious with me . . . quite rightly so, I'm afraid, for I said some dreadful—"

She was interrupted by the sound of a door slamming. This was immediately followed by low voices and footsteps hurrying back and forth out in the corridor. Cassie looked at her hostess in alarm. "Good heavens," she gasped, "that can't be—!"

"No, no, don't worry," Lady Sarah assured her. "It must be Beecks, having a problem with the tea tray."

But the words were no sooner out of her mouth than the door of the room swung open and Jeremy stepped over the threshold. "Mama," he said impatiently, looking directly over to a cupboard just to the right of the doorway, "have you seen my *chapeau bras*?" He began hastily to rummage through the drawers. "Hickham says he can't find it anywhere, and I promised to bring it to Charl—"

He looked round at that moment, saw Cassie, and was struck dumb.

"Tell Hickham that I saw some headgear in the large wardrobe in the blue bedroom," his mother said calmly.

As he looked from Cassie's face to his mother's, Jeremy's expression of shock changed to tight-lipped fury. "Hang it,

Mama, what are you up to? I thought you'd given up this sort of high-handed meddling."

"I don't know what you're blustering about, dear boy," Lady Sarah said innocently, "but don't you see we have a guest?"

"Oh, yes. I see."

"She will think you obnoxiously rude, I fear." She turned to Cassie with an apologetic smile that did not hide the twinkle in her eye. "I do apologize to you, my dear. I cannot imagine what has gotten into my son. I can only surmise that he's taken too much wine with his luncheon. But let me introduce you. Lady Beringer, this rudesby is my son, the Viscount Inglesby. I believe you've met him before. Do you remember him?"

Cassie, feeling trapped and desperate (for this was not at all how she'd planned her meeting with Jeremy to proceed), had a sudden inspiration. "I'm not sure," she said with a tentative smile. "I have a problem with memory. A dysfunction, I think it's called. I can't remember anything since a certain night when I stood with a gentleman—one who looked quite like your son—in a room in a turret."

"How very interesting," her ladyship observed, looking from one to the other with eyes brimming with amusement.

But her son was far from amused. If Cassie, who was obviously trying to make amends, believed she could so easily cozen him into forgetting how badly she'd maligned him, she had much to learn. "Lady Beringer's memory lapse is not 'interesting' at all," he snapped. "I'd call it *convenient*."

"Convenient?" Cassie eyed him worriedly. She'd never seen him so angry, not even that night when she'd made all those insulting accusations. Perhaps she shouldn't have come. Had she made a dreadful mistake? "I don't know what you mean," she said fearfully, her heart pounding. "In what way convenient?"

"I mean, ma'am, that if you've so conveniently lost the memory of the sins you committed during that time, you are then able so conveniently to avoid having to atone for them."

"Oh," Cassie said lamely.

Lady Sarah, finding delicious enjoyment in witnessing this exchange, would have liked to remain in the room to hear how matters developed, but she knew her presence would only exacerbate the tension between her son and this woman whose mere presence in the room had so overset his equilibrium. "Well, enthralling as this conversation is," she said, starting toward the door, "I must excuse myself to see what's become of the tea."

"You needn't bother, Mama," her son said, flashing her a look that brooked no opposition. "*I'm* the one who's leaving."

But his mother would not be cowed. "No, you are *not*," she said, drawing herself up and returning his glare with a dagger look quite equal to his. "No son of mine will desert a guest in that unmannerly fashion. You will behave like a civilized creature, no matter how unfamiliar you apparently are with civilized conduct. You will sit down, behave like the gentleman you were reared to be, and converse with Lady Beringer until I return." And with head high and skirts swishing, she stalked out of the room and slammed the door behind her.

Jeremy stared at the door for a moment, his teeth and fists clenched. Then he whirled around. "Damnation, Cassie," he raged, "what the devil do you mean by this? What are you doing here?"

"I'm not certain. I didn't expect . . ." Her throat tightened and she could not go on. Nervously, she dropped her eyes from his burning glare. She had to find the right words to get through the fury that was making a wall between them. But what were the right words?

Taking a deep breath, she lifted her eyes bravely and threw him a tremulous smile. "Perhaps I came to atone . . . for those sins you spoke of."

"Then take yourself to church," he retorted cruelly. "You'll not get absolution from me."

"But, dash it, you're the only one who can give it." She rose from her chair and took a step toward him. "Please, Jemmy, don't glower like that. You're terrifying me."

"And what do you imagine you're doing to me?"

"I don't know. Tell me."

"Never mind. I have no wish to tell you anything." He wheeled about and strode toward the door.

"Jeremy, please, can we not even speak?" she asked in a desperate attempt to stop him.

He put his hand on the doorknob but did not turn it. "No, we cannot. Conversation with you—even your presence in the room—brings me too much inner turmoil."

She took a bit of hope from those words. "Perhaps, if my presence is so upsetting to you," she suggested softly, "it means that you are not indifferent—"

"Indifferent?" He threw her an ironic glance over his shoulder. "What a joke!" And he slammed out of the room.

"Jemmy!" It was a cry of despair but too choked to be heard outside the room. Cassie stood staring at the closed door, heartbrokenly wondering what had been wrong with what she'd said, and what, if anything, she should do next. She shouldn't have come, she realized. She'd probably ruined everything.

But she couldn't just stand there trembling. She still had a vestige of pride; she would keep her head high and take her departure. If Lady Sarah took offense at her failure to say good-bye, well, it couldn't be helped.

She started toward the door but had only gone a step when it opened again. Jeremy stepped over the threshold, shut the door and leaned against it. He stared at her with an expression of angry defeat but said not a word.

Her heart began to pound so loudly she thought he surely must hear it. "You've . . . come back," she whispered.

"Yes," he said stiffly. "I find I'm quite unable to turn my back on you."

"You are not indifferent, then?" she asked timidly.

"Anything but." He threw her a glowering look before crossing to the nearest chair and throwing himself down upon it. "Even after you call me a liar and a cheat," he said, dropping his head in his hands, his voice hoarse with self-disgust, "my pulse still runs amok whenever you come into my line of vision."

Her hands flew to her mouth to stifle her gasp. "Oh, Jeremy! How *lovely!*"

He opened his fingers just enough to reveal one glaring eye. "Oh, yes," he grunted. "Lovely."

Her heart opened in her chest like a flower. She knew that she could win him now. "You aren't a liar or a cheat, of course," she murmured, joyful at being given this opportunity to apologize.

"Oh?" He looked up, one eyebrow raised in icy sarcasm. "When did you discover that?"

"When Cicely told me that you offered for her."

He sneered. "So she told you at last, did she? Did you think I would be pleased by that news? The only thing that might have pleased me would have been your taking *my* word for it."

"I know." She came across the room and stood before his chair. "I've behaved dreadfully to you ever since my memory returned. I've been a fool. I know that now. Will it be somewhat of an atonement if I promise never to doubt your word again?"

"Somewhat, I suppose." His tone was grudging, but his expression had softened. His eyes gleamed with a questioning hopefulness. "What else are you offering?"

"My heart." She knelt down beside the chair and took his hand. "My whole heart."

"Confound you, Cassie," he groaned, pulling her to him, "I love you so. Don't do this to me unless . . ."

"Unless—?"

"Unless you intend to marry me."

She slipped into his lap and nestled in his shoulder. "I want to, my love, I truly want to. But are you sure it's what *you* want? Cicely told me that you said I'm too old for you."

"So I did," he acknowledged, tightening his hold on her and gazing down at her with a look that told her all she needed to know. "But the agony you put me through has aged me sufficiently to make the discrepancy acceptable."

She giggled like a girl. "Coxcomb!" she murmured, lifting her face to his. "Cicely would not believe that those are the words of a lover."

"I am no longer concerned with what Cicely believes," he said as he slowly closed the distance between his mouth and hers. "I hope, ma'am, that you'll refrain from mentioning her name to me for at least an hour. If there's anyone I do not want in my embrace at this moment, it's Cicely's mother."

"I'll just be Cassie," she murmured against his lips. "Only your Cassie. No one else, I promise."

They sat together, kissing and murmuring endearments for a long, long time. And they would undoubtedly have remained in that blissful state much longer had not Lady Sarah come barging in. "Now, *that* is the sort of civilized behavior I like to see," she said, chortling at the sight of them entwined in each other's arms. "And all because I was wise enough to renounce my sworn pledge. I hope, Jemmy, that you finally appreciate the delightful benefits of my maternal interference."

"Good God," her son muttered, shaking his head in disgusted resignation, "mothers!"